The Supernormal Legacy:

Book III

Emerge

by

LeeAnn McLennan

Dedication

To all the lovely, wonderful folks who have stuck
with Olivia through the first two books:
Sorry about the cliffhanger in *Root* and for making
you wait to find out what happens next.

To my husband, Andy McLennan:
You give me the space to dream my dreams. I
couldn't do it without you, old bear!

The Supernormal Legacy:

Book III

Emerge

Chapter I

The hard metal examination table was cold under my back, the heavy restraints bit into my arms and legs, and the bright lights made my eyes water. None of that discomfort mattered as much as the pain I felt looking at my cousin, Emma.

"Hello, Olivia. Welcome to Mountain of Ash." Emma's greeting echoed in the room.

I managed to find enough spit in my dry mouth to speak. "What the hell, Emma?" I tried to sit up, vainly pulling against the straps. Not one of the four people watching me reacted; obviously they were confident I was secured. I felt spacey and weak, most likely from drugs to weaken my abilities.

Emma glanced at the smiling man standing across from her, acknowledging a signal I missed. She placed a hand on the table and leaned over me. "Be a good listener, cousin. You don't deserve the offer you're about to hear, but …" She shrugged like it didn't matter, but her eyes showed resentment. "… I suppose it doesn't hurt to ask."

"What do you mean?" I didn't want to talk to anyone, especially not a creepily smiling man. All I cared about was getting free of my restraints, finding Kevin and Anna, and rescuing Ben.

Emma gave a sweeping wave of her hand as she stepped away from the examination table. Everyone else in the room seemed to fade into insignificance when the short, lithe white man moved closer. His gray sweater and dark pants along with his ash gray hair worn in a Caesar cut made him look like a businessman out for a casual lunch in downtown Portland. Not a menacing presence in a scary room in who-knew-where.

He ran a finger along my forearm, and I couldn't stop the shudder that lifted the hairs on my skin. His smile got wider, stretching to Joker-like proportions. He laid a hand on the front of my shoulder, adding one more restraint to the ones holding me down on the table.

"Hello, Olivia Brighthall. My name is Isaac Milton."

If I thought I fought my bounds before, it was nothing compared to how hard I yanked on them when Isaac Milton introduced himself. It wasn't the words themselves but the fact that he didn't say them out loud.

"I've followed your progress for a while."

2

Isaac Milton had the same ability as Ben. I twisted my arms against the restraints, barely noticing they cut into my flesh.

But no one else other than Ben had the mind control ability, not now, at least according to The Council and every other supernormal I knew. Ben was the only mind reader in the world.

I fell back on the table, exhausted, my heart beating rapidly. I called flames to my hands, but whatever they'd drugged me with earlier reduced my fire to feeble sputters.

"I'm here to make you an offer." Isaac Milton continued as if I was a eager audience. "You have a valuable ability, disintegrator." He narrowed his startling bright blue eyes to a laser-like focus on me. "I'd like you to use that ability to help us."

Help him. Okay, interesting. "Help you do what?" I spoke aloud.

His warm voice flowed through my head, "We're going to get rid of some clutter that's jamming up our planet. It's much too crowded, isn't it?"

I nodded. There were too many people in the world. "Yes, it's too crowded." Images of crowded sidewalks filled my head. Busy airports, long lines at movie theaters. Roads clogged with cars. Normals in my way, taking resources that should be mine.

Isaac smiled, and I felt a surge of happiness. I'd pleased him.

"We have a plan to make it better. Scorched Earth. And you could be a part of our plan." I felt the warm touch of his hand on mine. "I can't wait to see you in action, using that marvelous fire to disintegrate anyone in your way."

A flutter of uncertainty ran through me. Did he just say–

"When I heard that you were a disintegrator..." He smiled at me as if he'd created me. "Well, I knew the Brighthalls were a strong bloodline, though it's a shame most of them have quaint beliefs." He paused, his smile fading before it came back full strength. "Well, never mind."

I nodded slowly, the sense of disquiet bubbling under the warm sensation his words gave me.

"Still, I had my doubts. Most of the Brighthalls are so, well, wholesome. With some exceptions," He flicked his gaze at Emma, who stood at the front of the examination table with an impatient look on her face. Feeling smug, I decided he hadn't included her in our private conversation. He focused back on me. "But, oh my goodness, you certainly showed us what you could do, back in that barn."

The flutter of fear turned to a distant alarm. I had a flash image of a woman, dark hair whipping around her face, her clothes, her body aflame. "No, I didn't mean to kill her. It was an accident." I protested, feeling shame— about killing the woman, about disappointing Isaac because I didn't want to keep killing—I wasn't sure why exactly.

"Oh, but it was beautiful. Didn't you feel it? The joy of unleashing your ability. Using it without judgement or fear."

Under his words ringing in my head, I caught an echo like a subliminal reinforcement urging me to accept what he told me.

I sucked in my breath. He was using his ability to make me want to join them. Well, that wasn't going to happen.

Frantic to push Isaac out of my head, I threw up my mental shield to stop him from getting into my mind. I was stunned that it hadn't been my first reaction.

"Ah, I see I struck a nerve." His voice sounded in my head, fainter than it had been, as if I was hearing him through a window. I could hear him, but I didn't feel his persuasion putting the whammy on me like it was previously. "Don't worry, we won't ask you to use your ability on our kind, only normals."

I gritted my teeth, pouring more force into the mental shield. I didn't want him anywhere in my head. Despite the drug they'd used to weaken my abilities I was able to summon the strength to build a shield. Apparently, Uncle Alex was right when he explained that mental walls had nothing to do with abilities. Even normals could erect them.

"Olivia, you really can't expect to keep me out—" His voice cut off and I gasped with relief while keeping a guard on my shield.

Isaac looked astonished, eyes wide. Emma leaned forward, one hand outstretched, not quite touching him, "What happened? Are you okay?"

He put a hand on his head, speaking aloud. "It's been a long time since someone was strong enough to push me out of their mind." His voice was higher than it had sounded in my head.

"Really?" Emma glared at me sourly, straightening up to cross her arms.

"Stay. Out. Of my. Head." I lifted my chin, even tied down to an examination table I was determined to exude defiance and strength.

Isaac tapped a finger on his lips thoughtfully for a moment before saying, "Olivia, imagine a world where we don't have to hide what we are. Where we don't have to overprotect normals. Mountain of Ash will make that a reality." He bent forward, staring into my eyes. "I know you're afraid, and you think we're the bad guys. I don't have to be a mind reader to know that."

"I will never join you." I hissed the words, as I pulled on the restraints.

His gentle smile never wavered. "No, I suppose you won't, but I thought I'd try. I figured, if one Brighthall joined us, then maybe another one might. It would be such poetic justice to get the younger generation." I wondered what he meant as his smile faded into a stern expression. "I should have guessed that your sympathies don't align with ours since you had a normal with you. And, like most Brighthalls, you're delusional about normals. Emma says the normal is actually your friend." He shook his head as if the idea of friendship with a normal was unimaginable.

Fear for Anna surged through me. "Leave her alone." My breath came in short gasps, "Don't hurt her." The word had echoed sounding as if Anna wasn't alive, and I felt my heart pound with fear for my friend. "Where is she?"

Still bent over me, Isaac studied me as if I were a curiosity, "Interesting." He unbent, not even bothering to answer me. "Emma, please have your cousin put in a cell until we can decide what to do with her."

"Emma, where's Anna?" I begged her to answer, "And Kevin, and Ben? Please at least tell me they're okay."

Emma ignored me to ask Isaac, "Do you want her bound?"

I wanted to scream at her to answer me, but I didn't understand her question. Wasn't I was already bound? I pulled on the straps holding me to the table in case they'd suddenly disappeared.

"Yes." Isaac brushed lint off the sleeves of his jacket. "When you're done, join me and the others upstairs."

Emma nodded. I noticed her face was expressionless. I knew that look, it was the 'I'm seriously pissed but want to hide it' look. What could she be mad about now? I sagged on the table, exhaustion sweeping through me as Isaac left the room.

"Peter, Paul, bind her and get her ready to be transported down a level." Emma spoke briskly.

I'd almost forgotten about the other two men in the room. My fear of Isaac's abilities caused me to lose focus of my surroundings, and other men in the room had faded into insignificance. Now they stepped forward, moving in unison, twin Asian men wearing white lab coats that reminded me of doctor's coats. Without speaking, one twin pulled out two metal cuffs. He caught my left wrist, fastening the first cuff around my wrist too quickly for me to pull away even if I weren't restrained.

I felt the cold metal wrap around my flesh. As it did, I felt the connection to my abilities dim.

"Hey!" I struggled, "Stop it!"

His twin easily caught my flailing right arm and reached for the other cuff, but I managed to knock it out of his hand as his brother passed it across my body. Emma retrieved it with an exasperated sigh and handed it back the twin who clamped over my right wrist.

When the metal touched my other wrist, I gasped in shock as my abilities faded away to nothing.

The room seemed to dim as my super sight was leached away. The noises around me dulled as my super hearing was muffled.

Whatever was in the cuffs left me with the same feeling I'd had inside the damping field at Ley Prison when I'd visited Emma and Ben. But that took large quantities of the alloy to achieve the suppression effect. Whatever was in the cuffs was much stronger, so much so that I didn't feel like a supernormal at all. Unlike being within the field in Ley Prison, I couldn't even sense my abilities.

I panicked, screaming, fighting to free an arm to tear off the cuffs. I'd barely moved before one of the twins stuck a needle in my arm. I slipped into unconsciousness with the image of Emma smirking at me.

Chapter 2

I blinked my eyes open to a new room, this one dim and cold. I was on my back on a chilly, rough surface. I jerked up into a sitting position, grateful to discover I wasn't strapped down, but my fleeting relief was followed by a horrible feeling of loss in the pit of my stomach. I still couldn't feel my abilities. When I'd refused to use my powers for seven years I'd at least known they still existed, which gave me a connection to my mom. Now I couldn't feel even a spark of power. I felt like half of my brain had been turned off.

"Oh, Ollie, I'm so glad you're awake," Anna interrupted my brooding, her voice rough.

Relief washed over me at the sight of my friend, even though she huddled on a rough metal bed like the one I was on. She was dirty and disheveled, streaks of dried blood covered the left side of her face, but she was alive.

"Hey." I forced myself to my feet and gave her a hug. "Are you okay?"

She held me tightly, betraying her fear, even though she spoke in a steady voice, "I woke up here alone, but after a while some big guys dragged you in and then came back with Kevin." She pointed to another metal bed on the other side of the room. "I haven't seen anyone else."

Kevin lay flat on his back, eyes closed, and his arms stretched out by his sides. I wasn't surprised to see the dim light glinting off the cuffs on his wrists. He was as disheveled as I was, clothes dirty and soot-stained, a healing cut under one eye, but he didn't appear to have been tortured.

I stumbled over to check his pulse. It was steady, and his chest rose up and down at regular intervals. I shook his shoulder, but he didn't stir. "I bet he's under the same drug as I was." I looked at Anna, "Let's give him a little longer before we panic." I said the words to ease Anna's worries as much as mine

"Yeah, okay." She sighed, "At least you're awake now. It's been kind of lonely and creepy watching you guys sleep, or whatever."

I sat down beside her, leaning against her shoulder, taking some comfort in the warmth of her body. I looked around our cell, assessing the situation as objectively as possible, like I'd been taught by Uncle Dan.

Well, this place sucked. It looked like someone had read an instruction manual on how to make a cell as gloomy and awful as possible. Built of dark gray concrete which leached all warmth figuratively and literally from the room, the cube held four beds, if one could call a narrow metal slab a bed. The toilet hunched in the corner, facing the solid metal door. And that was it for furniture. There were no windows and the narrow door was solid metal, not even a tiny window to peer out of so I could get an idea of what was outside our cell.

Anna was watching me take in the view, "Yeah, they went all out on the ick factor, didn't they?"

"They just need a skeleton chained to wall and a few rats to complete the scene," I joked weakly.

"Yeah, they really missed an opportunity to make it even spookier," Anna tried to laugh but it ended with sniffles.

"Oh, Anna, I'm sorry." I rubbed my head with a sigh. "I shouldn't have gotten you into this situation."

"Sorry for what?" she asked. "You didn't make me come along, I made that choice. You didn't capture me, that was those Mountain of Ash people. I'm not saying I'm happy to be here, pretty much the opposite, but it's not your fault."

She sounded so much like herself that I smiled at her, feeling a tiny bit more cheerful.

Kevin chose that moment give out a long groan.

"Kevin," Anna and I hustled over to the metal block where he was struggling to sit up.

He let out another groan, hands going to his head as he stared at us with confusion. "What the hell?"

I wrapped my arms around him, "Hey, glad you're awake."

Kevin held on for a minute before releasing me. He pushed up to sitting, looking dazed. He ran a hand over one of the cuffs, frowning. "I feel weird." He paused as his eyes unfocused, then he said, "I can't feel my powers." His voice broke, and he stared around with a freaked-out expression.

I held out one wrist, showing him our matching cuffs. "Yeah." I lifted my hand, palm up, swallowing back fear when no spark of flame appeared. "Somehow they're temporarily blocking our powers." I hoped it was temporary. *Please let it be temporary,* I thought. I curled my fingers over my palm and let my hand fall to my side.

"You don't have your powers?" Anna's voice hitched. "I've waited for hours for you guys to wake up so we can get out of this shithole." She gripped her purple streaked hair with trembling hands, "What's the point of having friends with superpowers if they can't use them?" She paced around in a circle angrily before slumping on her bed.

"Anna, I…." I trailed off, uncertain what to say. Assurances of rescue sounded lame. I wasn't even sure Zoe and Lange were safe. And if they were, did they know we'd been caught? Had they made it home to tell the 'rents where we'd been? And where were we anyway? I didn't know if we were near Andrews, Oregon, where Mountain of Ash had waylaid us, or if we'd been taken somewhere else. We could be anywhere in the world.

It probably wasn't the best time to mention that to Anna.

Frantic to get free of the cuffs, I yanked on the one on my left wrist, trying so hard to pull it off over my hand that my bones started to crack in protest. Kevin grunted as he tried to pull off his own cuffs.

No matter how hard I tugged, the cuff wouldn't budge. I ran a finger over the smooth burnished silver surface of my bonds, twisting my wrist to look at the closure. It was a black clasp, and nothing I did budged the fastening.

"Here," I held out my arm to Kevin, "Try to pull off mine."

His eyes lit up, "Good idea," He stood up, bracing his legs as he grasped my arm and the cuff. "Hold on to something."

I looked around for something grip. The walls were featureless except for the exposed plumbing pipes around the toilet. I wrapped my arm around the pipes. Anna watched from her perch on the bed, leaning forward eagerly as if she could lend her strength to Kevin.

I met Kevin's eyes, "Okay, pull."

His hand tightened on my cuff and I gritted my teeth, ready for a powerful jerk on my arms. Kevin stepped back, pulling and pulling on the cuff as I held onto the cold, damp pipes.

As Kevin pulled, the cuff tightened around my wrist and the blood was being cut off from my hand. "Stop!" I gasped out, sweating, quivering in agony.

He let go, stumbling back a few steps from the force of his efforts. I relaxed my grip on the pipes and fell to the floor, holding my throbbing hand to my chest. I tried not to sob with pain, but it hurt more than I was accustomed to, and with my powers cut off, my super healing abilities weren't kicking in like they should.

Anna ran to my side, wrapping her arms around me, "You're okay. Thank you for trying. I'm sorry I yelled at you," she said in a rush.

Kevin crouched down beside us. "This blows, guys."

Gasping as if I'd run a marathon, I shuddered and fought the impulse to curl up and cry in fear.

Anna stood up, putting her fists on her hips as she turned her head, gazing at the room. I knew that look; she was trying to kick into 'Anna solves everyone's problems' mode. Her eyes narrowed as she chewed on her lower lip.

"Um, so, I," Kevin shuffled his feet awkwardly, "I know we need to figure a way out of here but I have a more pressing problem."

I pushed up onto the bed closest to me, "What?"

He glanced at the toilet, making a face.

"Oh." I gave a short laugh, while Anna turned red. "Well, I guess we can turn our backs. It's not like we can go anywhere." I shifted; now I was thinking of my own full bladder. "You might want to hurry. I'm next."

We turned our backs as Kevin peed. I crossed my legs, willing him to hurry. When I heard the toilet flushing, I turned around, "Okay, look at the wall."

Peeing in front of friends and family in a cell was somehow more humiliating than being unable to get the cuffs off. When I was done, I gave Anna an inquiring glance.

She said, "Oh, well, you guys were passed out for a long time. I'm good."

I joined Anna on her bed again while Kevin wandered around the room peering at everything. After several minutes of brooding silence, I said, "Kevin, have you been unconscious since the fight?"

Kevin shook his head, "No, I woke up tied down on an examination table in a lab or something." He swallowed. "I saw Emma for a little bit right before they brought me here. She told me this is Mountain of Ash's hideout." He grimaced. "Well, she didn't say hideout, but whatever..." He trailed off, rubbing his eyes tiredly. "Some guy named Wesley came in and tried to talk me into joining Mountain of Ash." He shook his head, "Dude was crazy, so happy. He kept calling the Mountain of Ash people Ashers. I guess that's their name for themselves." Kevin took a shaky breath and stood up straighter. "So, yeah, what's been going on with you? Have you seen Emma? What about Ben? Any idea if he's here too?"

I chewed on the inside of my cheek, working myself up to tell Kevin about meeting Isaac. "Yeah, I, ah, well, I saw Emma too."

"Shit." Kevin glared at the door to the cell. "It sucks, knowing she really is one of them. I guess I always kind of hoped...."

I nodded, feeling the same sadness knowing Emma was here by choice. It shouldn't have been a surprise, but somehow, seeing with my own eyes how willingly she let

Isaac Milton question me forced me to truly accept that Emma was on the side of darkness.

"Did you talk to her? What did she say? She didn't tell me much." Kevin asked, "Do you know where we are?" He paused, then asked with anxiety in his voice, "Are we still in Oregon?"

I drew in a deep breath and let it out slowly until I could speak over my own fear. "Emma wouldn't tell me anything. She wouldn't even tell me if either of you or Ben were alive. Emma really didn't say a whole lot. She mainly showed up to introduce me to someone." I stopped talking because I didn't want to describe the man Emma introduced me to while I was strapped helpless to the gurney.

Kevin waited a moment. "Who did she want you to meet?"

I paused, collecting my thoughts, trying to find a way to tell Kevin. Finally, I looked at Kevin. "Isaac Milton."

Kevin's expression was confused for a moment before clearing, "That's the guy the lymph monster told us about, right?"

Anna had her head angled, listening intently. "But Ben's the only one with his abilities alive right now." I told her, "We fought this super gross creature at the Hawthorne Theater a few nights ago. He told us some guy named Isaac Milton is the one sending the monsters to Portland. The 'rents didn't know who he was." To Kevin I said, "Yeah, Godfrey was right. Isaac Milton seems to be the leader of Mountain of Ash." I waited a moment, letting the scene with Emma and Isaac Milton replay in my head while I tried not to shudder.

"Ollie? What did he say? What was he like?" Kevin leaned forward to peer into my eyes, worry mingled with dread on his face. "Did he hurt you?"

"No, not like you're thinking." I spoke quickly, afraid if I stopped I'd lose my nerve. "He wanted to meet me, to talk to me." I reached for Kevin's hand, taking comfort in the touch of a friendly person. "Kevin, he spoke to me in my mind."

"He's like Ben?" Kevin looked shocked. "I thought Ben's the only one with telepathic abilities in the whole world."

"Apparently not. And Kevin, Isaac is so strong." I clenched a fist, my stomach churning at the memory of Isaac trying to force me to betray my family, to turn against normals, to reject everything I believed in as a supernormal. "He tried to make me join them. He tried to make me think I wanted to join them by trying to control my feelings."

"How did you resist him?"

"Using what Uncle Alex taught me about shielding. And, well, when Ben and I were in contact he told me the best ways to shield against his ability." I unclenched my fist with an effort and laid it flat on the metal bed. "But it was really difficult. I don't know if I could keep him out for long."

"Why does he want us to join him?"

I meet Kevin's concerned gaze. "Who knows? Maybe he's starting a Brighthall collection or something. He talked a little bit about that plan, Scorched Earth. Remember it? The one Emma went on about last year?"

"Scorched Earth? Yeah, I remember." Kevin frowned. "What in the hell does that mean?"

I shrugged, afraid to say that I thought it involved a lot of fire and devastation, given the name. Next to me, Anna shivered.

Kevin gritted his teeth, straining against the cuffs blocking his ability, obviously trying bounce away. He stopped after a few tries, panting and shaking. He tugged at the cuffs but had the same results I did earlier when we tried to find a way to release the restraints.

"How are these attached? I was unconscious when they put them on me." He peered at the metal as he turned it on his wrist. "I don't see a seam. Just this." He pointed to the black clasp adorning each cuff.

I stared at my wrists, "They snapped them on me like they were regular bracelets, but maybe they need special tools to remove them?"

"Mmmm." Kevin ran his fingers all around the cuffs before finally sighing and slouching down.

I shifted; my rear was getting uncomfortable from sitting on the hard metal.

Anna shifted as well, frowning. "Do we know if Ben is really here?"

"Oh, that would suck; we're here but he's somewhere else." I rubbed my head, thinking. "I think he's here," I decided. "Emma was very smug, and I know her enough to think it was for more than us being caught."

"Ok," Anna said, "What about—" I squeezed her arm, giving her a quick head shake. Kevin glanced at me, seeming to understand we had an unspoken agreement not to mention Lange or Zoe. We didn't know if the captors knew our cousins had been in the ghost town of Andrews, Oregon with us. It was nice to hope our family was working on a rescue right now, but more than likely, we were on our own.

Kevin tapped a finger on his cuff, biting his lip. "If they have Ben, do you think they would try to use his abilities?"

I shrugged, "Before I met Isaac Milton, I would have said yes, but since that guy has the same powers…"

Kevin nodded. He gazed off into space while I fidgeted. Anna dozed off after a while.

I jolted when the door to the cell scraped open. Without thinking, I reacted by lunging forward, but suddenly Emma was there, yanking my arm behind my back. Kevin fought uselessly in the grip of her other hand.

I realized she'd used her ability to stop time for a few seconds so that she was the only one who could move in the pocket her ability created around her.

Her fingers dug into my skin as I fought uselessly to pull away. She sneered at my forced weakness. "None of that. You're all coming with me."

Anna charged forward, assuming if Emma's hands were full, she wouldn't be able to stop Anna, but Emma was too well trained to let a normal get the best of her. As Anna ran past, Emma simply stuck out her leg, sending my friend sprawling into the corridor.

I yelled, "Anna!" as I tried to get free of Emma's grip.

Anna scrambled to her feet, but a hulking white woman strode into view and put Anna in a headlock. The woman bared her teeth at us, and I had a horrible moment where I thought she going to break Anna's neck.

"Lottie," Emma spoke in a commanding voice, "Not yet."

Lottie looked disappointed but shifted so she was holding Anna by the waist in the crook of her elbow. Anna dangled, her feet inches off the ground. I kept my gaze on her face, watching a tear trickled down one cheek.

"Don't hurt her," Kevin said, "What did she ever to do you?"

Lottie gave him a puzzled look as Emma said, "Come on." She dragged us after her as she left the cell. Lottie and Anna followed.

I glanced around as I stumbled along, assessing my surroundings. We were in a bland, white corridor with a door across from our cell; if the locks on the door were any indicator, it was also a cell.

Emma pulled me along like an unwilling trailer, passing a few more doors. Some were partly open. I saw medical equipment in a few of the rooms. We passed a room with what looked like a tank like the one my cousin Hugh used to train in … before Emma murdered him, of course.

When we reached the doors at the end of the hallway, Emma pressed a button and the doors swung open. She pushed me and Kevin ahead of her, and Lottie followed. I had a moment to see there was a man sitting at a desk on the other side of the door. I assumed he was a guard.

Emma didn't halt until we were upstairs in a small room with a couple of couches and a coffee table in it.

She shoved me and Kevin down on one of the couches. Lottie tossed Anna face first onto the other couch.

"Hey, stop—," I cut off my words as Emma and Lottie marched out of the room, slamming the door behind them.

"What the hell?" Anna sat up, looking scared and mad.

I shrugged, at a loss to explain why we'd been hauled out of our dank, dark cell to this rather comfortable room.

I was lurking near the door when it was pushed open by Emma. I reacted quickly, charging towards the opening, but she kicked out, hitting my leg, and I slammed down on the floor. Shaking with surprise at the force of the blow and resulting pain, I almost huddled in a protective ball, but I gritted my teeth, willing my normal-level weak body up to my feet.

Emma stood, framed in the doorway, hands on her hips. To distract myself from the discomfort I was feeling, I really looked at her for the first time since I'd arrived. She was dressed in tan pants, with a tight military-style jacket buttoned to her chin. Her hair had been trimmed into a tidy pageboy since the most recent vision Ben had sent me of her.

Kevin hadn't moved since Emma's second arrival. Now he nodded at her almost casually. "Hey, Emma, you're looking snazzy." His angry expression was at odds with his calm voice. Then his voice took on a hard edge when he thought of his brother. "Killed anyone lately?" His rage over Emma killing his brother made his voice crack..

Emma let her hands drop to her sides, "Kev, if you knew the endgame, you'd understand why I've done the things that I have."

"You lost the right to call me Kev when you killed Hugh." Kevin got to his feet, balancing on the balls of his feet as he was ready to fight Emma despite her advantage of active abilities.

Emma looked stricken for a moment, but then her expression went back to the cold, calculating one she'd been wearing when she came into the room. "As you wish, *Kevin*." She glanced behind her and shifted, making room for a woman to walk past her in to the room.

I jerked back, and Kevin gripped my shoulder.

It was Black Gaea. In person.

Chapter 3

Black Gaea had also cleaned up since I last saw her in Ben's vision of Emma destroying the Clark Planetarium in Salt Lake City. She was dressed similarly to Emma. Her blond hair was twisted into a bun at the base of her ivory neck. She still made me think 'white suburban soccer mom.' Except for her crazy eyes. There was no compassion in those blue eyes, just glee and something else … maybe anticipation?

"Well, hello there, Brighthalls." She greeted us with a wide smile, her words almost friendly in her heavy Southern accent. "I swear, y'all are like weeds, you keep popping up all over the place." She smirked at Anna. "And you bring your pets along."

I crossed my arms, tucking my shaking hands under my elbows, as I shifted to stand in front of Anna. "What do you want?" I was genuinely curious why this woman, who was part of the trifecta of Mountain of Ash leaders along with being responsible for one of the worst US droughts in recent years, would bother visiting three imprisoned teenagers.

Black Gaea mirrored my stance, except her fingers tapped restlessly on her elbows. "Just satisfying a curiosity." She cocked her head in Emma's direction. "I wanted to meet Emma's dear cousins. She was kind enough to bring you to a more pleasant place for our get together. I do hate those dank cells, don't you? And I heard that Isaac was impressed by Olivia's shielding abilities, but then I suppose you had private lessons, didn't you?" She trailed off with a leer.

I tightened my shoulders to stop the involuntary shudder at the reference to Isaac's mind controlling abilities. I reminded myself I'd shielded from him once, and I could do it again. "What do you mean private lessons?" I held my breath in the hope they would tell us about Ben. Was he here? Was he held in another cell, maybe the one across from where Kevin, Anna, and I were held? I felt panic budding inside of me. What if he was in that cell, and I had missed my chance to find him?

Emma annoyed me by grinning widely while Black Gaea tsked. "Isaac was in your head, and he did a bit of digging while he was there, before you kicked him out."

My breath caught in my throat, and I stared at them in panic. What else had Isaac seen? Did he know that Lange

24

and Zoe had been with us? Did he know the 'rents didn't know where we'd gone? I tried to read Emma's expression for any clues, but I couldn't decipher her grin.

Kevin spoke up, "Stop screwing around and let us go."

Emma snorted with derision, rolling her eyes in such a familiar way that I felt my throat tighten with memory of her doing a similar eye roll when we were six and Uncle Dan was lecturing us on how we couldn't use our abilities in public. Back then her mockery was funny to me, but now my reaction was tinged with fear.

Black Gaea threw back her head and laughed heartily, dropping her arms to wipe away a tear. "Oh, bless you, darling. We can't let you go." The smile dropped from her face so abruptly that it seemed like it had never been there. "You'll leave here under our control or in a body bag."

I gasped at the outright threat, "Emma?" I couldn't help plead with her, "Please let us go, let Anna go, help us. We're your family." I glanced at Kevin and Anna before adding, "At least let Kevin and Anna go. I'll stay, as a hostage. Just let them go."

Kevin grunted in protest.

Anna said, "No." She gripped the couch cushion with both hands as if they would drag her away on the spot.

Emma's expression hardened, "Shut up."

I lurched forward, reaching out to her, making one last appeal, but Black Gaea shoved Emma behind her with a snarl.

Raising her arms, the woman lost all semblance of a soccer mom as she widened her fingers, holding up her palms to the ceiling. Her skin paled to virtually white, and her hair burst out of its tidy bun to fly around her face in a halo. She kept her gaze on mine as the air pulsed with electricity.

"Holy shit!" Kevin shouted, grabbing my arm. I looked back to see he was staring up at the ceiling with startled eyes. Anna whimpered, covering her mouth with both hands.

A swirl of dark gray storm clouds filled the top of the small room, flashes of lightening dancing through the darkness. For a moment, we were all as motionless as a freeze frame while lightning crackled in the air, fizzing and snapping above us.

I yelled at Black Gaea, "Stop!" but it was too late. Lighting slashed down, three strikes aiming for me, Kevin, and Anna. Kevin pushed me aside, but I was already leaping to protect Anna. As I fell, knocking Anna back on the couch out of the way of the strike, I realized I was in the center of a wild lightning storm but I wasn't being struck by the jagged flashes of energy.

I held up a shaking hand, watching as sparks flew within millimeters of my skin but never quite touching. It was as if there was a defensive shield around my body.

Emma screamed at Black Gaea, "Don't kill them!"

Black Gaea growled at Emma who stepped back quickly, bumping into the door. Black Gaea lifted her hands again. I scrambled up, but it was too late as she pulled more lightning from the electricity in the room, sending all of it directly at me. I raised both arms, crossing them in front of my face in an instinctive move to fend off the lightning. The slashes of energy struck the cuffs on my wrists.

I heard a soft *snick* as the cuffs slid off my wrists, falling to the floor with a clatter that resounded through the room.

I sucked in a breath of air as awareness of my abilities once again flooded my body. Without hesitation, I summoned ice, forming two balls in my hands. I threw them straight at Emma and Black Gaea. It was incredibly satisfying to knock them both back to land against the wall. Both women lay still.

I switched to a blast of flame, blowing open a hole in door, and yelling at Kevin and Anna, "Come on!"

They charged out the door with me following. Two guards were in the hallway. One was on the floor, shaking his head as if he'd thumped it on the wall when he was knocked back by my blast, but the other one was alert. He raised his fist, aiming at Anna, but I hit him with more ice, knocking him out.

Kevin grabbed Anna's arm as I took the lead. For the moment, the hallway was quiet, but I doubted that would last. Someone probably heard the door blasting open.

Kevin said, "What happened in there? How did your cuffs come off?"

Anna answered, "The lightning must have released the catch. I wonder if they're held closed by a current of electricity?"

I glanced at my cuff free wrists, "Probably," I gave Kevin a sympathetic look, "We'll figure out how to get them off you as soon as we can, okay?"

"Yeah." He gave me a half smile.

I peered around the hallway, looking for the best exit. I saw an empty room and through it a window. My heart leaped at the sight of rays of sunshine slanting through. Kevin pushed the door open. No one was in the room, so we darted in. Anna closed it after us. I looked outside. My view was limited by the side of another building, so I couldn't tell if anyone waited for us outside.

Bam! The door behind us slammed open. I didn't waste any more time, turning up my heat to disintegrate a large hole in the wall. Fresh air rushed in as Kevin and Anna darted out, avoiding the stilling glowing hot edges of the ragged hole.

I heard shouting behind me as I jumped outside. We were between two white metal buildings. I could see more buildings beyond; it looked like they created a square. On a small hill behind the building directly across from me, I saw a large yellow Victorian house. The gable and gingerbread structure looked strangely out of place in contrast to the plainer, utilitarian buildings.

Kevin and Anna were already sprinting as fast as Anna could across the open grassland. Despite the fact I was being pursued and was frantic to get away, I was ecstatic at being able to use my abilities. I ran after them, easily catching up. Slowing my pace to match theirs, I scanned our surroundings.

The countryside was rugged, with low trees all around us and mountains in the distance. The predominant colors were brown, yellow, and gray. With a tremor of relief, I saw the three trucks parked alongside the buildings had Oregon license plates. Based on the plates and the terrain, I decided we were probably somewhere in Eastern Oregon, which was known for its rugged, dry environment. I wondered if we were on one of many ranches dotted throughout the region.

It was all open flat land. Only the occasional clump of trees sprinkled the landscape, but otherwise there was nowhere to hide. I felt panicked. Was our escape attempt already doomed?

Kevin said, "There," and pointed to a huge building in the distance. "Maybe we can make it there? Get out of sight for a while?"

"Okay." It wasn't the greatest plan, but I didn't see anywhere else to go, and we were completely exposed out here.

I spun around, hearing whizzing sounds behind me. Dozens of projectiles flew at us. I raised my arms as I moved, sending a stream of fire at the objects. They dissolved into dust in the time it took me to drop my arms. I looked for our attacker but didn't see anyone.

"Come on." Kevin grabbed Anna's hand, pulling her in the direction of building. I took several backward steps, still scanning the area, but no one appeared. I turned, running to catch up to Kevin and Anna. Moving faster than they could, I dashed around, looking for signs we were being followed.

As we drew near the building, I saw it was a hangar large enough to house several airplanes. The huge rolling doors were closed, and there was an air of privacy around the building. In a way, it reminded me of the warehouse in Portland. I swallowed hard at the rush of homesickness flooding my body, telling myself not be distracted by thoughts of home when I needed to stay focused on escape. Homesickness was replaced by anxiety.

When we reached the airplane hangar, Anna bent over, bracing her hands on her knees, gulping air. Kevin looked out of breath, but he was straining to hide it.

I turned to stare back in the direction we'd come, and my stomach clenched when I saw figures milling around the buildings. Without talking, we started walking along the side of the building, searching for a door. We found one on the far edge.

I pushed it open just wide enough for us to slip inside, with no idea what to expect on the other side.

It was dark inside, the only light coming from several large skylights in the roof. It was enough for me to see the hangar was one enormous space, so large I could barely see the far end. The walls were lined with a sturdy material that looked like heavy burlap, and the floors were concrete, except for what looked like a sandbox the width and length of a soccer field at one end of the hangar. Scattered across the sand were dozens of figurines of turtles, dogs, giraffes, large spiders, people, and many other figures—made of stone, metal, or clay. It looked like a creepy convention of garden statuary. I didn't have time to puzzle out its intended purpose.

A massive timer was mounted on the wall opposite the large hangar doors. The glowing yellow numbers showed a countdown—as I watched the numbers flipped from 10 days, 5 hours, to 10 days, 4 hours.

We didn't have time to wonder what the countdown was for because the middle of the large hangar doors rattled and started to rise. As it slowly opened, I saw a pair of feet in the middle of the opening and hands gripped on the bottom edge—the doors were being lifted by a supernormal with super strength.

"Crap," Anna muttered. I looked around frantically for a place to hide, but the only ones I could see were obvious hiding spots.

Kevin nudged me, catching my attention, before he headed for a section of tables and computer screens that looked like the classroom back in our warehouse. Another echo of home. We ducked under a table just in time. The doors were high enough that several people bent over and rushed into the hangar. The overhead lights snapped on, flooding the hangar with light and chasing away any shadowy corners to hide out in.

I peered out from our dubious hiding place. There were about ten Ashers searching the hangar, and they were coming closer and closer. I glanced back at Kevin and Anna; both were wide eyed with fear. I probably looked the same, but at least I had my abilities.

I had my abilities.

I looked at the approaching danger, then at Kevin. He read my intentions in my face because he frowned and shook his head fiercely. I nodded and pointed back to the door, trying to make it clear I wasn't going to argue. Anna looked puzzled by our silent exchange.

I didn't look at Kevin any more, trusting that he would at least run to save Anna. Still crouching, I ran silently behind the tables until I was out of direct line of sight from Kevin and Anna. I ignored screaming thoughts of 'Stop it, you idiot!' as I stood up straight and jumped up on a table.

I stood, legs braced apart in a fighting stance. "Looking for someone?" I shouted as defiantly as I could, raising my flame covered hands.

Heads swiveled in my direction. My heart pounded so hard I was sure everyone could hear it. I risked a quick glance and saw Kevin and Anna darting outside.

I brought my focus back on my audience as a large guy of about twenty said, "You've had your fun." He crossed his arms, revealing bulging biceps, and surveyed me with a cold expression, his ice blue eyes startling against his coffee brown skin, "Time to behave."

I rolled my eyes. "Whatever." I had to buy Kevin and Anna as much time as possible.

With my hands still lit up, I leapt off the table, landing solidly on the floor. "Come on. Come at me." I let fire swirl over my entire torso.

The group surveyed me for a moment before another guy stepped forward. He had to be related to Bulging Biceps guy because he had the same eyes and complexion. Both guys were tall and stocky with short, dark brown hair. Both were dressed in what I was coming to think of as the Mountain of Ash uniform—tan and brown outdoor clothes.

The second guy was younger, closer to my age. In fact, I thought he was the youngest person in the group. He bared his teeth at me in a cocky grin, holding out his hands as flames licked the tips of his fingers until the fire covered his torso, mirroring my flame pattern exactly.

My breath caught in my throat. I had wanted to meet another firestarter since my ability manifested. It felt unfair that the first one I'd met was someone I was about to fight.

He let the flames ebb until they outlined his hands, then he reared back and threw a ball of fire over my head. I ducked, my gaze following the path of the fire ball until I realized it was aimed at one of the large overhead lights. As the fire sliced through the fixture, sparks and metal rained down on me. I darted out of the way, aiming my own fireball at a spot in front of the ten Ashers.

The woman's face from the barn flashed through my head. I sucked in air through my nose with shock at the memory but kept my flames steady. I didn't want to kill anyone again, so I made sure I didn't aim to hit anyone, just to keep them from getting me.

As I fought, I tried to angle towards the door, so I could run after Kevin and Anna if possible.

The young firestarter was a good opponent. He never aimed directly at me, always using his fire to create obstacles in my way like I was doing to everyone.

His brother had no such reservations, landing a few punches to my ribs when I was dodging more falling debris from another exploding light. I punched him in the jaw, barely knocking him out of my way. He spat out blood while I tried to ignore the pain in my ribs.

"Enough! Logan, don't damage her. Zander, it looks like she's a match for you." A man's voice shouted, startling me so that the firestarter was able to grab my arms and pin them behind my back. I struggled, fire in my hands, but he was clearly immune to burns like I was. Not all firestarters were, something else I'd discovered back at the barn.

I stopped struggling for the moment and looked up. At some point, more Ashers had arrived. I was surrounded by about fifty people, dressed in the ubiquitous brown and khaki. They stood in tidy lines, unnervingly quiet, watching me. I quivered under such massive scrutiny, feeling very exposed.

Emma shouldered her way past the front line, glaring at me. Black Gaea followed Emma. Black Gaea's appearance was tidy again, as if she'd never had a temper tantrum. She watched me with barely concealed rage, and I tensed, expecting another attack. Instead of attacking, Black Gaea crossed her arms, waiting as the crowd parted for Isaac and another man I'd never seen before now.

At the sight of Isaac, I instinctively checked my mental shield. With the cuffs off, I needed to shield my thoughts.

Isaac smiled, "That was an impressive display back there."

Black Gaea was grinning maliciously now, her expression scaring me as much as everything else in the room. Anything that Black Gaea was excited about was probably bad news for me.

The other man had a wild shock of gray hair which looked odd in contrast to his unlined brown skin. He stared at me avidly, commenting to Isaac, "It really is too bad. I'd enjoy training a new disintegrator."

Isaac also stared at me. "I understand, Wesley, but maybe she can still be useful."

"No, I can't. You should let me go." I knew it was a pointless request, but I wanted to be very clear that I had zero intention of helping Mountain of Ash. Maybe if I said it enough, they would let us go. I knew that wasn't going to happen, but it helped to keep stating my position.

Isaac simply turned to the silent crowd behind him, raising his hand. At his signal, the middle ranks stepped to one side, revealing several Ashers dragging Anna and Kevin towards me. Anna's head drooped, her long, purple-streaked hair skimming the ground.

Kevin gave me a bitter grimace as if to say, 'We tried,' as he was tossed to the floor with Anna falling into him. They both shifted into sitting positions.

I gritted my teeth, frustrated that our escape attempt was thwarted so easily. I tried to pull away from the firestarter, Zander, but he muttered, "Don't, or they'll hurt your friends."

Oddly, his comment sounded more like a caution than a threat.

Isaac said, "Wesley, Gaea, I think we should make an example, a warning if you will. Shall we use the normal?"

He didn't wait for their nods before continuing, "Logan, if you will?"

Logan hauled Anna off the floor, squeezing her arms so tightly that her flesh bulged out from his grip. I was really starting to hate that guy. I tried to go after her, but Zander tightened his grip. Kevin surged to his feet, but a small woman kicked him down easily.

Unable to follow Anna, I assessed her condition. Dried blood crusted over a cut on her check. Her eyes were red and there were tear tracks in the dirt on her face, but she managed to smile at me as they dragged her to a heavy wooden chair. The guards busied themselves with strapping her to the chair with chains, and the smile faded from her face to be replaced with dread.

"Let her go." I tried pulling away from Zander again, but he tightened his hold on my arm, muttering, "You can't stop what's about to happen."

I watched, anxiety curdling my stomach, as Isaac circled the chair while Anna twisted around attempting to keep him in her sight. He stopped in front of the chair, using one finger to stroke her cheek just under the cut. He looked at me. "Emma tells me this normal is important to you." He grabbed Anna's chin, turning her face side to side. "Normals are so fragile, aren't they? So easy to break."

I fought harder to pull away from Zander, flames sparking from my skin, my head spinning with terror that Isaac would break Anna's neck, but he let her chin go with a shove. Anna swallowed and kept her eyes on him. I could feel the fear coming off her in waves.

Isaac signaled to a tall woman in the front row. The woman walked over to a large barrel standing near the chair where Anna was held. Without looking at Anna, the woman pried off the top of a barrel and flung it aside. She dipped her hand inside and when she pulled it out water clung from her fingers like a ribbon. She lifted her hand higher, the water like thick ropes trailing through the air.

The woman spun her hands catching the water in both sets of fingers. She moved gracefully, slowly spinning her hands as the water flowed around Anna's feet. The water swirled up Anna's ankles in response to the woman's motions, gradually encasing my friend's calves.

"Water is such a contradiction, isn't it? Giving life but also taking it." Isaac watched as the woman wove water past Anna's knees. "It doesn't take much to fill the lungs, cutting off breath." His eyes glittered with anticipation. "Every minute an agony. Carol is a master at weaving water."

"Stop it." I fought uselessly against Zander's hold. "Anna's never done anything to you. Leave her alone. She can't hurt you."

Isaac chuckled, putting a hand to his belly as his great rolls of laughter echoed through the room. "A normal hurt *me?*" His amusement was echoed in chuckles and giggles throughout the crowd. He wiped his eyes, "Oh Olivia, thank you for the joke. I needed a laugh." Wesley chuckled while Black Gaea continued to grin at me like the Joker.

Isaac sobered, chopping his hand through the air. The crowd instantly silenced. "It's not so much what the normal can do to me, it's what you can do for me. Agree to give us what we want willingly, and *this* normal will remain unharmed."

Ribbons of water glistened in the air as the water weaver pulled liquid from the barrel to her fingers to swirl over Anna. I swallowed hard against the lump in my throat as the water wrapped around Anna's chest.

Anna's eyes were wide as she looked down at the glistening cocoon encasing her body. Her clothes were dark with water, and dirt turned to mud on her trapped arms. She raised her eyes and looked at me. Our gazes locked for moment before she shook her head, mouthing the words, "No, don't give in."

I licked my lips, hesitating to say no again. On one hand, Isaac could be bluffing. A part of me didn't believe they would kill Anna yet, not if they wanted to use her for leverage.

On the other hand, the water was at her chin, and there was no sign of the water woman stopping its rise.

As the water touched her lips, Anna choked, "Ollie, don't give in." She spat out a plume of water, tilting her chin so her mouth was slightly above the line of water.

The water weaver twirled her hands faster until water flowed around the back of Anna's head, over her scalp, covering her face like a cowl until only her eyes and nose were free.

Anna's eyes were wide, and her chest heaved as she tried to breath in as much air as possible through her nose. I winced as the water crept closer to her nose. Soon, she wouldn't be able to breathe, drowning in the middle of a dry room. I looked at Isaac for any sign he was relenting but he simply watched me with a small smile on his face.

I turned to plead with my cousin, "Emma, you can't let this happen. Please make them stop."

Emma stepped forward, and for a moment I hoped she was going tell Isaac to stop but she gave me a shove, forcing me to look at Anna. "Don't be a weakling." She snapped out the words.

When I looked back at Anna the water had encased all but her eyes. She stared at me with terror.

I shouted, "Stop, just tell me what you want from me! Don't hurt Anna anymore."

"Excellent. Release the normal." Isaac smiled at me with pleasure as Carol spread her hands wide, scattering the water from Anna's body to land in pools on the floor.

Chapter 4

Zander released my arm, and I ran to Anna's side, grabbing and tugging on the chains. I grabbed a chain between my hands and pulled it apart as if it were paper. I immediately unwound the rest from Anna. She lurched out of the chair, into my arms, almost knocking me to the floor.

We hugged tightly, her wet hair and tears cool on my face, until Logan yanked her up by the back of her shirt, ripping it in the process. He twisted the material to get a better grip. I got to my feet, holding out a hand for my friend to grab. "It's okay, Anna." Still holding her hand, I looked at Isaac, "I've agreed to what you want, so don't hurt her anymore, ok?"

Isaac didn't answer me, giving Logan a wave that the bulky guy interpreted as an order to haul Anna over to the Ashers who'd brought her in earlier. As her grip was ripped from mine, I felt as if the last comforting touch of a friend was gone. I watched, wrestling with misgivings, as they escorted her out of the hanger. Agreeing to what Mountain of Ash wanted was the only way to keep her safe for now, but I didn't know if I could trust the overlords to maintain the status quo.

Kevin shouted, "Where are you taking her?"

Isaac said, "Logan, take Kevin Brighthall away. We'll find a use for him later."

Kevin lifted his chin defiantly, "I won't leave Olivia."

Emma snorted at his pointless statement as Logan simply slung my tall cousin over his shoulder and marched off with him dangling down his back.

"All right!" Wesley clapped his hands, startling me out of my apprehensive thoughts. "Let's get moving. We've got so much to do."

I narrowed my eyes. Was this guy for real? He was so freaking peppy, I wondered if he was on something, but his eyes were clear.

"What do you want from me?" I asked, fighting the urge to flame up and run. Breaking out had a body count, one I couldn't bring myself to accept. Guards lining the walls, rank and file in the middle—yeah, I wasn't getting out of here alive if I tried anything.

Anyway, there was no point in fleeing if I couldn't take Anna and Kevin with me. And we still didn't know if Ben was here.

Wesley circled around like he was measuring me while Isaac answered, "We'd like a demonstration of your disintegration ability. To judge your strength."

I was sincerely puzzled by his request, "Why? Didn't you see enough just now?"

Isaac spoke sternly, "We require a demonstration. It's not for you to question why. As to where," He nodded to Wesley, "that's easily handled for the moment."

"Olivia." Wesley opened his arms, and I stepped back, afraid he was about to hug me. "Looking forward to the demo." When he started towards me, I tensed, but he clasped my hands in his and began pulling me gently but firmly across the room. I tried to pull away, but he didn't even have to tighten his grip to keep his hold on me. I reminded myself not to burn him, Anna's water-logged face flashing through my mind.

I heard rustling behind me. Glancing behind, I saw the crowd marching after us. I guessed they were coming for the show.

"What are you doing?" I managed to keep my voice from shaking but inside my heart thudded in my chest.

"Showing you where we want you, of course." Wesley pulled me to stand in front of the weird sandbox I'd seen earlier. He gestured at Zander and another man who'd come forward to stand beside the sandbox, "Zander and Trent can provide directions if you need them." Trent brushed aside strands of blonde hair from his forehead. He was nice looking in an unremarkable way, but the gaze from his brown eyes held an unmistakable lecherous shine. I felt a creepiness that had nothing to do with being surrounded by evil supernormals. This was a universal fear inherent to being a woman.

Zander took Wesley's request as an order, taking up a position next to me at the edge of the sand field. He spoke softly while looking over the statues, "These are our targets." Turning his ice blue eyes to meet mine, he continued. "It's fairly simple: Fire at the target with the intention of disintegrating it. Think you can manage that?" Without waiting for my answer, he aimed a shot of flame at a clay giraffe. After a moment, it crumbled to ash, not as quickly as I could do it, but not too bad.

"Now you try it." Zander pointed to a clay giraffe.

I couldn't believe it. They wanted me to use my disintegration abilities. It had to be a trick of some kind. I lifted my hand while watching Zander, Trent, and everyone else for signs they were going stop me.

I watched hungrily as flames outlined my fingers. Despite my dire circumstances, joy kindled in my heart at the sight. How quickly I'd gone from rejecting my abilities to accepting they were a core part of me.

As if echoing my thoughts, Isaac said, "Feels good, doesn't it? Feels right. You shouldn't have to hide who you are. We shouldn't have to conceal ourselves from the normals."

I looked at him, still holding flames in my hands, the sound of his voice reminding me to check my mental shield, blocking him from entering my mind. My shield was strong since Ben had trained me in hiding my thought from his mind reading. I could feel Isaac pressing against the mental shield, his face briefly reflecting frustration before assuming his calm expression.

He appeared very relaxed for someone standing in front of a girl holding fire, especially one who could turn him into ash in seconds.

Movement around me caught my eyes. Several hulking supernormals lined the walls, all watching as if daring me to run. I curled my fingers into my palm, extinguishing the flames.

I focused on the sandbox, the one with the creepy figurines of turtles, dogs, giraffes, and other statues made of stone, metal, or clay.

"Olivia, if you would?" I flinched when Isaac put a hand on the small of my back, guiding me closer to sandbox. I walked quickly to get away from his revolting touch.

I lifted my hand, intending to send the hottest flame I could achieve at the target, ready to show off what I could do. Then I hesitated. Did I want to reveal my full strength? Or could I be canny enough to hold back? I couldn't explain it to myself, but some instinct told me to try to hide my power. I still had no idea why they wanted to know how much I could do with my fire ability, but I was certain I wouldn't like the reason.

I stretched out my hand, aiming it palm forward at the giraffe. With a quiet breath, I paused to make sure my mental shield was in place before letting a few fake thoughts trickle to the surface. *Can I disintegrate the target quickly enough to satisfy them?* I thought loudly. *Will I be good enough to do what they want?* When Isaac frowned, I wondered if I'd laid it on too thick, so I cleared my mind.

I'd decided to be just a smidge better than Zander. I felt strange, holding back my power, like I was betraying the 'rents. With a jolt, I wondered what they must be thinking. Was Uncle Dan still in disgrace or had they called him back to help search for us?

Wesley frowned, impatient, "Come on Brighthall, show us what you've got."

Yeah, yeah, I thought. I raised my hand again and let a stream of bright, hot fire hit the clay giraffe. Seconds later, the head and neck crumbled into ash, followed by the rest of the body. Smoke rose from the tiny pile of ash, circling up to the ceiling. It felt good to use my ability, and I had to force myself to stop, curling my hand down by my side.

The room was quiet for a moment.

Isaac said, "Interesting. Faster than Zander, our strongest disintegrator, but somehow disappointing." He pursed his lips, "My sources claimed Kate Brighthall was over the moon with excitement about how powerful you are." He turned his gaze to me, now smiling gently. "Kate Brighthall is many things, but she's never been a fool or a braggart." He stepped closer, his smile gone, his eyes cold. I swallowed hard, pouring more power into my mental shield. He pointed at a large metal spider. "Show me your aunt truly isn't a fool nor braggart or your normal friend will receive another visit from Carol. And this time there will be no stopping her."

Fear shuddered through me at the mention of the water weaver. I had zero doubt Isaac meant what he threatened. Without a word, I spun around, arms raising as I moved, sending a tiny spurt of fire at a hulking metal spider on the far side of the sandbox. It dissolved into a thin dusting of ash in the time it took me to drop my arms.

The profound silence following my performance was punctuated by soft pops as the ash cooled. Then a babble of excited voices rose around me. Isaac simply smiled while I clenched my hands into fists at my sides. I wanted more than anything at this moment to send a sweep of flame around the room and run away as fast as I could. However, all the reasons for not escaping yet were still true. I turned to glare at the ash, tears of shame blurring my sight. I blinked them away before they could fall. Zander made a soft humming sound in his throat, either in approval or annoyance.

"Magnificent." Wesley's voice came from directly behind me, irking me with his gushing tones.

"Yes, Wesley," Isaac sounded indulgent. "I've always been confident we'd find a way to help us make the scorchers stronger than they are now."

"What? How?" I demanded in astonishment, that was what he wanted from me? Make supernormals stronger? "That's impossible. No one's abilities get stronger after thirteen."

"Well, that's not quite true is it?" Wesley rubbed his hands together. "You didn't manifest your significant ability until you were fourteen, did you?"

I stared at him, my mouth dropped open. He was right but, "That was a special circumstance. I'd suppressed my abilities. I'm lucky they manifested at all. But that doesn't mean they will get stronger or that I can do...whatever, to make your people stronger." I felt panicked, afraid Anna's well-being depended on me doing the impossible. What did they expect me to do—some special way of training? I felt my breath hitch in my chest as panic flooded my body. I fought to hide my fear from everyone else, but Emma gave me a smirk, clearly enjoying my discomfort.

"Oh, we don't need you to *do* anything." Isaac said.

"Then what do you need from me?" I asked in desperation.

"Blood, my dear," Isaac answered. "We need your blood."

Chapter 5

"What?" I asked, freaked out by Isaac's statement, "You need my blood?" All around me Ashers muttered, some looking at me eagerly while others, like Emma, regarded me coldly.

I wasn't aware of any vampire supernormals, so why would anyone need my blood? My mind spun, visualizing scenes from vampire movies—people chugging down chalices of blood, fanged creatures ripping out the throats of innocents, and Angel from *Buffy the Vampire Slayer* buying bags of blood. None of the images gave me a clue as to why Mountain of Ash wanted me to bleed for them.

I stepped away from Isaac until my calves hit the sides of the sandbox. I flexed my hands, ready to fight back an attack. A thin line of smoke from the destroyed spider drifted past me.

Isaac smiled, clearly guessing my train of thought even without being able to read my mind through my mental shields. "We only need a little. Just enough to make a serum."

A serum from my blood? The idea was so bizarre, I expected Isaac to start laughing and tell me it was a joke. Instead he nodded at two hulking Ashers, indicating they should approach me.

Instinctively, my hands filled with flames. I trembled, fighting to hide my fear, while crouching into defense mode.

"Olivia," Isaac chided me as if I were a naughty child, "think of your normal."

"Anna isn't a pet." I snapped out the words, but I acknowledged the warning by relaxing my posture and extinguishing my flames. The hulks grabbed me. I fought internally to hold back my fire while everything in me screamed to fight back. I succeeded only by tapping into my less frequently used ability—ice—until a fine layer of frost coated my hands.

Wesley laughed with delight, "I didn't know she was an icer as well. Paul, if you would?"

The doctor I remembered from the lab I had awakened in just hours ago came towards me with a needle and vial in his hand. I reared back, but instinct kicked in again and I lit up, the layer of frost melting from my skin. Both hulks yelled and dropped my arm, one waving his burned hands in the air. The other one kicked me to the ground, jarring the teeth in my head as I landed. He planted his foot on my back to keep me down.

"I'm sorry, it's instinct!" I cried out. "Don't take it out on Anna!"

To my surprise, Isaac said bitterly, "Of course. You've been trained by Daniel Brighthall, he's a very skilled combatant. He would have taught you not to give up without a fight."

Emma winced at the mention of her father, lifting her chin in anger when she caught me watching.

Isaac pointed at Zander and Trent while I wondered if he had ever met my uncle. Something about the way he said Uncle Dan's name left me certain he had interacted with my difficult uncle, but I didn't have time to fully process this.

Zander and Trent replaced the hulks, Zander reaching down and pulling me to my feet. He gently turned my arm and pulled my sleeve to expose a vein, murmuring, "This is will be quick if you don't fight too hard." He glanced at the other guy, "Trent won't hurt you, will you?" It sounded like he was warning Trent not to hurt me as opposed to reassuring me. Trent's reaction was to shrug non-committedly.

"Why aren't you cuffing me?" I asked. "Not that I want to be cuffed." I spoke quickly, my chest tight at the idea of being cut off from my abilities again.

Zander answered, "The theory is that your ability must be active when they take your blood." He shrugged. "Something about it being charged up."

"So, they've tried to make a serum before?"

Trent spoke for the first time, "Yep, many times." He gave me a defiant look. "Hasn't worked yet, but it will."

I tried to hide my horror as I realized I had risked Anna's life on a long shot, but Zander seemed to understand, "They've gotten close. Here's hoping your blood is the key."

"Sure," I said unenthusiastically. Compliance kept Anna safe, but it also potentially gave Mountain of Ash more power. I was sure Mountain of Ash achieving more power was a bad thing.

Paul came forward again, ready to take my blood, and inevitably I lit up. This time the fire didn't bother my handlers. I already knew Zander was a firestarter who was immune to fire, and Trent must be as well because he didn't react or get scorched.

Without a word, Paul handed the needle and vial to Trent. In the back of my mind it occurred to me I hadn't heard Paul or his brother, Peter, speak.

Trent jerked my arm around, stabbing painfully at my fire-laced flesh until he found the vein. I bore down on my desire to jerk away as the vial filled with blood. My blood in the vial appeared to flicker slightly.

When the vial was full and the needle was out, I tried to pull away, but Zander and Trent held on. I struggled as hard as I dared, knowing that too much resistance meant pain for Anna. I hissed as Paul set the vial on the table and came back with the cuffs in his hand.

He locked the awful bracelets in place. My stomach felt hollow as the cuffs touched my skin, cutting off any sensation of my power. I reminded myself that the cuffs were only temporarily denying my fire and ice, but it didn't ease the horrible sense of loss.

I pulled free of Zander and Trent, knowing I only got away because they let me. Everyone was staring at me. I sneered back, a useless gesture that made me feel worse.

I thought Isaac was done with me. After all, he'd gotten what he wanted. To my dismay, he told Zander and Trent to guide me to stand on one side of him. I forced myself not to shiver with exhaustion. After being drugged, losing then regaining then losing my abilities again, seeing my best friend tortured because of me, and having my blood drawn, I was near collapse. I refused to let any Asher see how frail I felt, so I stiffened my back and stood tall as I could.

Isaac spoke sorrowfully to the crowd, "You all know I expect the best from you at all times. We are the chosen people of this world, and we must always show how we are the strongest, the most elite of all creatures. I cannot abide failure or weakness among you. It must be found and snuffed out." His words sent a ripple of shuffling and heavy breathing through the crowd. I saw some Ashers exchange looks of fear while others stared straight ahead as if afraid to move. On my left, Zander stayed perfectly still while Trent grinned cruelly on my right.

"You all know the penalty for failure," Isaac continued as the squeak of rolling wheels came from the back of the crowd. The crowd parted down the middle with Ashers stumbling back hastily. I saw two women using steel cables to pull forward a large refrigerator-sized metal box on wheels. The door of the box was held shut by a heavy padlock. It was clearly a prison, and I was very sure I didn't want to know what was inside.

The women's appearance contrasted with each other—one woman was dark skinned with pale hair floating around her shoulders, and the other woman was so white that her skin looked translucent with jet-black hair of equal length, the contrast making their appearances seem more dramatic. Both women had the same expression, almost gleeful. Their obvious enjoyment of their task was odd among the fear emanating from the rest of the Ashers. As the cage came closer, the tension increased in everyone except Wesley and Isaac. Wesley was bouncing on the balls of his feet with excitement while Isaac stood serenely.

The women hauled the box to the middle of the warehouse, letting the cables drop with a thud. Without speaking or acknowledging the silently-watching crowd, the women each unsnapped their cable from hooks on either side of the prison and dragged the cables aside.

The pale-haired woman walked the set of cabinets lining one side of the warehouse, and she returned carrying four objects shaped like traffic cones. She handed two to her black-haired companion, and they set the cones at four corners, creating a box with the prison in the middle.

All of this was done without speaking. I could feel questions crowding in my mind, but I couldn't bring myself to break the oppressive silence.

Once they were done, the two women faced Isaac, folding their hands in front of them with their heads bowed.

Dread permeated the crowd like a dense fog. When Isaac clapped his hands, some Ashers let out shuddering gasps. Through the still-parted crowd, two men were dragged in by guards. I gasped as well; these were the two guards I'd knocked out in our failed escape. Both men wore identical expressions of complete terror. Their eyes shifted between staring wide-eyed at the prison box in the middle of the square and at Isaac, who watched them with a grim expression.

The guards shoved both men into the square. The men looked at each other, then bolted in opposite directions, but members of the crowd grabbed each man and tossed them back into the center of the marked off area.

I didn't want to speak up but couldn't seem to stop myself. "What's going to happen to them?"

Isaac didn't take his eyes from the offending Ashers. "Failure is unacceptable and must be punished." He spoke to the women who'd delivered the box. "Please release the device of reckoning."

All around me, the crowd seemed to shudder, but the two women simply bowed in response and turned back to the prison. In contrast to the fear on the faces around me, they appeared eager to greet whatever was inside.

I couldn't take my eyes off the box as the both of the women took a key from a chain around their necks. They inserted their respective keys into the two locks on the padlock and turned together. The room was so quiet that I heard the *snick* of the padlock opening. Both women put their keys back around their necks, and one woman removed the padlock, slipping it into her pocket.

No one moved as the other woman swung open the door, revealing a compartment inside where a creature stood still. It looked like a tall, willowy human woman dressed in a black leotard with unnaturally long arms crossed over its breasts. I suppressed a startled scream when I saw its face. Where I expected to see two eyes, a nose, and a mouth there was nothing but blank, pale white skin framed by black hair like strands of seaweed. Where there should have been ears were only slits like gills. It was like looking at the head of a smooth Q-Tip.

The monster didn't move, but it was impossible to tell if it was awake or not. Its stillness with the door open made me think it wasn't awake. Yet.

"What...?" My voice faded as one hand twitched.

Wesley said, "Isn't it beautiful and horrible at the same time?" I decided not to answer. "It's an Anone, a fearsome fighter."

One hand dropped to its sides, followed by the other one. The women stepped slowly, reluctantly back, past the edge created by the defining cones. They were barely past the edges when the cones all lit up and beams of red light shot between them to create a true boundary. One of the men shrieked and ran to escape, but when he hit the red line, there was a flash, a spark as he was tossed back into the middle of the stage.

"Ahhhhh." The sound emitting from the metal prison was like a yawn of someone waking up from a deep sleep. The Anone stretched out its arms, lifting its blank face as if looking around the room. Its face turned to look directly at the two women who minded it. Both women moved as if to go back inside the ring, but Wesley murmured, "No, my dears," and the women's movements subsided.

The Anone waited for a moment, but when it was clear the women weren't coming into the stage, it turned its attention to the men who both stood as if frozen. The Anone finally stepped out of the prison, causing everyone in the room to step back except for Isaac and Wesley. It dropped into a crouch with its too long arms in front, hands flat on the ground, and face angled downward. It began to shift slowly from side to side in a hypnotic movement.

"Ashers, what is their failure?" Isaac spoke the words as if they were part of ritual.

The crowd answered him with variations on, "Letting the prisoners escape," confirming my qualms that these men were being punished for failing to stop us.

Isaac nodded, accepting the answer, "I hereby declare their punishment is death by Anone."

I tried to shout out, "No!", but my throat felt constricted with dismay.

As if the Anone had been waiting for permission, it scuttled forward. One man screamed and stumbled backwards, hitting the forcefield. When it flung him back, he ran at it again and again until he was tossed back to lie still on the floor.

Meanwhile the other man went on the offensive, hitting and kicking the Anone. The Anone didn't seem bothered by the strikes as it skittered around the man until it was behind him. Then it reached out with one arm and wrapped it around his neck, pulling him into an embrace. I thought it was going to strangle him, but my stomach dropped in horror as the Anone pulled the man to its chest. Holding the struggling, screaming man firmly, the Anone went still as a slit opened from side to side under its chin. I swallowed in revulsion as I realized that was probably its mouth. The notion was reinforced when it engulfed the man's head until he abruptly stopped screaming. The slit closed, snapping off the man's head. His body slid to the floor with blood pooling under the gaping wound where his neck once joined his head.

"Holy hell," I breathed out the words, horror curdling through my stomach. "All they did was get knocked out. It's not like they helped us escape."

Isaac gave me a pitying smile, "Olivia, there are no second chances when there is no room for mistakes."

I didn't have a comeback for his weird justification, so I gazed around the hanger. Most Ashers were watching the Anone with a kind of fascinated relief. There were a few folks who looked down as if they couldn't stand to watch.

Zander caught my stare, returning it with an expressionless face. I searched for Emma and saw she was leaning forward, staring at the Anone with keen interest like she was recording its every move.

The Anone sat back, throat bulging and convulsing as it chewed its gruesome meal. A thin line of blood dribbled down its neck. I tried not to gag but I had to turn away, breathing deeply before I could stomach another look. I regretted it immediately, the Anone loomed over the other man, stretching its neck mouth over the man's head. I thought the unfortunate guy was already dead, but as the monster closed its mouth, the man's legs kicked out before collapsing when the monster chomped on his head.

Once again, waves of greasy nausea rippled through my body, making me break out in a cold sweat. I heard someone behind me choking for just a moment.

When the Anone finished its second helping, it scuttled around the perimeter of the stage. Everyone tensed as the creature came closer, its head down, stringy hair hiding the featureless face. It swung its head from side to side, and for a moment I worried there might be eyes in the back of its head. After all, it had a mouth in its neck, so apparently anything was possible when it came to the creature's anatomy.

Isaac stepped closer to the fence, speaking firmly while staring intently at the Anone. "You will return to your containment unit. You have fulfilled your duties well, but you must rest now."

The Anone hesitated, twisting its body as it resisted Isaac's command. Isaac kept his gaze on the creature while saying, "Nancy, Paisley, some assistance, please."

I pushed down the slightly hysterical laugh bubbling up in my chest at learning the names of the two guardians of the monster. It seemed wrong that they should have old-style names. If the world made any sense, these women would have menacing names like Sinstera or something.

The women had acquired ropes at some point, and now they swung their ropes, easily lassoing the Anone around its long neck. Working in tandem on opposite sides of the creature, they pulled the ropes taunt, forcing it to hold up its head.

Isaac narrowed his eyes, no longer speaking, and I realized he was using his ability to control the monster. My mind spun as I understood this was how he'd controlled the monsters he sent to Portland to torment my family.

The Anone let out a frustrated yowl, fighting the ropes but unable to move its head. It started to back away in the direction of the metal prison. Nancy and Paisley, I didn't know who was who, let the ropes slide through their hands.

Isaac spoke in his soft, forceful voice, which I assumed was for our benefit since I knew he didn't really need to speak his commands aloud. "You will rest now. Soon you will be released to fight for us, but now you must rest."

Slowly, the Anone backed into the cage. Then Isaac waved for the two women to release one of the force fields. As they moved toward their charge, Isaac continued staring at and talking to the monster. I saw a bead of sweat run down the side of his face.

The women moved quickly as they secured the Anone back into the cage, and as the door closed, I saw the monster start to slump down, but a bar snapped shut across its chest, forcing it upright.

Once the cage was locked shut, I heard soft sighs of relief from several people in the room. Isaac clapped his hands and all eyes turned to him as he gave a resounding shout of "Mountain of Ash united!" and I shuddered when the crowd roared back, "As one!"

Thankfully, this slogan appeared to break up the meeting, as the assembly then broke into smaller groups, leaving the hangar in clusters. I jumped at a grinding sound, but it was only one of the garage doors opening to let out the smoke from the fight and the demonstrations.

Wesley ordered some unfortunate Ashers to clean up the mess left by the Anone's gruesome meal. I saw a couple of them turn pale and sweaty as they grabbed mops and buckets and began scrubbing at the blood. Two other men grabbed the headless bodies and began dragging them away.

Blood dribbled from the corpse's necks and made a trail out of the hangar. So that was what Mountain of Ash was all about. A trail of blood. Theirs, and now mine.

Chapter 6

I didn't move; my limbs felt weighed down by the fact I'd inadvertently caused the horrifying deaths of two men. Even though they were on the side of evil, I didn't think letting prisoners escape warranted death.

Weaving through my guilty feelings was another emotion—despair. I knew Mountain of Ash used monsters. After all, they'd sent several to harass my family in Portland. But I didn't expect to see the creatures used to mete out punishment as if they were tools.

"Are there more?" I spoke aloud to whoever was listening.

"Yes." Zander answered in a flat tone. I raised my eyes to meet his, and for a moment I thought he looked unhappy, but the moment passed and he muttered, "So keep that in mind should you decide to escape again."

I swallowed and nodded. Nancy and Paisley had already attached the cables to the metal prison and were rolling it away. Through the open doors, I saw a waiting truck with a lowered lift. "Are they all kept here?"

"Yeah." Trent gave me an evil grin. "In fact, you and the creatures are neighbors. Most of them are a few floors down from your cozy nook."

Well that's creepy, I thought but I didn't want Trent to know I was scared, so I gave him a sharp nod to acknowledge his statement. He smirked at me before walking away.

All around me, Ashers were dispersing, going off to whatever they did at the Mountain of Ash lair.

Emma darted over to catch up with Trent, leaning in closely to him as they walked out. The haze from the smoke blurred their figures as they stepped into the sunshine.

Black Gaea gave me a perky smile as she joined a handsome man who wrapped his arm around her. They disappeared with a flash.

Zander was staring at me thoughtfully, tapping the fingers of one hand on his thigh. I thought he was going to speak, but he simply gave me a little finger wave before leaving.

I watched him catch up with a couple of guys, one who was gesturing dramatically as he chattered. Zander seemed to be focused on the conversation, but he gave me a last backward glance just before stepping outside.

I was left with Isaac and Wesley. Wesley took my hands and peered into my face, his eyes alight with excitement. "Olivia, I know you don't want to be here, but you are a part of an extraordinary mission that will change our world forever. We will finally—"

"That's enough, Wesley." Isaac spoke softly, but I caught the warning in his tone. Wesley dropped my hands, his earnest expression smoothing out into a placid smile. Isaac continued, "Gentlemen, return her to her cell."

One of the guards slung me over his shoulder, à la Logan, while the others led the way back to the cluster of four buildings.

To my frustration, they didn't return me to the cell I'd shared so briefly with Kevin and Anna; instead they tossed me in a tinier cell. Same grim look and feel, just on a smaller scale. And this time I was alone.

The light was courtesy of a single dim bulb in the ceiling. As I watched, it flickered a few times, threatening to die out altogether, but it didn't. Yet.

I paced around, thinking furiously about what I'd seen and heard. My arm ached where Trent had bruised it while taking my blood. My very being ached at being cut off from my abilities. I couldn't stop from trying to use my fire or ice abilities. It was like poking at the spot of a missing tooth.

Questions spun through my mind. Isaac had at least one disintegrator, Zander, and I assumed at least some of the other Ashers were also powerful, so why didn't he try to use their blood for a serum? Had he tried and failed as

Zander had said? Or did he really think my blood was special just because I'd come late to my abilities? Was this his big plan? Create supercharged supernormals? To do what exactly? Clearly, whatever it was required a great deal of power, though nothing Isaac or anyone had said gave me a clue about what kind of power.

My steps gradually slowed until I sat on my hard bed.

As bad as my outside reality was it didn't compare to what was going on in my inner world. My thoughts tumbled and twisted around worry and fear. And shame.

Worry for Zoe and Lange. Did they escape? Were they okay? Did they know Anna, Kevin, and I had been cornered in the barn and hauled away? Did they have any idea how to find us?

Worry for the 'rents back in Portland. We'd left them with little warning and no support in the event of more monster attacks. And now that I knew there were more monsters at the ranch, I was sure there would be more monsters sent to Portland.

And worry for Dad. We hadn't parted on the best of terms, but I knew he'd be frantic with anxiety.

Fear for Kevin and Anna. Had they been stuck in equally tiny cells, too? I hoped so, since it was better than some of the alternatives I imagined. In the eyes of people like Isaac and the other Ashers, Anna was a lesser being, so I was terrified they would hurt her with as much emotion as stepping on an ant.

Fear for Ben. Was he here? Was he okay? Had he met Isaac? How had Ben reacted to the existence of another mind reader? A thread of colder, deeper fear wove through my thoughts—would Ben be seduced by the idea of openly using his ability? I shoved the unwanted thought away. No, Ben *knew* it was a violation to use his ability. He had to know Isaac was malevolent and would only use his power for evil. Didn't he?

And fear of Isaac. He scared me, not only because he was a mind reader, but he seemed to know a lot about my family. His glee at having swayed Emma to the dark side along with his excitement over having me and Kevin in his possession felt personal to me. His words about Uncle Dan sounded like he'd had experience with my uncle.

I squirmed on my bed as shame came in waves when I tried very hard to avoid thinking of the woman I'd killed in the barn in Andrews. Isaac's cold delight over the unnamed woman's death made it worse somehow. He hadn't expressed any sadness or dismay over losing a member of his group. Even though she'd been a member of Mountain of Ash, she wasn't worth his grief.

I grieved for her, because even though she was an evil Mountain of Ash member, she didn't deserve to die a fiery death.

I also grieved because in killing her, even by accident, I'd stepped over a line. The same line Emma had once stepped over. A person no longer existed because of my actions.

I rubbed my hands on the fabric of my grubby, smoky jeans. I stank of ash and burned wood. My senses were filled with the evidence of my crimes, and in this bleak cell there was nothing to distract me except for more worries.

I sat on the bed with my arms wrapped around my bent knees for what felt like hours, occasionally rubbing my fingers over one of the cuffs on my wrist as I pondered the discovery that this device not only blocked my own abilities but also prevented another supernormal's abilities from touching me. As Uncle Alex often said, there was some good in every bad.

In my head, I replayed the attack from Black Gaea that released my cuffs. Her lightning must have broken whatever force kept the cuffs secured. It was good information to have, and more importantly, I wondered how I could recreate the scenario. Could I provoke Black Gaea again? Was she that impulsive?

A scraping sound jolted me out of my reverie. I sat up straight, dropping my knees to a cross-legged position.

I stared at the door as a small tablet sized hole appeared at the bottom. After a moment, a tray of food slid through the opening. Once the tray was inside the room, the opening melted shut. All of this occurred in less than a minute without anyone speaking to me.

I gaped at the food while my stomach growled, reminding me it had been hours since I ate. I was mildly surprised that the spaghetti and meatballs with salad and bread looked good. A part of me had expected either no food or horrible food at best. The delicious smell of meat and pasta made my mouth water.

Was the food safe to eat? I was so hungry, I resented thinking the question, but Uncle Dan's teachings about caution in dangerous situations were etched in my head. I forced myself to think logically. Would they try to poison or drug me? What if they needed more of my blood? Zander had said they'd had several unsuccessful attempts at making the serum. It made sense that the Isaac was cautious enough to keep me in good health in case they needed another sample.

I gave in after a few minutes, feeling weak but too tired to argue with myself anymore.

I was right: the food was good. I scraped up every piece of pasta before setting down my tray by the door. And I was right that it wasn't poisoned or drugged, at least as far as I could tell. Usually I would have relied on my super senses to guide me, but now all I could depend on was the fact I didn't feel any different.

The next time the door rattled, I didn't move. I waited to see if the door would open, but as it had when the food arrived, a small opening appeared to melt out of the metal, this time at eye level. This time, I saw hands pulling the metal apart as if it was a curtain. Voices murmured, too low for my dulled senses to catch the words. Finally, a face appeared, framed by the opening.

It took me a moment to recognize the face framed in the narrow opening, but the familiar green eyes gave me a clue. I sat up, joy giving me strength.

Ben smiled tentatively. "Hey." He looked strange with his black hair cut extremely short instead of flopped in his face.

I could only gape at him, unable to speak over the lump in my throat at the sight of him. He was the reason we'd left Portland, to rescue him from Mountain of Ash. The sight of him safe, talking to me, smiling at me, was

almost too much to handle. I was painfully aware of my filthy clothes and body. I ran a hand over my hair, feeling rough knots in my short curls.

I scanned his features for signs of injury, but except for his short hair, he looked like he always did. Then a flitter of fear crept up my spine; he did look different. There was an air of lightness around him as if a burden had been lifted.

"Hey, Ben." I fought to keep my voice level, "What are you doing out there?"

In a heart wrenchingly familiar gesture, Ben shoved nonexistent hair out of his face. "Well, I'm here tell you I joined Mountain of Ash."

Chapter 7

Ben's words seemed to bounce around the tiny cell, getting louder with each reverberation. I longed to snatch the words out of air and throw them back at Ben.

"Joined Mountain of Ash? What the hell?" I asked in a choked voice. "Ben, why? Why would you join the people who killed my mother?" I forced my words around the breath caught in my throat. "You know what they've done. You've seen the destruction."

I didn't say what I really wanted to say—how could you hurt *me* like this?

Ben nodded solemnly. "I understand why you're concerned, but do you know what their mission is?" He smiled, his eyes shining, and a tremor ran through my body. "Freedom to be who we are without limits. Imagine it: the world will see us for who we are. We can go to school and train in plain sight without having to worry." He grinned. "Think of how transportation will change when everyone can ask a transporter or a slicer to take them somewhere. Empaths can heal anyone, so there will be no more suffering. Our world will be the paradise it's supposed to be, not the craphole it is now."

"And what role will a mind reader and controller have in this paradise?" I could barely get the question past my lips. "Will you be the one convincing the rest of us it's okay to remake the world for supernormals to rule?" My chest was tight with anger.

Ben's eyes narrowed, and his lips pressed together. I was glad of the protection afforded by the cuffs, though he could probably gather my thoughts just by looking at my face. At least he couldn't read my mind and see the humiliation I was feeling. I believed he was a good person in spite of the fact he'd broken the law by using his abilities more than once. I'd hoped for a relationship that was more than friends, but all of these feelings seemed foolish now.

"I thought you disagreed with the restrictions on my abilities?" Two spots of red appeared on his cheeks.

"I thought you'd been treated unfairly, but then I met Isaac." I spoke fiercely, remembering Isaac's face as he used his ability to try to coerce me into joining Mountain of Ash.

"Isaac is the one who will free us." Ben spoke with fervor, his eyes shining with enthusiasm. "He knows how oppressed we've been. Having to hide our abilities from the normals so they don't take advantage of us. Having to be less than we are. Getting forced into captivity, blocked from my abilities just because people are scared of what I could do with them, it's not fair." Ben took a shaky breath. "Isaac gets it. He's read minds of people planning terrible things and stopped them. He's acted to save supernormals and normals more times that he could tell me."

"What do you mean?" A horrible suspicion crept into my head.

"Ollie, you don't, you can't know what it's like. To know what's in someone's head, to know they plan to do something to hurt people. When I read Emma's mind, just that one time ..." He swallowed hard, eyes dark with painful memories. "It was all I could do to control her without killing her." He leaned forward, his forehead touching the top of the opening. "What if I could have stopped her before she started killing by remaking her? By changing her thoughts?" His green eyes were intense. "Hugh would still be alive. Emma would never have been put into Ley Prison."

"Is that what Isaac did?" I asked without trying to hide the revulsion I felt. "He changed the minds of people *he* decided were bad, without judge or jury?"

Ben's gaze dropped for a moment, "He took a simpler route. He killed them." I inhaled sharply, and Ben met my glare with an earnest look. "Yes, I'm working through my issues with that choice, but I hope to show Isaac that there are less lethal ways to use our abilities. At least he

71

isn't trying to stop me, like everyone else has been for the past three years since my mind control ability manifested." Enthusiasm showed in his face again. "He's training me. His abilities are a little different than mine. He can only get into your mind if he's looking at you, but he's way more powerful than me once he does. He's got so much to teach me."

I remembered how intently Isaac had stared at the Anone while controlling it.

Out of all the excuses to join Mountain of Ash, I empathized with Ben's pleasure in finding someone to train him properly. Ever since my fire and ice abilities manifested, I'd been asking the 'rents to let me train with someone with similar powers. I had my grandfather's notes on his fire ability which helped, but it wasn't the same as physical training. And he'd only had the fire ability, not ice. Aunt Kate kept promising to find someone to train me this coming summer.

My stomach clenched — thinking of my future that may not come to pass while trapped in this place was disheartening. I pushed down any sympathy for Ben. He could have chosen to find a way to help me, Kevin, and Anna escape. Instead he joined the bad guys. No matter his reason, he was aligning himself with evil.

"What's Isaac's plan?" I couldn't keep the cynicism out of my voice.

Ben gazed at me for a moment before answering, "You're not ready. You're too mired in the way we do things now." He turned his head to look at his companion who must be the supernormal with the power to handle metal. Ben nodded in response to a murmured comment. When he looked at me, his green eyes showed regret. "I'm sorry they put the cuffs on you. They're like the ones at Ley Prison, though I think these might be stronger. But now maybe you'll understand how much it sucks to be deprived of your abilities. I'll see you soon."

With that parting statement, Ben disappeared from the oblong opening, and the hands pushed the metal back into a solid wall too quickly for me to react.

Fury surged through me, and I punched the door. I gasped at the pain that shot through my hand. I held it out, slowly moving my fingers, worried I'd broken them, but they were only bruised. I slumped on the bed, cradling my hand while my thoughts spun over Ben's betrayal.

Tears trickled down my cheeks, and I wiped them away irritably. I couldn't believe Ben had turned. It was worse than finding out Emma joined Mountain of Ash. I hadn't spent time with her since we were little, so I didn't really know her when I rejoined the Brighthalls. Her betrayal had been shocking, especially compounded by Hugh's murder, but I hadn't felt the same void inside me as I did now that Ben had announced his alliance with Mountain of Ash. I knew I was feeling more than a loss of friendship; after all, I'd let Ben into my head willingly with the belief it would bring us closer. I rubbed my chest, wondering if the tightness I felt was heartache.

Had I been too naïve to fully understand how rough life as a mind reader was for Ben? Never getting to use his abilities, politely ostracized, always under suspicion. And when he did use his abilities to save most of the

Brighthalls during Emma's attack under the Hawthorne Bridge, he was punished horribly for it. I remembered the anguish on his face when he was told he had to endure a five-year coma for using his abilities.

I swallowed down the sick feeling in my throat, imagining what Ben must've felt when he met another mind reader. Especially one who wasn't obeying the restrictions put in place two hundred years ago when the first Benjamin Hallowfield used his mind control ability to kill eighty percent of the supernormal population globally. But, still, to join Mountain of Ash? The terrorist group who was responsible for Mom's death and for the deaths of countless others over the years?

I huddled on my cold hard bed, brooding over Ben. When my dark thoughts about the Ben situation got too repetitive, my mind tossed in replays about the moment I burned up the woman in the barn. For seasoning, I fretted about Kevin and Anna's safety. At first I was certain Anna was okay because I thought Emma wouldn't hesitate to hurt me with the knowledge that my friend was hurt, or worse. Then I worried, would Emma even think to tell me if something happened to Anna? I gripped my hair with both hands, wincing at the reminder of my injured hand. I flexed it a few times, noting that it was healing but more slowly than if my abilities hadn't been suppressed.

I wondered if Ben had visited Kevin. I imagined Kevin's reaction was like mine, minus the tinge of heartbreak. I wished my cousin was in my cell so we could talk about it.

Thus, my cycle of gloomy thoughts began anew.

It was so quiet in the cell that the silence pressed against my ears.

I didn't know how long I sat, locked in feverish brooding, when an opening melted into the bottom of my cell door. Moving as fast as my stiff body was able, I unfolded and darted to the door, calling out, "Hey! Hey!" I flattened my body on the floor, trying to see outside.

No one answered, unless a tray of food shoved into my face counted. I jerked back as the tray slammed into my nose, spilling hot soup up my nostrils. I snorted and sneezed, backing away as the opening melted closed.

I grabbed the cloth napkin and wiped away the liquid, blowing diced carrots from my nose. I sighed and sat for a moment before pulling the tray over beside me on the floor. I spooned up vegetable soup, knowing I needed to keep up my strength. It was a small relief to have something to do other than agonize.

Once I finished dinner or lunch—I wasn't sure which meal since I had no idea what time it was—I shoved the tray over by the door. My phone was gone, either lost in the fight or taken from me when I was captured. Assuming I'd only been unconscious a few hours, my guess was I'd been here for about a day.

In time honored prisoner tradition, I used the edge of one of my cuffs to scratch a line in the wall next to the door. Day one of captivity.

Restless, I got to my feet, pacing around the cell. It took me three paces to walk the width of the cell and five to go the length. I alternated pacing the width then the length, occasionally mixing it up by walking the perimeter, skirting around the bed and toilet.

To distract myself, I considered what I knew about Mountain of Ash. Ever since Emma's betrayal, imprisonment, and subsequent escape, all my thoughts around Mountain of Ash had been focused on wondering why Emma joined them. Now that I was caught in the belly of the beast, I found myself wondering who they were. And what they wanted. What was the Scorched Earth plan?

Still pacing, I mentally ticked off what I knew about Mountain of Ash. Last fall I'd found out they'd been the organization behind the explosion that had killed my mother seven years ago, but I didn't know why they'd attacked that building. At the time, all I'd cared about was that Mom was never coming home. When I asked the 'rents about the explosion last fall, they didn't know much except that there were some government offices in the building.

The other fact I knew about Mountain of Ash was they recruited Emma and required her to do some terrible things as her initiation.

Stopping in the middle of my cell, I closed my eyes and remembered a dark day last winter after Emma's sentencing. The 'rents sat me and my cousins down to discuss how we were handling Emma's duplicity. Zoe had stormed around the room, yelling, "How could Emma be part of that sick group? Doesn't she know what Mountain of Ash has done?"

Aunt Kate had tried to calm her daughter. "Zoe, I don't understand it either, but we need to focus on how to move forward."

Zoe waved her arms around, pacing as she ranted, "They're worse than a normal terrorist organization! Normals don't have any way to fight them, and they don't even know about Mountain of Ash." She spun around, planting her fists on her hips, "Someone would have to have a black soul to want to be a part of something like that."

I was huddled on the couch, my own soul feeling gloomy, when I realized I didn't know much about Mountain of Ash. "What else have they done?" When Zoe and Lange stared at me in astonishment, I said defensively, "Hey, out of the loop for seven years, remember?"

Even as I recalled the conversation, Zoe's irritable shrug annoyed me. Lange glanced at his mother as he answered, "Mountain of Ash used to be the boogeyman of organizations. You know, the one you hear about but there's not a lot of evidence they really exist. That changed about five years ago." He spoke to Aunt Kate, his brow furrowed. "But I don't remember exactly why. I just remember everyone talking about Mountain of Ash and being certain they did exist."

Uncle Alex had answered Lange's question, sitting on the couch, twisting an exercise band in his hands, "There was a bad drought in the Midwest." He was speaking slowly, exhaustion soaking every word. I recalled he'd left not long after this meeting for the first of many retreats

LeeAnn McLennan

to help manage the overwhelming impact of being an empath surrounded by suffering family members. "The Council tracks events, natural and human made, that could be supernormally caused, and they saw signs that this wasn't a natural drought. The weather patterns were clearly being manipulated. They tracked it to a supernormal who goes by the name Black Gaea."

I remembered how I'd been amused at the idea of a supernormal using a nickname like a comic book character. "Why doesn't she use her name?"

Zoe muttered, "Cause she's a psycho."

Uncle Alex shushed her, "I don't know why. After they caught her, she claimed to be a member of Mountain of Ash, declaring their intent to bring supernormals out of hiding. For the next couple of years, the Council kept an eye out for any incidents they could attribute to Mountain of Ash." He paused.

"Did they find any?" I prompted; even in my memory, I felt the worry coming from Uncle Alex.

He shrugged, "There were a couple but nothing concrete."

Kevin spoke up, "What were some of the ones they thought could be Mountain of Ash?" He was slumped in his chair, and I was surprised to hear him speak since I hadn't thought he was paying attention. His brother's death was still so fresh in all our minds, but I knew he was feeling the loss more than any of us with the exception of his parents.

Aunt Kate gave him a concerned look as she answered, "There was a strange disease that killed a lot of people in some small towns in Idaho. The Council thought it could be Mountain of Ash because some of the symptoms matched a disease they'd seen a few years ago."

"And there was an actor who played a lot of action roles. He claimed to have been kidnapped by people who could fly." Uncle Alex had given a half smile at my startled laugh. "Yes, most people thought he'd gone on a drug-induced vision quest or something, but the Council had him discreetly questioned. They seemed to think there was some truth to the story."

"Wildfires." Uncle Dan spoke in clipped tones. "There were several that seemed like they could have been started by firestarters who were untrained, undisciplined."

I'd perked up at the mention of firestarters. "How did they know—"

Aunt Kate spoke over me. "Remember that none of these were ever pinned to Mountain of Ash for sure. We still only have circumstantial evidence they even exist."

Behind her, I saw Uncle Dan frown. I had a feeling even without his daughter's confessed alliance to Mountain of Ash, he was sure they existed.

I opened my eyes, replacing the comforting view of the warehouse with the cold gray walls of my cell. I felt cold inside as well. Even in my darkest fears, I never imagined I'd be a prisoner of Mountain of Ash.

I must have slept because I woke up to the sound of the door creaking open. I felt muzzy-headed and out of sorts, and it seemed like too much effort to attempt rushing at the door. I shifted to sit up, and saw Emma framed by the doorway. She was flanked by two guards on either side, each carrying whips. The sight of the whips made me think of Zoe. Before my mind could follow the thought, Emma spoke.

"Hello cousin." She surveyed me with a smirk on her face, clearly enjoying my woeful state. "Been enjoying your quiet time?" Then she laughed, "Oh right, you've had a special visitor, haven't you? Isn't it sweet, seeing Ben all happy? It reminds me of, well ..." She gave me a wink to go with her smirk. "I guess, it reminds me of when he and I used to be closer." She emphasized the word 'closer,' drawing it out to mean so much more.

Anger surged through me, and I gripped my hands on the edge of the bed, feeling my shoulders tighten with the effort of not punching her in her smug face. "What do you want?"

Emma flipped her hair. "No need to be pissy, Olivia. I'm here to fetch you for a command performance." She gave me a come-on wave. "Let's go."

I hesitated. I was eager to leave the tiny room I'd been in for hours, but anywhere Emma was excited to take me didn't bode well.

"Walk or be dragged," Emma spoke coldly, her joking just-us-girls tone gone. "I don't care."

I tried to hold back. "Where are you taking me?"

Emma shoved me out the door into the hallway where I came face-to-face with Wesley. "Well, Olivia, it looks like that blood sample wasn't quite the ticket."

Relief washed through me — Isaac's plan wouldn't benefit from me after all.

"However, we're not quite done." Wesley waved to the guards who grabbed me. "I've got a few tricks up my sleeve to charge up your blood even more." He held a syringe in his hand.

I hurled myself away from him, stopping when the guards tightened their grip. The syringe was full of liquid; clearly, he wasn't getting ready to take more blood. I felt a numbing fear down my spine when he plunged the needle into my upper arm. Why the hell did they need to knock me out when I was already powerless?

The last thing I saw as I faded into unconsciousness was Wesley's stupid smile.

Chapter 8

I crouched behind the table in the bank lobby, cradling Jack in my arms as I watched the robbers yell and wave their guns around. One of the masked men slapped a bag in front of the teller window and demanded all the money in the cash drawers. Another man wearing a gray ski mask shoved the bank manager toward the vault. The security guard lay dead in front of the bank entrance.

Blood dribbled down the side of Jack's face where one of the robbers had clobbered him for refusing to give up his cell phone. I glanced at the bag holding our cell phones in the middle of the floor and then at the robber yelling at the teller. I was sure I saw blood on the barrel of his gun.

The woman next to me was crying and saying over and over, "Someone make them stop." She wailed at me, "This is *your* fault. You could stop them and save us."

I gasped as if she'd punched me in the stomach. How did she know I had supernormal abilities? My head spun with confusion. Wait, no, I didn't; I'd rejected my heritage seven years ago. I flexed one hand, noting it felt hot and swollen.

My eyes strayed to the last robber who stood near the ATMs. He had barely moved since the robbers had burst into to the lobby. What was he waiting for? This was a robbery. Shouldn't he be robbing? Instead, he glowered at me. "You're so lame, Olivia. You can't even get it up to save innocent people."

Wait, what? How did he know my name? Or that I was supposed to have abilities?

My heart leapt when Jack groaned, and his hand tightened in mine. His eyes fluttered open, and we stared at each other for a moment before he said, "Ollie, what the hell?"

I tried to smile but failed. I kept my voice soft. "Do you remember where we are?"

He tried to turn his head to look around but winced. He looked at me with panic. "The bank, right? It's being robbed." His eyes narrowed. "And you could have stopped them from killing anyone, but you're too selfish, too afraid to be your true self, aren't you?"

Stunned by his accusations, my mouth dropped open. I let him slide away from my numb arms. I stayed crouched on the floor, looking up at him as he slowly stood up, muttering, "Whatever, Olivia. *I'll* stop them before they hurt more people."

I tried to grab his hand to pull him down before the robbers saw him, but he jerked his arm out of my reach.

"Hey!" Jack yelled, commanding everyone's attention. The gray masked robber circled around, eyes wide through the holes in his mask.

I struggled to get to my feet, but my legs felt like they were made of cooked spaghetti. "Jack, no."

"Be quiet, Olivia, and see how heroes are made. Even though I don't have supernormal abilities, at least I'm doing something useful."

I shook my head, thoughts running through my mind, *Jack doesn't talk like that. He doesn't know about my lineage.*

Gray Mask said, with a sardonic quirk to his mouth, "Don't be a hero, kiddo." He hefted his gun, pointing it at Jack's forehead. "Especially a dead hero."

Jack balled his fist up and swung it at Gray Mask, surprising him enough that Jack landed the punch in the robber's gut. Gray Mask grunted and slammed his gun into Jack's shoulder. Jack staggered back but kept his feet.

I managed to get to my feet, though my legs still felt rubbery. I stood, swaying slightly.

Jack didn't so much as look at me as he darted forward, fist raised to hit Gray Mask again. This time, Gray Mask didn't give him the opening, raising the gun and firing it right into Jack's forehead. Jack jolted back as the bullet hit flesh and bone with a sickening sound. He seemed frozen in place for a moment, then he was falling like a tree to the floor. His body sprawled out on the floor, blood pooling behind his head.

I started screaming and felt my body grow strong, all limpness dissolving in my agony over Jack's death.

I breathed in anguish, and the pain filled all the corners of my body. In the space of that breath and the next, I begged for help from my dormant powers, demanding vengeance, drawing on the faint stirrings I'd ignored for so long and asking for more.

As I breathed out, power filled me as if the breath leaving my body made space for it. I felt electric. Everything, even the air around me, was sharper and clearer than anything I'd ever experienced. I had awakened my powers, and I felt complete, like the last puzzle piece had been put in place inside me.

Gray Mask snapped out the words, "What now, another baby hero?"

I looked at him, feeling hatred and contempt for this normal. Heat flowed through my body, and for a moment I wondered abstractly if this was my significant ability manifesting. I didn't feel happy or excited about it, only satisfied that I might have a weapon to destroy the normals.

Following my body's urgings, I raised a hand and pointed it at Gray Mask. All the heat in my body centered on my palm as fire blasted out of it. Gray Mask lurched as flames wrapped around his body, his mouth opened as if to scream, but his body dissolved into ashes before he could articulate his pain.

A remote corner of my mind reacted with shock at murdering a person, normal or not, but the rest of me felt triumphant. Without hesitating, I shot disintegrating fire at the rest of the criminals in the bank, quickly destroying them one by one.

I was dimly aware that the rest of the hostages were screaming and scrambling to get out of my line of fire. Annoyed by the screaming and aware I didn't want any witnesses to my use of powers, I lifted my other hand, adding more flame to take out all the normals in the bank. A stray thought drifted through my consciousness: Wasn't it wrong to kill innocent people? But the thought faded as I marveled at my skill, noting how very precise I was at hitting only what I targeted without demolishing anything around it.

The screaming gradually stopped as I picked off the normals until all that was left were little piles of ashes littered throughout the room. And Jack. I couldn't bring myself to disintegrate the body of my boyfriend.

Dropping my hands to my sides, I knelt beside his body. Confusion reigned inside me as adrenaline faded. I closed my eyes tightly, then opened them to stare blankly at Jack. How could he be dead?

It didn't happen like this before. The words whispered through me. I shuddered, lifting my gaze to the piles of ash dotting the room. I ran a hand over my face as if I could wipe away the sight, but the shameful reminders of my actions remained.

This is wrong. I never killed anyone in the bank. The background voice was getting more strident. *Jack didn't die.*

The piles of ash shifted, blowing around as the bank doors burst open. Cops charged through, wearing armor and carrying guns. They halted at the sight of an empty lobby with me next to the only body left in the lobby. With a clattering sound, all guns were aimed at me, with shouts of "Surrender!" resounding through the room.

I stood up, feeling my skin harden like armor as bullets ricocheted off me. I shot out flame to disintegrate the police, but the internal voice began screaming, *This is wrong! You would never do this!*

I hesitated, brow furrowing in confusion. The voice was right — killing normals, even bad guys, went against everything I believed in. Why was I so eager to kill? What was wrong with me? I felt like some of the dark thoughts weren't mine, in particular the cold view of normals. No one in my life had this contemptuous view of normals.

I heard a new voice say, "Olivia, you took longer than I expected to catch on."

I looked around the bank lobby seeking the source of the voice, but the cops, the bullets, and the bank faded away. I blinked at bright lights shining in my eyes.

My flame tipped hands were stretched out in front of me. For a moment, I relaxed. I was whole again. Everything, getting caught, being cuffed, and forced to give blood for a serum, it all was a dream. Wasn't it?

Bewildered by the abrupt shift in scene, I struggled to figure out where I was.

I tried to move, but straps held me in place. I looked around, realizing I was in a large empty room. The only furniture seemed to be the chair I was strapped into. The walls were solid along three sides, but a large mirror and door lined the fourth wall. I saw my reflection, eyes wide, clothes and hair dirty and disheveled. An IV ran from my inner elbow to a bag attached to the side of the chair. Blood with flickers of fire filled the bag.

I was still a prisoner of Mountain of Ash. And it appeared I was contributing more blood for another serum attempt.

A spritzing noise from overhead shifted my attention to the ceiling where I saw several sprinkler heads like the ones installed in buildings in case of fire. Instead of water, a light mist sprayed out of the nozzle directly over me. Certain I didn't want to breathe in whatever was in the mist, I held my breath. However, as the mist settled on my skin, I felt my focus fade. I tried to burn away my restraints, but my flames were weak and only charred the metal.

The mist faded away, leaving me disoriented and unable to focus enough to call up my abilities.

I blinked, watching muzzily as the door opened and one of the twins, possibly Peter due his slightly shorter hair, came into the room. I felt my arms being lifted. I struggled uselessly as cuffs were fastened around my wrists. All feeling of my abilities was cut off again. Oddly, my head had cleared from the effects of the drug they'd given me.

Peter removed the IV and released the straps from my body without looking at me. I sat up, rubbing my arms that ached from fighting the straps.

"What happened?" I croaked, my throat parched. I licked my dry lips.

Peter murmured, "The procedure can leave one thirsty," as he handed me a bottle of water from his lab coat pocket. His voice was rough, as if he rarely used it.

Isaac stood near the door, thoughtfully rubbing the side of his mouth, looking like he needed a mustache to twirl. "Peter, show me what you found."

I twisted the cap off the water bottle, draining the contents. I set down the empty bottle, asking again, "What happened?" I glowered at Isaac. "What did you do to me?"

Peter handed Isaac an iPad, which Isaac looked at while answering me. "Like Wesley told you, the first serum we took wasn't adequate to increase existing abilities in our test subjects." He handed the tablet back to Peter. "Peter and his brother think the results would be better if we took your blood while you were using your disintegration abilities at their strongest." He lifted his gaze to the wall I'd been facing when I woke up. "So, you can see, we needed a way to trigger your power and take your blood at the same time. While keeping you under some modicum of control."

I peered around to see where he was looking and gaped at the scorch marks and ash-filled holes peppering the wall.

"Yes, well, most of it was in your head, but you did emit some fire." He smoothed down his jacket.

"What the hell was all of that revisionist history?" I was slowly cluing into the realization Isaac had been in my head. I tried to fight off the repulsion long enough to demand answers.

Isaac smiled at me. "Just my way of activating your abilities. I find it's helpful to work with a known scene from someone's past. And give it a little twist."

"You made me remember it like you would have handled the robbery." I spoke carefully, afraid I'd break down crying over the tainted memories he'd left me with of a moment I'd been proud of until now.

"If you'd been trained properly, by supernormals who understand the real meaning of power, you wouldn't have hesitated to save yourself by destroying the entire bank." Isaac said in a pitying voice. "Not to worry. In the new world to come, no normal would ever dare threaten a supernormal, no matter the situation. They'll understand their place as inferior beings in our world. But you'll see that soon enough." He opened the door, pausing to give me a last glance. "If you live to see that world."

Chapter 9

Isaac's parting words left me quivering inside, but I forced myself to get up from the chair. Peter ignored me, busily working on the iPad. I stood beside the chair, uncertain if I'd been dismissed or not. Peter looked up with a smile creasing the lines in his face. For a moment I started to smile back, automatically thinking the smile was for me, but it was for his brother, Paul, who came in carrying a printout. They bent over the pages, not talking, but seeming to communicate.

Something about their interaction made me wonder if they shared thoughts like the Octad. I hadn't bothered to find out if the hive mind called the Octad were unique in the supernormal world. Thinking of the Octad made me wonder how Six was doing. Was she still in a coma induced by Three's death? What had happened to her sisters? Were they in the same situation, shocked into unconsciousness? I hoped they all, especially Six, recovered from losing a member of their hive mind. I didn't really know the rest of the women, but Six had seemed to be enjoying herself during her time with my family.

I shook my head to get rid of thoughts of home. I needed to focus on the now. In particular, right now. I took a few steps towards the door, expecting Peter or Paul to stop me When neither twin acknowledged my movements, I hastily left the room.

I peered around the outer room, noticing it was set up with monitoring equipment. Clearly it was a lab. I guessed the room I'd come from was a training room of some sort. Or maybe it was more deserving of the name 'torture chamber,' considering what I'd just been through.

Any feeble hope I had of trying to escape was cut short when I saw Emma. She leaned against the exit from the lab, arms crossed in an attitude of casual annoyance. "About frigging time." She pushed off the door to stride over, grabbing my arm. "I thought I was going to have to come in and get you."

"Dammit." I hooked an elbow over the frame of one of the shelves lining the wall, forcing her to stop dragging me along. I was still shaken up from the rewritten version of the bank robbery and, even more importantly, I was so over people carting me around like a sack of dirt. "Let go of me."

Emma merely reached over and broke my grip. I could tell she enjoyed exploiting my weakness. She shoved me in front of her, but at least she didn't try to carry me. I knew she was strong enough, but she seemed satisfied with giving me occasional pokes in my back.

"Emma, why are you doing this?" The words burst out of me. We were alone for the first time since her escape from Ley Prison. I had to ask the question that had burned in my gut ever since we'd found out about her betrayal. "What made you join Mountain of Ash?" I spun around, facing her.

She poked me in the chest, "Keep going."

"Are you afraid to answer the question?" I tried sneering though I was too shaky to give the expression much potency.

"Fine." She snapped out the word, "I'll tell you." She pushed me around, forcing me to keep walking as she talked. "I joined Mountain of Ash because they are strong. From the first time I met Cassie, she taught me to be proud of my abilities."

I remembered Emma's trial, where she'd confessed to meeting a woman named Cassie in Forest Park. In the year leading up to her entrance into the warehouse at thirteen, she'd snuck off to do extra training late at night because she'd been so afraid of not measuring up to Uncle Dan's expectations.

"They made me feel powerful, not like Dad, who just made me train all the time like I was too weak to make it. Cassie taught me all kinds of ways to use my ability, and she always told me how amazing I was." Emma gave me an extra hard poke in my back. "Not like the 'rents. All they cared about was assessing our skills. But what was the point, if we had to hide our abilities from the normals?"

I started to answer, but she rolled right over my words. "And then *you* decided to come back." Contempt dripped from every word. "First you leave! All, 'Oh woe is me, my mom died, and I don't want my abilities anymore. It's too hard, poor me.' You were such an idiot. You were already so strong at seven. Even Dad talked about your abilities. After you left, all the 'rents did for weeks was talk about how hard it was to lose you and how much they hoped .you would come back." Her voice shook as she continued, "I was angry, too, but then I was *glad*. If you didn't care about your heritage, then screw you. I was going to be stronger than you ever could have been."

Her hatred no longer surprised me, but I hunched over at the anger in her voice, momentarily afraid she would do more than jab at me. She drew in a deep breath. "Everything was going great until you decided you wanted your powers after all. I remember the day you came out at the bank robbery. Cassie had just given me the news that Mountain of Ash wanted me to prove my allegiance. I was excited and nervous. Then Aunt Kate told us what happened."

She paused, opening the door to the stairs that led down to my cell. "You just came swanning on back, expecting everyone to treat you like you were so special. 'Poor Olivia, she's had a rough time of it. Everyone help her get acclimated to her powers.'" She did a fair imitation of Uncle Alex's kind voice with her twist of disdain laced through it. "Well, I was glad you had trouble manifesting your significant ability. It served you right." She pushed me so hard I almost fell down the stairs, but I caught the handrail in time.

"I wanted to join Mountain of Ash even more than I had before. Cassie met with me and encouraged me. She even introduced me to Wesley, but they both told me I couldn't meet Isaac until my tasks were complete." She laughed, "It was hilarious when everyone thought you were setting the bombs. I knew the truth, and I knew I was going to succeed."

We reached the door to my cell. I regretted asking her why she'd joined Mountain of Ash. I was worried that her anger would cause her to ignore Isaac's directive against hurting me. I tensed when she opened the cell door while still spewing out how much she detested me. "You were so confused and upset. So lame. You even believed just a little bit that you were the culprit." She shook her head while shoving me into the cell. I faced her, staying silent but watching her for an attack. I didn't know what I would do if she did.

To my relief, she braced a hand on the door, preparing to close it. She met my watchful gaze, her face flushed. "When you manifested your ability, I was furious, but I knew I had Mountain of Ash on my side. I just had one last trial." Her eyes were livid. "And you had to screw that up, didn't you? But never mind, it seems to have all worked out as it should. Now I'm the one closing the cell door in your face." She looked regretful. "I still wish I'd been able to blow up the Hawthorne Bridge, though."

With that parting statement, she slammed the door. I sat down, legs shaking so much I couldn't stand on them anymore. My head pounded, either an aftereffect of the flashback or from the strength of Emma's anger, I couldn't tell.

The cell door opened again. I flew to my feet, trembling fearful of Emma coming back for more. I hated that I was afraid of her, but, in my reduced state, I knew I couldn't fight her.

I sagged on the bed when Zander came through the door. It closed behind him, but I thought I saw the shadow of someone moving outside.

Zander raised an eyebrow at my reaction. I didn't bother explaining. "What do you want?"

He grinned a little at my blunt question. "I wondered if you'd be willing to talk about how you were trained?" His expression turned sober when I just stared at him. "I know you can't use your abilities right now, so you may not want to talk about them but..." He cast a shy look at me. "You're the most powerful firestarter I've ever seen." He looked at his hands. "And I feel like I have so much more to learn."

I felt my mouth drop open as feelings of incredulity ran through me. Did he really think I'd be willing to sit and chat about my abilities when he was a member of the organization holding me prisoner? I was also astonished that he felt there was more to learn from me when he'd clearly been training with other firestarters. And under all of my churning thoughts was a thread of wonder that he thought I was the most powerful firestarter he'd seen.

"You're kidding, right? You seriously think I want to talk to you about training?" I held out my arms, the metal on my cuffs glinting dully in the dim light. "Go ahead, take these off and I'll show you everything I know."

He gave me a shrug and a half smile. "Yeah, I knew it was a longshot."

"Does Isaac know you're here?" I couldn't believe Isaac would approve of this idea.

I was surprised when Zander looked recalcitrant. "Despite what you seem to think, Isaac may be the leader of Mountain of Ash, but he doesn't dictate my every move." He shuffled his feet. "Initiative within reason is encouraged."

I tilted my head. "Is that in the handbook? Did you memorize that line?"

He scowled at me, his blue eyes bright against his caramel-colored skin.

With a sigh, I sat down. "Look, I don't want to talk about training." I hesitated, realizing Zander *had* been relatively nice to me. Not that it was saying much when he was being compared to the likes of Emma and Isaac. Still, I was getting fed up with sitting alone in my cell or being hauled off on a whim by Wesley or Isaac. "Can we talk about something else?"

He looked startled by my request, "Uh, sure, I guess." He shoved his hands in his pockets. "What do you want to talk about?"

"Well, I guess..." I fumbled for a topic before asking, "How long have you been with Mountain of Ash?" I was suddenly curious how a guy who seemed nice enough could a part of a terrorist organization.

"Oh, my parents joined about seven years ago. I was eight, and Logan was eleven." Zander's expression was unreadable as he dropped his gaze to the floor.

"They let kids join?

He poked the toe of his boot against the foot of my bed. "Not usually. In fact, I'm the youngest Asher." He looked thoughtful, "Until Emma, I guess, but she was still older than we were when we joined."

"Why'd they let your parents bring you here?" I couldn't keep the judgement out of my voice. I couldn't imagine parents wanting to bring kids to a place that locked up and tortured people.

Zander picked up on my disapproval. He looked at me, raising an eyebrow. "It's a long story, and pretty much none of your damn business." He stepped back and knocked on the door, "Maybe you'll feel like talking about training later."

I frowned after Zander as he left. There was something different about him. He didn't seem as all-consumed by Mountain of Ash like everyone else here.

Dinner arrived in the unwelcome company of Ben. He handed me a tray of food and sat down with his own tray settled on his lap. I stood staring at him, astonished by his audacity in thinking he was welcome to share a meal with me. "What do you want?"

He gestured to the empty seat beside him. "I wanted to see if you're okay." He shrugged. "I heard you had to give more blood."

I opened and closed my mouth a few times before I could find the words. "Do you know how they got my blood? Do you know Isaac got inside my head, twisting and warping my memories?" Bitterness made my voice rough. I felt a sharp pain in my hand and saw I was clenching my fists so tightly that my fingernails cut into my palms. I curled my hands against my chest.

Ben nodded, looking stoic. "Olivia, it would help if you would accept that you're helping a great cause. There's so much we can do to help the world, we just need to be free to do it without interference." He sat his tray on the bed, giving me such an earnest look that I felt my heart twist with regret.

"Ben, how can I accept that anything Mountain of Ash does is okay? They killed my mother. You were there when they killed Three. Six was in a coma last time I saw her. They've caused so much death and destruction. You know what Emma did for them!" I leaned forward, wishing for the first time I had his ability, so I could force the words into his head. "Remember how she didn't care if she killed people when she blew up Portland landmarks? All she cared about was making an impression on Mountain of Ash." My voice caught in my throat. "How she killed Hugh and tried to kill Uncle Alex?"

Ben took my hand in his. I tried to pull away, but he held on tightly. "Olivia, they want to free us from having to huddle in the shadows. They want us to rule the world like we should have been doing all along." His grip tightened as his voice grew more fervent, repeating his justifications for joining. "No longer will we have to worry about normals and their needs. No longer will any supernormal have to suppress their urges. No longer will a supernormal be punished for using his power." He peered intently into my eyes as if he could break through the damping force of the cuffs and use his mind control ability to force me to understand. "We're going to eliminate the damage caused by the normals and make this world the paradise it was meant to be for supernormals."

Tears trickled down my cheeks at the pain he was causing to my hand. I managed to say through fear frozen lips, "Where are the normals in this paradise?"

Caught up in his dreams of a supernormal ruled world, Ben answered, "In their rightful place, serving supernormals in return for a safe world."

A flash of my father's face, smiling at me over a joke we'd shared, went through my mind, piercing my heart with fear for him. Homesickness wound through my body.

I finally managed to yank my hand away. "Get out!" I pointed to the door. "Now. Don't come back."

Ben's gaze snapped to mine, realizing he'd gone too far. With an overly casual shrug, he picked up his food tray and rapped on the door, calling out, "Ready to go."

A slit unfolded in the door. I saw a pair of eyes darted this way and that; clearly the doorkeeper saw nothing of concern because the door swung open.

Ben stopped in the doorway, saying without facing me, "You may disagree with Mountain of Ash's plan, but I hope you'll understand that I won't suppress my abilities any more. Being here with another mind reader to train me is a dream come true."

"Go away!" I shouted, picking up my tray and hurling it at him. Food splattered all over the hallway as the tray whacked the door opposite mine.

As the door slammed shut, I sank back onto the bed, drained of energy and sick at heart. I covered my head with my arms, wishing I could wipe the image of Ben's joy from my thoughts. There was a time where I would have done anything to see a smile on his face, but I'd never imagined his happiness would come from joining Mountain of Ash.

Chapter 10

The Hawthorne Bridge loomed over me, flashing car lights creating shadows and lights. A low spotlight sat in the dirt, illuminating the horrible sight of Uncle Alex hanging from a long chain by his arms. I was forced to re-experience Emma's attack on our family, but this time Kevin, Zoe, Lange all died along with Hugh. And instead of stopping Emma, Ben helped her kill Uncle Alex. And I used my ability to kill Ben. The shock of killing him woke me from the mind screw.

Once again, I was in the cold room, strapped to the chair. I relished the feeling of my power running through my body until the nozzle above me spewed out the fine mist that dusted my body, dulling my abilities. This time it was Paul who came in and snapped the cuffs on my wrists. I looked up to see Isaac watching me through the observation window.

Isaac entered once I was cuffed, smug while he watched me shudder over the memory of my family dying in front of me and of killing again. I knew it wasn't a real memory, but it felt real enough to leave me with a lingering sensation of horror and shame.

I managed to smirk through my mental anguish. "Still not able to get the right charge in my blood for the serum?"

Isaac stayed calm, "It's a journey. I'm confident we'll find the right kick to make your blood work." He laid a hand on my thigh. "But the journey is certainly more enjoyable for me than it is for you."

My skin twitched under his touch, trying to cringe away in revulsion. I sighed softly with relief when he left the room to look at the results on the doctor's iPad.

When Isaac moved away I saw Ben through the observation window. He was frowning until he saw me staring at him. He pressed his lips together and joined Isaac and Paul's discussion. My stomach roiled with disgust at the sight of Ben huddling with my enemies, and I closed my eyes to block out the view.

I felt the straps loosening, and I opened my eyes with a jerk. I realized Logan had come into the room and was unstrapping me. He grabbed my arm, yanking me to my feet. I staggered on weak legs but gripped the chair to keep from falling. I shrugged his hand off my arm, knowing I only shook him off because he let me.

Logan said, "Come on, back to your cell."

I expected Isaac and the doctor to comment, but they'd moved out to the main lab to a table filled with beakers, machines, vials, and other apparatuses. I was clearly dismissed. Ben gave me a quick sidelong glance before turning away.

Logan shoved me out of the room into the hallway. As we walked away from the lab, I studied him. Like his younger brother, he had dark skin that contrasted with his icy blue eyes. He was shorter and stockier than Zander, and his expression held none of the glint of humor that softened Zander's face. However, Zander had been friendly enough, so maybe I could convince Logan to be a little nicer. I didn't have a specific plan, but I felt like it was a good idea to build some sympathy for me among the Ashers. "So, you and Zander. You joined with your parents?" I asked.

Logan gave me a suspicious look. "What do you know about that?"

"Oh, not much, it's just something Zander told me when he visited me in my cell."

Logan raised an eyebrow and smirked a little bit. "Zander visited you?" He snorted. "Got a little crush on a fellow disintegrator, does he?"

I flushed with embarrassment. "I don't know, maybe he thought we had something in common."

"Yeah, well, you don't have anything in common with me, so don't get any ideas." Logan nudged me forward.

I cast about for another way to reach him. Then I remembered. "Well, we do have one thing in common."

Logan sneered at me incredulously. "Really?"

"The monsters," I stated.

"The monsters?" Logan looked perplexed. "What about them?"

"According to Godfrey," I waved around, "you, I mean Mountain of Ash, are partnering with them instead of trying to dominate them. You don't believe the monsters are all animals."

"Who's Godfrey?" Logan's brow crinkled with confusion.

"You know, Godfrey, the lymph monster Isaac sent to Portland? To, um, attack my family." I couldn't keep the bite of anger out of my voice.

Logan stared at me for a moment before breaking into uproarious laughter. He laughed so hard he bent over, bracing his hands on his thighs. Finally, he stopped laughing, giving only the occasional chuckle. "Oh no, that's too funny. Come on."

I tried to pull back, but he dragged me along easily. "Where are we going?" I demanded.

Logan didn't answer as he shoved open one of the doors. Inside was a small room with TV monitors lined up along one wall facing a desk in front of them. I couldn't see what was on the monitors. Past the desk was a heavy door with several locks.

A woman sat at the desk, typing away on a laptop. She looked up with a puzzled expression, "Hello Logan."

Logan nodded back, "Hey Hallie." He jerked his head at me. "Olivia here thinks we're friends with the creatures."

Hallie's eyebrows drew together in a V. "Why would she think that?" She regarded me as if I was demented.

"Seems like she's been talking to monsters." Logan sounded disgusted as if he'd caught me doing something gross, like eating chewing gum off the ground.

"Hey, I'm right here!" I snapped.

Logan gave me a pitying look before saying to Hallie, "So, can I show her?"

Hallie grinned viciously. "By all means." She pressed a button, and one by one, the locks on the door snapped open.

Even without Logan and Hallie exchanging conspiratorial grins, I had a premonition that I wasn't going to like what I saw on the other side. I didn't have time to worry because Logan put his hand on my back, thrusting me through door. I almost fell down the steps but managed to keep upright while I stumbled down. There was another heavily locked door at the bottom which opened automatically when we reached it.

My stomach was already clenched with apprehension as I entered the room. I got three steps in before I froze.

I stood in an enormous room filled with clear cages set in four rows leading away from me. Bright lights flared over the glass and metal cages, and everywhere I looked I saw horrible monsters locked inside the cages. Some stood or sat resignedly, but others paced around in agitation. My nostrils flared at the stench of stale urine and other funky smells permeating the air.

The cage closest to me contained a squat goblin who glared me through eyes narrowed against the strong light. Spittle dripped from a fang overlapping its lips. As I watched, the goblin leaned forward while staring directly into my eyes and drew a stubby finger across its throat. I shuddered and turned away.

"Gah!" I jolted back, staring into the malevolent gaze of a huge snake. Then I saw its body was that of a horse. It expanded its hood, and I found myself mesmerized by the swaying motion. I felt my body relax as I swayed in response.

I jumped when someone punched me in the arm. "Hey!" I rubbed my arm, frowning at the woman who held her hand in a fist, obviously ready to punch me again if I showed signs of falling under the spell of the snake again.

The woman said gruffly, "Watch out." I recognized her as one of the women who'd escorted the Anone. At that thought, I scanned the room until I saw the awful blank-faced thing in a cage near the other end of the room.

Logan laughed, "Nancy and her companion are somewhat possessive of their charges." He glanced over to where the other woman, who must be Paisley, lurked around a cage that was filled up halfway with what I thought was goo until the mass shifted and a tentacle slapped the side of the container. The tentacle slid down the wall, retracting into the goo.

I stared at the tiny inhabitants of another cage as they fluttered around. At first glance, the cage seemed to be filled with dozens of small, beautiful butterflies flowing up and down the sides of the cage. In the room of monsters, this appeared to be an anomaly. As I looked closer, my breath caught in my throat; though the creatures had butterfly wings, their bodies were tiny lizards with fangs.

Nancy snorted at my reaction. She opened a plastic container and used a set of tongs to pull out a large squirming rat from inside. Without taking her eyes off me, she opened a port in the side of the lizard butterfly cage and dumped the rat inside.

I barely had time to exclaim in revulsion before the lizard butterflies swarmed the rat, fighting it and each other as they killed and devoured the remains within seconds. Soon all that was left was the skeleton, but the monsters worked together to break open the bones and gnaw on the marrow.

My voice shook with horror. "What are those things?"

Nancy stroked the side of the cage, her face rapturous. "These are tiny rustlings. They are rarely seen, though often heard." She looked directly at me, her lips pulled back in a leering smile. "Ever heard a soft noise in the woods but can't find the source?" She gestured at the cage where the monsters had finished their meal and fluttered around their prison. "Tiny rustlings doing their thing."

"Oh my god." My legs felt weak, and I wanted to gag, but I took several shallow breaths before asking, "What is this place?"

Logan looked around his eyes bright with glee, spreading his arms wide. "Welcome to the monster library." He turned to me with a smirk. "When Isaac or anyone needs a dirty job done, we can check out a monster and have Isaac do his whammy to control it."

"His whammy?" My lips were almost numb with horror. I wasn't so naïve to think some of these creatures were good, and I knew several would try to kill me if they could, but that didn't stop me from feeling sick at the idea of them being used as tools by Isaac.

"Yeah." Logan eyed the cages around the room, his gaze stopping on one where a little blond boy sat slumped against the side of the cage. Paisley moved over to bang her hand on the side of the glass, and the little boy looked up, his blue eyes narrowing with hate. I stumbled back into Logan as the boy's head shot up as its neck elongated. The thing hissed through rows of needle teeth, its forked tongue darting out. Nancy and Paisley both laughed as the creature's neck shrunk back, and it resumed the appearance of a dejected little boy.

The women gave matching satisfied sighs. I frowned. "Why are they like that? Those two, I mean."

I was surprised that Logan looked uncomfortable. "They, um, they like suffering. When people or monsters hurt, they get off on it."

"They're empaths?" I asked feeling a twist in my stomach as I was reminded of Uncle Alex's ability.

Logan did smile at that, "Yeah, your cousin calls them sadistic empaths because they don't heal like your uncle does. They like inflicting pain, then they like feeling the pain through their empathy."

I felt revolted by the idea of the women hurting the monsters for their own heinous pleasure.

Isaac entered, pausing when he saw me with Logan. Logan spoke quickly, "Hello, sir. Olivia had the misconception we treated the monsters like equals. I brought her down here to show her how such creatures should be treated." He waved his hand around the room of horrors.

Isaac nodded. "Well, Olivia, you're in luck. I'm sending another monster to Portland. You have the privilege of watching me condition the creature."

As I watched, Isaac walked over to a device that reminded me of the exam machine eye doctors used. The device had the same forehead and chin resting places, but there were straps that I assumed were to force the creature to stay in place.

Isaac signaled for Nancy to go to the goblin's cage where she pressed a button on the side, flooding the inside with a white mist that reminded me of the mist they used on me post-Isaac mind invasion. The goblin slid to the floor, its eyes still open but its body clearly incapacitated. Nancy opened the door and grabbed the goblin by the back of its neck, dragging it out of the cage and along the floor, ignoring the bumps and bangs as its body hit cages and chairs along the way.

"Nasty little creatures, goblins," Isaac remarked as he fiddled with the machine. "Do you know how they kill their prey?" I shook my head numbly, balanced between fear of the monster and anger over the way it was being treated. Logan must have sensed my anger because he stood more closely behind me and took my arm in his hand.

Isaac waited while Nancy lifted the goblin, securing it into a heavy chair. "They are much stronger than their size indicates."

Nancy shoved the goblin's face into the chin support of the device. The goblin grunted but stayed limp while she strapped its head to the support. Paisley lurked on the other side of the chair, watching the work with a small, mean smile.

Isaac ran a finger along the goblin's lumpy chin. "This little guy may not look capable of it, but its favorite method of killing is to rip its prey apart limb by limb." He gave the creature an affectionate pat. "Very painful but effective."

I swallowed down bile. "Why are you sending it to Portland? Can't you leave my family alone? You've got me and Kevin. Isn't that enough?"

Isaac looked at me with so much hate that I stepped back, bumping into Logan, who pushed me forward. "Olivia, it's not all about you, young lady."

The goblin chose that moment to growl, thrashing against its restraints. Isaac turned back to the device, crooning at the monster, "Are you angry? Are you afraid?"

Nancy and Paisley crowded in behind the monster. Nancy's eyes were closed, and she looked ecstatic. Paisley folded her arms and smiled as the goblin struggled. I felt revulsion at how these women were perverting the empathic ability my uncle used to help people. Their obvious pleasure over the goblin's suffering contrasted with my memories of Uncle Alex's reaction to momentarily taking on another's pain during healing. I knew if he were here, he'd be furious.

"Hey, leave the goblin alone!" I sputtered, clenching my fists.

"This is a vicious being. You know it would kill you if it got the chance." Isaac raised an eyebrow, studying me with interest. Nancy opened her eyes and smiled, not at me but at my pain. I wished I could hide my feelings from her. It was gross to know she was enjoying my distress.

"Just, don't, it doesn't matter, you have to stop this!" I sputtered, struggling to express my dismay. "It's wrong to cage it, tie it up, and force it to do your bidding. It may be a vicious creature, but you're taking away any choice it has." I felt my face tighten in anger. "You're a bully."

Isaac stood up abruptly, his face flushed with sudden rage. "You have no power to tell me or anyone here what they can and cannot do." His voice was coldly furious, and I didn't have to be an empath to feel the anger radiating off him. "*You are nothing.* Soon you will be of less use to me than any monster in this room." He drew in a deep breath. "If I didn't enjoy the mind trips we take together, I would have already killed you and drained your body of the blood we need to find the key to the serum. It won't be as effective, but it would be better than dealing with an obnoxious child." He loomed over me, snarling. I wanted to run, but I was locked in place by Logan.

Isaac drew a deep breath before saying, "However, given your ignorance of true discipline ..." I knew better than to point out that Uncle Dan was all about discipline, keeping silent while Isaac continued. "I will allow this to pass. This time." He waited for me to nod. "Good."

I gritted my teeth to keep from slumping in relief when Isaac sat down opposite the goblin, dismissing me. I forced myself to take slow breaths to calm my pounding heart. Isaac's revelation that he didn't really need me alive to use my blood shook me to my very core. I was alive only because he liked screwing with my mind. I hadn't realized how thin a thread I walked on.

By the time I calmed down enough to focus on what Isaac was doing, he leaned towards the monster. The goblin fought its restraints frantically, but it was unable to break eye contact with Isaac. In desperation, the goblin closed its eyes, but Isaac simply waved a hand. Paisley reach over and used her fingers to force open one eye. She pulled down a lever and used hooks to hold the creature's eye open. As she did the same to the other eye, I was sure I saw tears slip down the monster's rough cheeks.

"They always try to close their eyes." Isaac shook his head. "So silly and futile." He waited for Paisley to finish. "Thank you, my dear."

She flushed, speaking for the first time. "Thank you, sir." Her voice was soft, almost gentle.

Isaac focused on the goblin, who had stopped fighting, slumped dejectedly. Isaac murmured, "All we need to do now is redirect all that rage and strength on the right target. Yes, that's right, see the images I'm putting into your mind. All those snotty Brighthalls, so superior, so kind to normals." He said 'kind' as if was a bad word.

I wanted to ask why he hated us so much, but I was still shaking from his outburst, so I simply watched him use his ability to turn the goblin into a missile directed at my family and Portland.

The goblin quivered as Isaac said, "That's good. You're fully primed. Now go to sleep, and we'll get you where you need to go. I promise you'll enjoy yourself."

The goblin gave Isaac a fawning look as Paisley removed the eye restraints. It made a slobbering sound that sounded like words, but I couldn't understand them. Isaac simply gave the creature an indulgent smile before standing up.

I watched as the goblin was carted off to a heavy transport cage like the one they'd used for the Anone. Logan told me, "One of our transporters will shift to Portland and release the thing."

I closed my eyes, wishing I could think of a way to warn my family. When Isaac spoke, I opened them to stare at him warily.

"Well, Olivia, what do you think of the monster library?" His cruel smile told me he knew what I was thinking.

Chapter II

Numb from what I'd witnessed in the awfully named monster library I let Logan lead me back to my cell. He wordlessly opened the cell door. I walked in, thinking the place wasn't any more welcoming than it had been before my latest trip down revisionist history lane, but at least no one was poking around in my head at the moment. And I wasn't face to face with a chamber of horrors.

I stumbled when Logan thrust me into the cell. I fell onto my bed, numbness fading as I twisted around to glare at him. "What the hell? I was going in."

He shrugged. "Not fast enough." He started to close the door, saying, "I've got more important things to do than shuttle around weaklings."

I held up my arms with their horrible bangles. "Take these off and call me weak again. I punched you once, and I'm ready to do it again."

He rolled his eyes as the door shut in my face.

I sighed, sitting down on the bed, exhaustion lending weight to my body. I was glad this latest attempt at a serum didn't work, but at the same time I dreaded having Isaac invade my memories again.

Stretching out, I wished for sleep to come, hoping to gain strength before whatever happened next. However, sleep didn't come; instead, when I closed my eyes, I replayed the new version of Emma's attack under the bridge, my stomach clenching at each death. My chest tightened, and my breath came in short gasps when the goblin's face flickered in my head.

I felt like my head was going to explode from the pressure of so much swirling in my mind. After suffering through the rerun several times, I gave up on trying to sleep. I needed a distraction, something to do other than brood.

I was a little sorry Zander didn't drop in again. Talking to him was an interesting distraction, and I suspected there was more to his story about life before his parents had brought him here. Something about him didn't fit the rest of the people here. He wasn't as arrogant. His brother had clearly chugged the Kool Aid, though.

I paced while I thought. Even though my mind was exhausted from the replays, my body missed the regular workouts I was so used to doing every day. I tried doing some jumping jacks, but I kept whacking my hands on the walls. Jogging in place worked better, but it was boring. Still, I managed to work off a little bit of energy, enough that I fell into a restless sleep, punctuated by nightmares, clearly the dregs of the revised flashbacks.

I woke up to what I dubbed my "food delivery service" sliding my latest meal through the floor-level slot. I assumed from the meal of eggs, bacon, and toast that it was morning. In accordance with my habit, I scratched another line on the wall to mark the next day. If my accounting was correct, I'd been here three days.

This pattern repeated itself for the next day and half. I'd wake up in the lab, shaking from the latest memory Isaac had twisted around to be more horrible.

I replayed the time I'd almost hit my school nemesis, Mindy Careen, in the school hallway, but this time I not only hit her, I burned her alive. And while she was screaming, I turned my fire on Jack, then the rest of my classmates.

That wasn't enough to charge up my blood, so Isaac dug up the fight with the Blattarian, aka the cockroach cluster. The memory was bad enough all by itself since Kevin had almost died from his wounds at the time. Isaac's special touch included Kevin dying in a swarm of Blattarian bites, along with Zoe and Harold, the homeless man who'd alerted us about the danger. And Isaac finished it off with the roaches crawling all over my body until I lit up with disintegrating fire, shedding the ashes of dead bugs as I fled.

I awoke, my skin quivering from the sensation of cockroaches all over my body. As usual, I was strapped to my chair. Resigned to what came next, I looked up at the nozzle above the chair, waiting as the mist to wafted over my body. Then one of the twins cuffed me. Logan was my grudging escort back to my cell. Emma hadn't appeared since the disastrous first day.

Sometimes I saw other Ashers going about their business, but very few of them acknowledged me. It was as if I walked in a bubble of silence.

That was preferable to the day we came face to face with Ben as he came into the lab just as I was leaving. He stopped, clearly uncomfortable to see me. His gaze skimmed me before he looked away and swallowed hard. All he said was, "Hello, Olivia."

I didn't bother answering as I let Logan lead back to my cell.

The flashbacks of my darkest memories still weren't enough charge in my blood to make the serum Isaac wanted, so he rooted around and found my memory of training with Ben, a memory I held sacred because it ended with him kissing me and ultimately me discovering my fire ability.

When the rerun started, I knew enough by now to be aware that I was in a replay. My breath grew short with panic as a part of my mind detached to watch the scene play out. "No!" I screamed, covering my eyes so I couldn't see Ben or the warehouse around me. "I won't do this anymore. It's too much." I screamed at Isaac, the puppet master of my horrors. "You're corrupting all of my memories."

"Olivia, need I remind of what will happen if you refuse to undergo the process?" Isaac spoke, his voice booming from all directions as if it was coming from the speakers set up throughout the warehouse.

"Ollie, make them stop, it hurts!" Anna's voice sobbed from the warehouse speakers, echoing around me. "I can't take any more—" She abruptly began screaming.

I cowered down, covering my ears, "Okay, Okay, I'll do it, just stop hurting her." Even though I couldn't be sure what I heard was real, any degree of uncertainty meant I had to comply with Isaac's demands.

Anna's screams died out, leaving behind silence. I stood up, opening my eyes and facing Ben, who was frozen mid-spar in front of me. I raised my fists, "All right, let's get it over with."

Without comment, Isaac plunged me back into the nightmare. In Isaac's corrupted version, the minute my lips touched Ben's, I lit up, literally on fire. My lips refused to leave Ben's as my flames covered his body. His lips were the last of him to burn away, leaving warm ashes clinging to my cheeks.

I yanked out of the flashback, not caring that tears ran from my eyes, down my neck to pool in the hollow of my clavicles. Listlessly, I watched as I was cuffed. I sat up, slumping in the chair while Isaac and Peter talked.

Isaac's only acknowledgement of my resistance was to say, "Remember, it won't be you who suffers if you refuse to cooperate."

"I want to see Anna. I need to know that she's really okay." I spoke softly, while looking him directly in the eyes.

Isaac paused before nodding. "A quick visit might help your attitude. Your escort can take you now."

Relief flooded my body, lending me the strength to get out of the chair. I slid out of the chair, my bones feeling like they'd been on fire, my joints aching and my head reeling with weariness.

To my surprise, Zander stood by the door instead of his brother, Logan. I'd grown accustomed to Logan's sullen attitude while shepherding me to and from my sessions.

Instead of glaring at me with resentment, Zander looked pensive. He flicked his eyes in Isaac's direction before coming over to stand in front of me.

"Hey," he spoke softly, "ready to go back?"

His words were the first gentle ones I'd heard in days. I raised my head to look directly at him, expecting a cold, judgmental gaze like I'd seen in Logan's eyes, but Zander looked back with sympathy.

But then I thought I'd imagined it, because Zander's eyes went flat when Isaac spoke, "Filling in for your brother?"

"Yes, sir," Zander faced Isaac, "Are you ready for me to take her back to her cell?"

Isaac regarded him for a moment before answering, "Take her to see her normal first. Make it quick, though."

Zander looked surprised but only said, "Yes, sir."

I followed Zander, grateful he wasn't shoving or pulling me along. He seemed content to stroll along at my sluggish pace.

"Where's Anna?" I asked, eager to see my friend even though my body was aching all over and I was bone deep weary.

"She's a level down from you." He guided me down the stairs.

Anna's cell was like mine, and it made me wonder how many cells there were. And why there were so many cells?

When Zander opened the door, Anna looked up with fear in her eyes, but it turned to shocked relief when she saw me. "Olivia!"

I threw my arms around her, glad she was alive. "How are you?" I held her out at arm's length, scanning her for any signs of injury. "Are they treating you okay?"

Like me, she was dirty, still wearing the same clothes she'd been caught in, and also like me, clearly, she hadn't showered in days.

She looked down at the floor, "Mostly, though sometimes they take me upstairs and run tests, but they don't hurt me."

"What kind of tests?"

"Like strength tests, that kind of thing." Anna scrubbed her hands through her hair, leaving it messier than it already was. "It's not awful. In fact it's nice to get out of the cell, but no one will talk to me so it's really awkward."

Zander said from behind me, "I'm sorry to cut this short, but I need to take Olivia back to her cell now."

"Can't we have a few more minutes?" I begged him, but he shook his head. I hugged Anna again, murmuring, "I'll try to see you again soon."

I saw tears in her eyes as Zander shut the door. I had to fight back my own tears.

I didn't feel like speaking, and Zander didn't seem to be in the mood to chat, so we walked in silence until we reached my cell. He opened the door, holding it while I walked it to sit tiredly on my bed. He regarded me for a moment before saying, "Get some rest."

Chapter 12

Logan guided me into the dining hall. I was still surprised that we'd come here instead of to the lab. Logan's only response to my confused question was to mutter, "Ben wanted to eat dinner with you, and Isaac said it was okay."

I'd spent the rest of the way to the dining hall trying to figure out why Ben wanted eat dinner out here when he could see me in my cell when he wanted. It wasn't like I had a full schedule or anything.

When we entered the large room, my musings were disrupted by sensory overload. Not only were there over a hundred people in line, walking between the tables, or sitting down, but the clamor of so many people was overwhelmed by the noise blasting from TV screens mounted on the four corners of the room.

I stared at the screen directly in front of me. On it, I saw people running in terror as a car careened into a crowd. The camera panned across the panicked throng, focusing on battered and bloodied men and women. Police officers ran through, trying to control the chaos.

The scene cut to demonstrators carrying signs protesting gun violence, while gun rights demonstrators marched down the opposite side of the street. All the marchers were shouting at each other while cops tried to form a line between. Before the image shifted, I saw the protesters charging towards each other.

The barrage of awful images continued with scenes from a recent shooting at a shopping mall. Scores of people were running, then crouching down with their arms over their heads. Mothers huddled protectively over their crying children as the camera panned across the bloody food court.

The next image and the next image continued to show normals at their worst.

The blaring commentary shifting between different announcers was worse than the images. *Normals have forfeited their right to be the dominant species on Earth— They've allowed climate change to go unchecked—They kill each other without regard for life—They cannot restrain their worst impulses because they are powerless, weak, useless.* The voices alternated between Isaac, Wesley, and Black Gaea.

I felt Logan's hand on my arm pushing me to the line for food, but I could barely focus on what was on the tray he shoved into my hands. I shivered as the words in the air seemed to invade my mind. Was this how all Mountain of Ash followers thought? Did they only see normals at their worst? I wanted to jump up on a table and shout out all the good things normals did to balance the terrible acts shown on the screens—donating blood and money after disasters, setting up shelters, and looking for ways to ease the pain of the victims. I wanted to get Anna from her cell and show them how awesome she was and tell these people how she was my best friend who stuck with me through all kinds of bad and good times.

I did none of those things. I was too afraid to expose myself in my powerless state. More importantly, I had Anna's wellbeing to consider when calculating any next move. Any rebellious act I took was likely to cause her to be harmed. Thinking of Anna, I scanned the room, relieved when I didn't see her. It was too awful to think about Anna being subjected to this onslaught of horror propaganda.

The volume from the TVs gradually decreased as more people found their seats and started eating. No one reacted to the subsiding clamor, so I guessed it was typical to be greeted with the cacophony but not have to endure it at top volume while eating. I still found it difficult to ignore the awful words and horrible images.

Logan led me to a table in the corner under one of the TVs where Ben sat surrounded by other Ashers. As we approached, I noticed most of the doting crowd was female. He was smiling as a woman used her ability to twist a napkin into the shape of a dinosaur.

He saw me and got to his feet. When I glared at him, his expression went blank. He looked so strange without his black hair falling around his face. I noticed his ears stuck out a little bit and hated myself for thinking it was cute, so I scowled at him even more fiercely. He was dressed in Mountain of Ash casual wear—tan and brown.

Despite my cold greeting, Ben said to his admirers, "Make room for Olivia."

The woman who'd presented him with the origami dinosaur gave me a resentful look as she slid along the bench. She wrinkled her nose, murmuring to the woman next her, "Move down more, will you? She reeks."

I started to retort that I'd like to see how she smells after a gritty battle then not getting to shower for days, but instead I said, "I don't need to sit there."

Logan shoved me so hard my knees banged into the bench, almost spilling the food on my tray. I growled under my breath but sat down, dropping the tray on the table loudly.

Ben winced but only said, "Hey, Ollie."

I shook my head, "No, don't call me Ollie. You lost that right."

Ben frowned but didn't respond. At a look from Ben, Logan grimaced and sat at the end of the table away from us, but still close enough to stop me if I decided to do something crazy.

I didn't speak, unable to imagine what I could say to Ben. The sight of him made my heart pound in my chest, and I felt tears clogging my throat. I didn't know if they were tears of regret or anger.

Ben kept his gaze on me, lifting his chin defiantly. I knew he could tell from my expression what I was thinking even though my cuffs protected me, preventing him from reading my mind. Then a shock went through me when I remembered he'd been able to send me visions from Ley Prison even though he'd been in a coma and behind ability-dampening walls. As a test to be sure the cuffs really were blocking him, I fiercely thought of the worst obscenity I could and called him it repeatedly in my mind. His expression never changed. I relaxed; at least this crappy version of Ben couldn't get in my head.

Ben reached for my hand, and I jerked away. He blew out an annoyed breath. "I'm not going to hurt you. I just wanted to make sure you're okay. And talk for awhile."

My mouth dropped open, aghast at his ridiculous words. "Am I okay? Oh sure, I'm just peachy. I mean aside from being locked up in a cell." I held up my wrists encased in metal cuffs, "Can't use my abilities. Can't see my friends and family." I yanked up my sleeve to expose bruising from the blood draw. "My blood being sucked out of me for a freaking experiment." I let out a choked laugh, saying recklessly, "And on top of all of it, the guy I was hoping might become my boyfriend is a traitor. So, no, I'm pretty much the opposite of okay, asshole." I spat out the last words as if I could burn him with them.

Ben didn't speak for a moment as he gazed at me before rubbing his hands over his face. He dropped them to his lap and blew out a breath. "Come on, Ollie. Maybe you'll get it when you know how Isaac plans to help supernormals." He gave me a pleading look, and I wondered why he cared if I accepted Isaac's plans.

I jumped when a tray was smacked down on the table across from me. Zander nudged aside two women who'd been watching the conversation between me and Ben avidly, and he slid onto the bench and took his fork in his hand. He scooped up mac 'n cheese and chewed while watching me and Ben.

Ben frowned. "Do you mind?"

Zander grinned, his expression sardonic, saying, "You tell me."

Ben rolled his eyes, "I'm trying to talk to my friend."

Rage bubbled up in my throat. "We're not friends anymore." I spat out the words.

"Oh, don't be so dramatic, Olivia." Emma walked up, sitting down on the other side of Ben. Even in my anger, I noticed he shifted away from her as if he didn't want to be any closer to her than he had to be.

All I could do was glare at her and say, "Shut up."

Emma smirked, resting her chin in her hand. "You know, Olivia, I just don't get it. All that power and you're just wasting it." Her expression was one of mock pity. "It's like you want to be a loser like the rest of the family."

I started to surge to my feet, wanting to leave, but Zander said, in a calming voice, "Hey, what's the fastest you've disintegrated something?" His gaze flicked to my cuffs and he said, now sounding uncomfortable, "If you don't mind talking about it, while…" He waved his fork at my wrists, dropping macaroni on the table.

"Um." I gaped at him for a moment before deciding to answer. "A metal hand weight in two seconds."

"Nice," Zander shook his head, "I'm not that fast but could do that in about eight seconds."

"That seems fast enough. There isn't much difference between two seconds and eight seconds when burning something." I propped my elbow on the table and leaned towards Zander, trying to shut out Emma and Ben. "Though, I honestly don't know a lot about disintegrators. I only just leveled up a few days ago."

"And you're already hitting two seconds?" Zander raised an eyebrow, looking impressed. "Strong work. You're damn powerful. Now I know why they were so psyched when they snagged you."

I felt a chill at his words. "As I told them, I'm not joining."

Emma spoke loudly, "Like you have the guts to be an Asher." I didn't have to look at her to know she was sneering at me.

Ignoring my cousin, I said to Zander, "I'm only agreeing to let them take my blood so they won't hurt Anna and Kevin." I narrowed my eyes at him. "Why do they need the serum? I mean, why do they want to make some of you people more powerful?" I didn't need Emma's derisive snort to know it was a lame question—who wouldn't want to be stronger? But I hoped Zander would answer the question in a way that gave me a clue about Scorched Earth, Mountain of Ash's big plan.

Zander shrugged, "They haven't told most of us why. I just know they need a bunch of us to have hotter flame."

"Why?" I poked my fork into the green beans on my plate. I noticed that Logan hadn't given me any mac 'n cheese.

Zander raised an eyebrow. "I would assume to destroy a bunch of things *very* quickly."

I made a face at his smart-ass remark. "But what? What do they want to burn?"

"Well, Olivia," Emma snapped her fingers to get my attention, "that information is on a need to know basis, and quite frankly you don't need to know. All you need to know is that Isaac, Wesley, and Gaea have everything under control. Lame asses like you aren't ready."

Ben frowned at her, "Emma, be nice." He turned to me, opening his mouth to speak but stopping abruptly as Isaac walked in.

The crowd around me went silent as if Isaac had used his ability to quiet them. Isaac strode to the front of the dining hall where a podium stood. I glanced over the adoring faces watching him. I decided that he had not used his ability on the crowd because he didn't need to make these people love him. They already did.

As Isaac greeted his followers, I scanned the faces at my table. Emma watched Isaac with an admiring expression, her lips slightly parted and her gaze locked on his face. I barely repressed a shiver.

Ben looked thoughtful, eyes narrowed, as he rubbed a thumb over his pointer finger in an absent gesture.

The most interesting reaction was Zander's. His face was perfectly blank. I might not have noticed the change if it weren't for the animation he'd shown while we were talking about our shared ability.

The crowd gave a collective gasp, and I tuned into Isaac's speech, "...there were no survivors of the brutal attack." He paused, waiting for the crowd to stop muttering. "This is another reason why normals can't be trusted to handle this world. Allowing an individual access to enough weaponry to kill because of a personal vendetta." He shook his head sorrowfully. "It's pitiful that they can't prevent these massacres."

I asked, "What happened?"

Emma shrugged as she answered carelessly, "Oh, another school shooting, I don't know where. A bunch of normals were killed, shooter killed himself. Same old story." She took a huge sip of water while watching my reaction.

I felt devastated at hearing there had been another school shooting. I tucked my hands in my lap to hide the fact I was gripping them together tightly.

Isaac was still pontificating, "If they can't manage to create laws to prevent these horrible incidents, then they don't deserve to govern themselves. They are like children who must be disciplined. They must face a reckoning."

"Stick'em in a camp!" Shouts rang out from around the room. "They need discipline!"

I knew the answer to Isaac's argument since I'd had it with Aunt Kate after a similar event. I'd passionately argued that, if normals couldn't solve their problems, shouldn't we help guide them? Or at least act as protectors since we couldn't be shot. Aunt Kate's response was that normals were not children, and that they needed to take responsibility for their problems and solutions. In the past, supernormals had stepped in to try to solve problems for normals, and every time it ended badly.

Clearly, the crowd hadn't had the advantage of Aunt Kate's level-headed discussion about collective responsibility. As Isaac listed more ways the normals were helpless to manage the word on their own, the crowd clapped and shouted suggestions.

"Give me a couple of normals—I know what to do it with them!"

"Kill them all!"

"Wipe the Earth of this scourge!"

"Pull the trigger on the final solution!"

I forced myself to look at the podium where Isaac stood smiling while the Ashers shouted out more and more inventive ways to subdue normals. His eyes met mine, and he looked menacing.

Isaac lifted one hand and the room went quiet. "Ashers, my people, we are so close to the day of the reckoning. Be patient, keep training, and our day will come!"

Ben drew a sharp breath, distracting me from Isaac. I looked at him, surprised when he lowered his head, giving me a brief glimpse of his distressed face. Confused by Ben's reaction, I kept a discreet eye on him. He kept his head down and his hands gripped each other under the table so tightly that they shook. Something had triggered a strong reaction in him, but I couldn't figure out what it could be. I assumed he'd heard Isaac's rants before; the actions of the Ashers in the dining hall felt like a common occurrence. And Ben had been calm until Isaac's last words. No one else noticed Ben's behavior because everyone's attention was on Isaac.

Finally, Isaac ended his speech with a resounding shout of, "Mountain of Ash united!", and I shuddered when the massed Ashers roared back, "As one!"

Thankfully, the end of Isaac's speech signaled the end of dinner. Ben drew in a deep breath and sat up, though he didn't look in Isaac's direction. Instead, he appeared as confident as he'd been when I'd arrived at the table, but because I was looking, I saw signs of stress around his eyes.

When Logan came over to escort me back to my cell, Ben said, "I can take her." Logan hesitated a moment before shrugging and walking away.

Zander stood up when Ben did. "I'll join you."

"No," Ben spoke firmly. "I can take her alone." He added sarcastically, "Unless you're worried I'll run off with her. You don't think my pledge to Isaac is good, do you?"

Zander raised his hands. "We're good here. Just offering to help out." He gave me an indecipherable nod before wandering over to talk to his brother.

Emma said, "Does that mean I can't join you?" with a simpering smile at Ben. I almost threw up.

He said kindly, "For now."

Emma huffed and stomped away with several of Ben's fan club following.

I was relieved to see Isaac was deep in conversation with Wesley and Black Gaea. None of them looked our way as Ben guided me out of the dining hall.

We walked along in silence until we got to my cell, where a guard opened the door. Ben gave the woman a long stare, and she nodded as if responding to a statement. I realized he'd used his ability to tell her something. When he followed me inside, I couldn't repress a shiver as the door closed behind him.

I spun around to face him, crossing my arms to hide my trembling hands. I stared at him fiercely through narrowed eyes. "Go away. I don't want to hear about how Mountain of Ash is going to save the world from normals and put supernormals out in the open. Not after seeing Isaac feed them all that propaganda, the brainwashing, the ridiculous one-sided view of normals. Not after hearing all the awful things they just said about what they want to do to normals. It was sick and disgusting." My voice shook with rage and fear. "How can you side with them?"

Ben didn't look at me, staring at the ground during my outburst. When I stopped talking, breathing in deep gasps, he said, so quietly I almost missed his words, "You're right."

I gaped at him, my rant derailed by his admission. He looked me in the eye, "Yes, they aren't good people, and they don't have the best view of normals." He reached for my hands, and numbly I let him take them. "But Ollie, I don't know what to do. As I saw it a few days ago, my options are to join the Ashers, and maybe try to soften their approach, or go back to the rest of the supernormal world where they'll just put me back in prison, back in a coma. And I really don't want to be in a coma for the rest of my life. I want a chance to—" He swallowed hard. "But now, at dinner just now, I saw what Isaac really wants to do, and it's—"

The door swung open. Isaac smiled benignly at us, but I saw tension around his eyes. "Come on, Ben. We have work to do."

Ben jerked, letting go of my hands as if my skin burned him, "Yes sir."

Chapter 13

After Ben left with Isaac, I sat down on my bed, deep in thought. What had Ben started to say before Isaac interrupted? It sounded like he was going to tell me about Scorched Earth, Mountain of Ash's big plan, the one that was coming soon if the countdown in the training hangar was any indication. And, based on his admission that I was right about how evil Mountain of Ash was, I didn't believe Ben was all that pumped about the plan.

I ran a finger over one of the cuffs on my wrist, wishing for the first time since I'd seen Ben in my cell and he confessed to joining Mountain of Ash that he could communicate mentally through the ability-blocking binds.

I ran my hands through my filthy hair, flattening the greasy strands against my head. My stomach rumbled, reminding me I hadn't eaten much in the dining hall. I'd been too upset by the normal-bashing and by the conversation with Ben. I sighed and lay back on the hard bed, lacing my hands behind my head as I gazed at the ceiling.

I didn't realize I'd fallen asleep until the sound of my door opening woke me. I sat up, feeling blurry from being pulled out of deep sleep. I muttered as my latest visitor entered, "Why is there even a lock on the stupid door if you guys keep coming in and out so often?"

Wesley smiled at me, "Good morning sunshine! If you joined us, there wouldn't be any reason to keep you here." He sighed, holding up a hand to quiet my protests, "Yes, I know, but I keep hoping. Anyway, that's a matter for another time."

I was too worn out to respond to his idiotic greeting, so I just stared back at him from my spot on the bed.

His smile faded when I didn't reply or move. "Come on, Olivia. Perk up a little. You're helping a good cause." He held out his hand. "I've come to give you a demonstration of what supernormals can do when allowed to thrive."

I turned away, sick of being dragged out of my cell at the whim of Ashers.

Wesley gave an annoyed humph, which I hoped meant he was leaving, but a moment later I was a foot in the air, my arms and legs flailing, kicking the edge of the bed until I floated to stop in front of Wesley's hand.

Clearly Wesley had the same ability as Aunt Kate, but his power was much stronger than her limit of five pounds. And, like Isaac, Wesley didn't honor the rules of polite supernormal society — it was very rude to use your powers on someone without asking. The only permissible exception I knew of was Uncle Alex using his empathic abilities to heal people.

Wesley made a lowering gesture, and I dropped to the floor with a grunt. I stumbled to my feet, bracing against the wall to catch my breath.

"Seriously?" I asked, unable to summon the energy to feel outraged but wanting to register at least some protest at being manhandled.

"Young lady, I'm offering you a chance to participate in history." Wesley opened the door wider. When I continued to stand still, he raised his hand again, spreading his fingers wide. I felt a tug in my stomach forcing me out the door.

"Okay, okay, I'll go," I spoke listlessly. "Just stop using your powers on me. Don't you know it's rude?" I didn't expect an answer, but when I didn't get one, a flash of indignation went through me.

Wesley led me up the stairs where I expected to return to the lab of twisted mind trips. Instead, he kept going until we stood outside. It was a respite to be out in the sunshine and fresh air, until I realized Wesley was leading me to the hangar. He slowed his gait to match my forced normal pace, ambling along with his hands in his pockets as if we were out for a casual walk. He'd regained his cheerful demeanor, chatting incessantly about how proud he was to be a part of a grand enterprise such as Mountain of Ash.

"Before I joined Isaac's grand endeavor, I was so disillusioned with life." He sighed dramatically. "I thought, what was the point of having all this power when I was hamstrung by the rules of noninterference." He shook his head sadly. "It was tragic to sit back and watch normals make such a mess of the world when they clearly need our guidance to help them. It was so tempting to give them a little help here and there." He gave me a sheepish smile that didn't hide his pride as he said. "Lighten a load for someone." He waved a hand, lifting me over a rock in my path.

"Stop it!" Annoyance was rapidly overwhelming my former lethargy.

Wesley gave me a mischievous grin as he lowered me back the ground. He kept talking as if I was a willing audience. "And of course, nudge a few normals out of the way of moving vehicles, or into the way."

I stared at him. Had he just nonchalantly confessed to killing people by using his ability to push people into the path of moving vehicles? "You've killed people?" I didn't know why I was surprised. Maybe it was the way he told me about it like I was certain to understand.

Wesley said, "Oh no, not *good* normals, just ones who were bad. If I saw someone steal and try to get away, I might make sure they didn't survive." He shrugged. "It was a public service, really, though no one knew about it, of course. Just one of my little pleasures."

"But you killed people without due process. Maybe there was a reason they stole. Were other innocent people involved in these accidents?"

Wesley rolled his eyes. "Why do you insist on protecting the normals?" He gave frustrated sigh. "As I was saying, I was so depressed." He lifted a finger as his face lit up "But then about ten years ago, I met Isaac! He was as frustrated as I was, but he had a plan. He knew how to save us all from the fiasco the normals were making of our world. It was so simple, so obvious."

He stopped talking, and I waited for a moment but when it was clear he was done yakking, I asked, "What is the plan?"

Wesley shook his finger at me, "No, no, you're not ready. You'll never understand until you stop believing normals need protection."

I frowned at him, "Then why are you taking me to the hangar?"

"Because you deserve to see how mighty unfettered supernormals can be." Wesley walked towards the hangar. For a moment I stood still, my eyes skimming my surroundings. Now that my stupor had been burned away by irritation, I realized I should take advantage of my time outside to scope out the area better than I had during our failed escape attempt.

Ranch land spread out around me as far as I could see. Fences crisscrossed the land, with the occasional herds of cattle milling about. Dirt roads ran along the fences, with gates interspaced at regular intervals. It looked like any other ranch in Eastern Oregon. And I couldn't see any way to escape, especially in my debilitated state. If I tried to run, any of the numerous Mountain of Ash folks could catch me as effortlessly as going on a light jog.

I felt a tug on my shirt by an invisible force. "Come along, Olivia," Wesley called out from where he waited in front of the hangar.

I sighed and walked down to join him, dreading the promised demonstration because it probably meant I'd see several Ashers.

Today the airplane sized hangar doors were open. I saw people inside training, and a wave of homesickness hit me amid my trepidation. I longed to be back in Portland, in my warehouse, training with my cousins.

Wesley guided me into the wide-open space, past roped off areas where people were fighting.

I saw a firestarter dodging water from a water weaver in one area. Nearby, a woman sped around the roped off square while another woman stood, hands tucked into her pockets while she tossed floating objects, attempting to hit the other woman.

The countdown clock loomed over the training area, down to 5 days, 10 hours. I supposed I should be glad my scratches on the cell wall were accurate, but depression hit me when I saw for sure I'd been a prisoner for five days.

After the silence and solitude of my cell, the noise was deafening, and all the activity was as overwhelming as the clamor in the dining hall had been last night. I took several deep breaths, calling on my own training with Uncle Alex to find calm in chaos. I was almost there when a huge kettlebell came hurling through the air at my face. I staggered back, trying to get out of the way, but my constrained muscles didn't obey me as quickly as I was accustomed. I panicked, falling over a rope and cowering with my arms flung out as if I could catch the weight.

A body darted in front of me, catching the kettlebell with one hand and sliding into a graceful stop a few feet away. I gaped at my rescuer, blinking for a moment before I realized it was Zander.

"Thanks," I managed to say, as I tried to breathe again.

Zander gave me a short nod before twisting to glare at a woman standing several feet away. "Cassie, not cool." He threw the kettlebell back to her, and she caught it effortlessly, letting her arm swing it a few times very casually before she looked away under the weight of Zander's stare.

The crowd around me laughed at my reaction, making jabs about weaklings, sayings things like, "She's so twitchy." My face flushed from embarrassment, and I straightened, trying to pretend I hadn't recoiled in fear. I looked at the woman, wondering if she was the Cassie who recruited Emma into Mountain of Ash. She saw my stare and curled her lip at me.

Wesley tsk-ed, saying, "High spirits, high spirits." He took my arm. "Come on, I must apologize for some of my compadres." He steered me towards the huge sandbox where I'd shown my skills the last time I'd been in the hangar. "I'm sorry to tell you the Brighthalls aren't very popular. Except for Emma, of course."

As if his words were a summons, we came face to face with Emma. She stood in the last training area before the sandbox, leaning against the ropes and observing me with a brooding expression.

My stomach jumped when I saw Ben stretching beside Emma. He noticed me. "Hi, Olivia." He spoke in a very stiff and formal voice. I tried to catch his eye to let him know I was still willing to hear whatever he'd been about to tell me in my cell last night, but his gaze seemed to slide past mine. He stood up and leaned next to Emma.

Stung and confused by Ben's cold greeting, I turned away. "What did you want to show me?" I asked Wesley, ready to see it and leave as soon as possible

He smiled. "Oh, you'll be impressed." He clapped his hands, and the activity in the hangar hushed. Only the sound of equipment being set down broke the quiet until all was silent. I stared back the way we'd come at the rows of roped off training squares. Everyone stood at attention, facing me and Wesley.

I hid the shiver that went down my spine at how quick they were to obey, but I couldn't hide my start when Wesley clapped again, "Firestarters and enhancers, front and center." His voice no longer sounded like a relaxed gentleman about town; now he spoke with the authority and confidence of knowing his commands would be fulfilled quickly.

Several people stepped forward until about ten of them were lined up in front of the sand. I saw Zander among them standing next to Trent, the creepy guy who'd helped them take my blood a few days ago.

Several men and women gathered behind the line of ten firestarters. I wondered if there were more firestarters waiting their turn, but the space was large enough that they could have all lined up around the sand pit, so it didn't make sense for them to hang back.

I shifted from foot to foot, my chest tight with anxiety. It looked like the firestarters were lined up to start burning the objects scattered around the sand. Many of the objects I'd seen a few days ago were gone, I assumed destroyed during training, but new ones littered the sands. I couldn't figure out why Wesley would be excited for me to watch the firestarters training since I'd been forced to disintegrate objects there a few days ago.

"Gaea, if you would?"

I jerked around, unaware Black Gaea was standing behind us. When had she arrived? She ignored me as she walked over to a monitor set up near the sandbox.

The crowd was silent with an air of anticipation. I caught Emma smirking at me.

A crashing noise from high up in the rafters caused me look up so quickly I wrenched my neck. Several large cubes, balls, and stakes were falling from the rafters. I forced myself not to duck, standing as still as everyone else, but it was hard as the whooshing sound of falling objects drew closer.

Zander and the rest of the people in his line all raised their right hands in unison. Wesley shouted, "Now!" And they all began shoot streams of fire at the objects. Ashes floated down around us as the objects disintegrated in the air.

I stared at the line of people, all disintegrators like me. Even though they were working for the bad guys, I couldn't help feeling a fellowship with them as they unleashed destruction around us.

Not everyone in the line was a disintegrator. I noticed several of the objects fell into the sand still flaming. In fact, I narrowed my eyes in consideration; only Zander and about two others were able to turn their targets to ash in mid-air. And I was sure I could have outmatched any of them. Zander was the only one who seemed close to my strength. Well, when I wasn't cuffed, at least.

After a moment, no more objects fell from the ceiling, and there was a silence as the firestarters lowered their hands.

Wesley said, "Now, stronger."

Puzzled by his command since I'd been told the latest attempt at the enhancement serum wasn't ready for testing, I watched as the second line of people stepped up behind the firestarters I'd pegged as not strong enough to be disintegrators. Each person in the second line put a hand on the shoulder of the weaker firestarters.

Wesley commanded, "Get ready." He raised his hand and dropped it. Black Gaea pressed a key on the computer and more objects fell from the ceiling.

Once again, the firestarters raised their hands and began firing at the objects. As I watched, almost all the objects disintegrated in the air. A curtain of ash drifted onto the sand.

My head felt light with memory. I'd seen this same sudden increase in abilities in a Ben-sent vision when Emma used her time stopping ability to blow up a planetarium in Salt Lake City. One of Emma's fellow escapees, Joshua Grenon, had given her a huge power boost to stop time long enough to launch a powerful explosive that blew up Clark Planetarium. And sure enough, as I scanned the line of enhancers, there he was in the line. I'd recognize his uneven eyes, flabby lips, and deep scars anywhere.

He was worse in real life than he was in the visions. In real life, his eyes, lips, and scars were accompanied by the stench of body odor, making me wonder if he'd bothered showering in the week since the prison break. Trying not to gag, though why I'd worry about offending such an offensive person was unclear to me, I took several wide steps away from him. He watched my reaction with a derisive smile, as if he was used to repulsion and maybe even enjoyed it.

So, not all the firestarters were powerful enough to disintegrate objects. This explained why Isaac wanted to figure out how to increase their strength. If what I was seeing was accurate, only two or three firestarters were strong enough on their own. I wondered if the line of enhancers represented all of the enhancers in Mountain of Ash. And, as I scanned the crowd of Ashers watching the demonstration, I wondered if there were even more firestarters among them who would reap the benefits of my blood.

The real question was: Why did they needed so many disintegrators at all? The name of the plan, Scorched Earth, sounded even more ominous as I began to get hints of the pieces. I chewed on the inside of the my lip, wishing

Ben had found a way to tell me about Isaac's plan last night.

After several minutes of mayhem, all the objects had been destroyed. Smoke filled the air, giving the scene an eerie, otherworldly atmosphere.

"What is the purpose of this?" Isaac strode into the room, the smoke parting before him as if it too was under his command. People shuffled out of the way, brows furrowing with worry when they caught sight of his livid expression.

Even Wesley looked apprehensive, spreading his hands wide in a conciliatory greeting, "Isaac, we were just showing Olivia what a supernormal can do with—"

"Wesley, I know you believe you can persuade anyone that our way is the true path." Isaac snapped the words out without taking his eyes off me. "But Oliva is a Brighthall." His disdain made my family name an expletive. "They've always been too holier-than-thou to accept the truth that supernormals are superior and need to come out of hiding. And they always will be."

No one spoke as Isaac grabbed my arm and dragged me out of the warehouse. I glanced back to see Wesley fidgeting and Emma scowling while everyone around them appeared to be very deliberately going back to training as if nothing had happened.

Ben had already turned back to weight lifting as if he'd not been interrupted.

The only other person who watched me go was Zander. His expression was hard to see in the dim light, but I thought he looked worried.

I stumbled. Isaac was pulling me along quickly without regard to my dampened abilities.

"Why do you hate my family so much?" I was sick of him tossing veiled insults at the Brighthalls as if we were some sort of pariah lineage. "They didn't even know who you were when Godfrey mentioned you," I managed to speak even though I was breathless from walking so fast.

Isaac's expression changed to puzzlement. "Godfrey?"

"Godfrey, the lymph monster you sent after us." I should have known Isaac wouldn't know the name of the lymph monster he sent to attack us in Portland. Not after the way he'd treated the monsters down in the monster library.

My memory of fighting Godfrey in the Hawthorne theater had been overshadowed by the events immediately following — Jack discovering my supernormal identity, Uncle Dan going off the rails, and Ben's capture by Mountain of Ash. Despite all those events, I distinctly remembered Aunt Kate's puzzled reaction when Godfrey taunted us with the identity of the person who sent it to Portland.

Isaac's expression changed to annoyance, "Oh, that creature." He waved his other hand in dismissal. "Never mind it, it wasn't in possession of all the facts."

"What do you mean?" I felt curiosity running through my fear. "What facts?"

He didn't answer as we drew closer to the compound. I wondered if he was taking me back to my cell or to the lab. Of the two, the cell was better, but I didn't want to go to either place. It was so good to be in the fresh air.

I tried to resist Isaac's drag on my arm, digging my feet into the dirt. I only succeeded in slowing down Isaac's momentum for a moment. "Stop it," I said. "I can walk. You don't have be such a jerk." I yanked my arm, trying pull away. "If this is how you acted around my family, of course they don't like you!" I didn't know if my family liked him or not. I didn't know if they really knew him, but I wanted to provoke a reaction to see if I could get him to tell me.

He stopped walking, holding my hand in his with a vise-like grip. I bumped into him but quickly stepped back, getting as much distance from him as I could.

"Ah, now you remind me of your uncle. Daniel Brighthall is always so certain he's better than everyone. Always *so* focused on improving his skills and ready to tell you what's wrong with your own skills." Isaac's eyes seemed to glitter with anger or sorrow, I couldn't decide which emotion.

I brushed aside the jab at Uncle Dan, briefly thinking it was true but resenting the accusations when Isaac said them. "How do you know Uncle Dan?"

Isaac glared at me with so much hate I cringed inside while tensing up, ready to fight back as best I could if he should attack me. After a moment that felt like hours, he turned away, hauling me along, only saying, "I met your uncles, aunt, and mother when I was twelve years old at summer camp." He didn't react to my startled gasp.

"That's where Daniel Brighthall ruined my life and helped me discover my ultimate purpose."

Chapter 14

"Come on class." Mrs. Baker, my first-grade teacher, stood up at the front of the school bus as it came to a stop near the Lan Su Chinese Garden in downtown Portland. The flags in front of the garden fluttered in the light early spring breeze as clouds chased each other through the sky, alternating overcast and sunny skies.

"Olivia, let's go." Mom smiled at me, resting her hand on my shoulder to guide me into the line of students exiting the school bus.

I'd been so excited when she volunteered to be one of the parent chaperons for my first-grade field trip to the gardens. I knew she usually spent the days I was in school training and handling other work with her sister and brothers, so it was a treat for her to spend the day with me. I was too young to hone my supernormal abilities, unlike my cousin Lange who already got to do training sessions with Uncle Dan when that branch of the family visited from San Francisco. My best friend and cousin, Emma, begged her dad to let us start drilling now, but he stood firm on waiting.

Mom looked pretty in what she called street clothes, which as far as I could tell meant she dressed like all the other mothers instead of in her usual training gear. She wore jeans, a light green V-neck sweater, and the always necessary in Portland rain coat. As we descended the steps from the bus to the street, the wind ruffled her short brown hair around her strong, tanned face.

Oh, this is particularly cruel, the thought wafted through my mind. I shook my head, confused.

Mrs. Baker went to the office to check in and returned with a small Chinese woman by her side. The woman greeted us and began telling us about the gardens as she led thirty kids through the ornate gates.

Mom took charge of the tail end of the line of children. I stayed near the back as well, wanting to be near my mother.

Wanting to savor every moment. I shook my head again, squeezing my eyes closed, then opening them, feeling dizzy with a sense of being out of place. *This is another flashback.* Dread curdled in my stomach. *A flashback with my mother in it. I know this day. It was the worst day.*

"Olivia, pay attention." Mom took my hand, bringing my mind back from listening to the weird voice in my head.

I grinned at her, squeezing her hand. "I'm glad you're here."

"Me too, sweetheart."

I gave her hand another squeeze before letting go and skipping ahead to walk beside my friend Isabella.

When the last child entered the garden, I glanced back to see Mom still at the entrance, her head tilted up as she scanned the street. Her body was taut, attentive, and my heart sank when she pulled out her phone. I fretted, worried she would need to leave for some supernormal related business.

However, after typing quickly, she pocketed the phone and turned to come into the garden. She caught my anxious gaze and came over to take my hand.

"I thought you might leave." I spoke softly, ever aware of hiding our identities.

"Not this time, kiddo," Mom smiled down at me. "I don't think there's anything to worry about, but I asked your Uncle Dan to check on something just in case."

We caught up to the rest of the class where the tour guide was explaining the significance of a statue.

I shifted from foot to foot, restless. I kept sneaking glances at Mom who peeked at her phone every so often. She also sent frequent glances back at the entranceway of the garden. I looked down at the flagstone path, kicking at the grass growing between the stones. As usual, her attention was elsewhere, even though she'd told me she was excited about my field trip. No matter what she promised, Mom was always thinking about supernormal stuff.

The ground shook, and for a moment I thought a large truck was going by until Mom shouted, "Get the kids under cover!" at Mrs. Baker who stared back in confusion at Mom's assumption of authority. "Olivia, stay with your classmates!"

"Mom!" I shouted after her as she dashed out the entrance, but my words were lost in the boom of an explosion. Mrs. Baker gasped and began herding my fellow students in the direction the tour guide was frantically waving. I wavered; I knew I should follow my classmates, but I urgently wanted to run after Mom.

Another boom rocked the ground, and I gave in to what I wanted. When I ran out of the garden into the street, I expected to see chaos everywhere, but it wasn't as crazy as I'd expected. There was a crowd gathered two blocks away in the direction of the river. Deciding that was where the action was, I ran down the street as quickly as my short legs would take me.

Stop it, stop it, I can't watch this again, I slowed down, bewildered by the voice that seemed to be mine crying out in the depths of my head. Then I remembered again in an agonizing burst—this was an Isaac-induced flashback. I was watching my past unfold again, and I should have expected unpleasant twists in the already awful memory.

Gunfire followed by shouting sounded from behind a squat building a few blocks away.

I hesitated. What was the point of subjecting myself to the replay? I tried to turn around and run down a different street, but the scene froze around me.

Olivia, behave. Isaac's voice rang through my mind. I thought I heard fingers snap, and I was back in the path I'd taken on that fateful day.

I tried to deviate again, but he forced me to keep following the sequence of events. I fought him, struggling to wake up, but I couldn't. As the replay continued, I kept forgetting then remembering it was a revision of past events.

I followed the sound of the explosion to find people standing behind a barrier. Using my small size to my advantage, I squeezed in between the bodies to come up against the barricade. About a half a block away, cops surrounded the squat, stone building. The building was an old-fashioned style with wide steps leading up to fancy doors. I thought it might be government building; I remembered my grandfather going there with paperwork or something.

My sensitive ears picked up the chatter on the police radios—the building had been swarmed by armed and masked attackers, there were ten hostages, no demands had been made yet. The police were mystified as to how the attackers had gotten into the building. The people who escaped claimed they'd appeared in the lobby out of nowhere.

A chill went through me. That's why Mom was here. The attackers might be supernormals like us. Well, not exactly like us; we didn't storm buildings and take hostages.

I stood on tiptoe, looking for Mom. I spotted her standing near the steps. None of the normals would be able to see her through the supernormal glamour, but I could tell she was peering up at the windows. I wondered if she could see the bad guys through the windows or hear them. She circled around the side, out of my sight.

I don't want to watch this again! My teenage voice shouted in my head, startling the six-year-old version of me who kept forgetting this had all already happened. However, I was stuck in the replay until Isaac got what he wanted.

Commotion near the steps recalled my attention to the police. Someone was shouting that the bad guys were rigging up bombs all around the inside. They still hadn't issued any demands and they weren't answering calls from the negotiators.

Teenage me was impressed that child me recalled so much from the scene. Isaac was mining every detail, making it all so much harder to live through again.

The next part was clearly etched in my memories. I'd replayed it on my own numerous times in the years since. I watched as Mom came running back around the building, darting up the steps.

I couldn't stop what happened next, even though I'd rewritten it so many times in my dreams.

"Mom!" I ducked under the barricade, running as quickly as a six-year-old supernormal could. I reached the steps before any of the normals reacted. My glamour was barely enough to help me pass unnoticed.

Mom's eyes widened. "Olivia, no, get back!" She frantically waved at me to leave.

My teenage self begged my kid self to grab Mom and make her leave, but my kid self followed the narrative by turning and running away.

A rumble under my feet stopped me. Dread tightened my throat as I turned to look behind me.

The stone building shook as blast after blast went off inside. I didn't see Mom for a moment, but then I spotted her framed in the doorway at the top of wide steps. Flames flared around her as the building exploded.

I froze with shock, waiting for Mom to walk clear of the rubble, but she didn't. Instead, a man wearing a dapper suit and neatly trimmed hair strolled out, brushing dust off his shoulders. He looked around and saw me. With a smile, he came over. "You know, if you hadn't yelled after your mother, she would still be alive. You made her hesitate just long enough to get caught in the blast."

Six-year-old me wondered who the man was, and teenage me muttered, *That's Isaac, he's the worst bad guy.*

In the background, Uncle Dan ran in from the direction of the Steel Bridge, arms outstretched as if he could reach in and yank Mom to safety. I wanted to watch Uncle Dan to see if he could find Mom, but Isaac shifted, blocking my view. "You killed your mother because you're selfish and weak. Isn't that true?"

I clenched my fists at my sides, glaring at him, wishing my child-strength abilities were stronger. Wishing I had my significant ability and that it was the ability to turn back time. It was a foolish wish for several reasons—six years was too young to manifest my significant ability and, anyway, the ability to turn back time didn't exist. The best I could do right now was to try to push past Isaac. "Let me go!" I shouted when he grabbed my arm.

"Olivia, you can't help her now. You will only be in the way of your family." He held my arm so tightly it hurt.

"Let go of me," I yelled, struggling to pull away, but he tightened his grip even more.

"Do you think you can fight me?" He taunted me, lifting me off the ground.

I kicked my feet at him, but I couldn't reach him. He laughed, white teeth flashing in the gloomy rain. "Come on, Olivia, you can do better than that." He swung me around, my feet flailing in the air, until I was facing the blasted building. Emergency personnel milled around the rubble. Over to one side, I saw Uncle Dan talking frantically on his phone, gesturing at the last spot I'd seen Mom. Tears glistened on his cheeks, and he wiped them away as he shook his head at whatever the person on the other end was saying.

The sight of my stern, fierce uncle crying punched through my gut like a lance. If he was sad, then Mom was really gone. "No, no, no." I twisted in the air, trying break the awful man's grip.

"Yes, she's really gone. And there's nothing you can do about it except know that you're to blame. If she didn't have to be a mother and do the silly things a mother must do to appease you, then she wouldn't have been here without backup." I stared at him, crying, hanging limply in his grip. "She wouldn't have been so worried about keeping you safe and stopping the attack that she would have waited for your uncle before going inside." His voice pounded against my ears, driving the words into my brain relentlessly. "She would still be alive, if it weren't for you."

I screamed, "Shut up!" as his accusation exploded in my head. I felt my body heat up from my core, the spark building and building until it burst out of my entire body. I was at the center of a supernova of fire.

As the flames swirled around me, so did complete awareness once again. I was in another flashback, courtesy of Isaac. Only this time he was in it with me, holding me, tormenting me. I knew this was a flashback because he was still holding me up in the air despite the fire that should have burned him.

I wasn't six going on seven anymore, with childhood weak abilities. I was fourteen, strong, trained by Uncle Dan, fully manifested with my significant ability. I couldn't change the past, but I could fight for a better present.

I gave a fierce grin, tucking my legs up, then kicking them out together, feet punching into Isaac's side, giving me the leverage to shove out of his grip. He grunted and staggered back in a most satisfying manner. I landed firmly on my feet, focusing my flames into my hands. I was no longer in my six-year-old body, somehow, I'd transformed into my current body as I'd fallen.

Eyes on the blaze, Isaac spoke to the air, "Peter, did you get the blood drawn?"

I didn't hear the answer, but it must have been yes because his next words were, "Olivia, it's been fun, but playtime must end now."

I didn't waste time arguing. Instead, I aimed a thick stream of fire at his head. Just as the stream reached his face, I was yanked out of the flashback.

I screamed in frustration, strapped into the damn chair, flames all over my body. With a flash of hope, I saw that the straps were slowly disintegrating. My abilities were suddenly strong enough to erode the supernormal flame-resistant material. I called on my power, demanding more heat as a frantic voice shouted out, "She's about to get free! Stop her!"

I fought harder as mist sprayed down more forcefully than ever before. I called for even more heat, more than I'd ever pulled. Sweat poured down my face. My hair clung to my head in sweat-soaked clumps. I coughed as I breathed in the mist settling over my body.

One of the straps gave way, dissolving under my onslaught, just as the effects of the drug in the mist hit me. My fire trickled down to nothing, and I fell back in the chair, unable to hold back my exhausted tears.

I didn't resist when Peter and Paul cuffed me. When they finished and removed the remaining strap, Paul looked at me, "Impressive. We'll have to figure out how to make the material more resistant to your flame." I was too dejected to care that this was the first time one of the twins had spoken directly to me.

Someone shifted near the door, pulling my attention to meet Ben's gaze where he stood with Isaac. A flash of rage surged through me at the sight of my former friend watching me be tortured. "Oh, hello." I let my anger fill my voice; it was my only way to express how I felt. "Come to learn from your new master? Come to be educated in the ways of mind torture?"

Ben blinked at me, his expression blank. He opened his mouth to answer, but Isaac said, "Don't let her bait you into thinking you must explain yourself." He moved to stand between me and Ben. "It's best to think of her as a subject, a means to an end."

Ben spoke dully, "Of course, you're right. Don't let emotion get in the way." His gaze lingered on me uncertainly before he left the room.

I was undone by everything—the flashback, seeing Mom so alive then reliving her death, Isaac's cruelty echoing my own guilt, along with almost getting free — it was all too much to handle. I lay listlessly in the chair, hardly aware as the twin doctors spoke in excited tones with Isaac, barely registering the news that they both seemed certain this flashback event had charged up my blood enough to make the serum.

Isaac leaned over me, and I gazed back, digging up enough energy to put the hate I was feeling into my glare. He said, regretfully, "I am sorry it had to come to that." He touched my cheek with affection as I cringed back as far as I could into the cushion. "You are magnificent." He withdrew his touch, and I sagged in relief. "It's a shame you're not on our side, but at least I can keep you from benefiting the Brighthalls anymore."

I gaped at him. Did he mean what I thought he meant? Before I could sputter out the question, he turned away, issuing orders to have me returned to my cell while they prepared and tested the latest serum.

Zander was waiting outside when the guards led me out of the lab. He didn't say anything as he escorted me down the hallway. I ached all over. My body and soul felt like I was a million years old as I hobbled along. I didn't care; nothing mattered. I'd had what was probably my best chance to escape, and I'd failed. And I was pretty sure Isaac had my execution scheduled if the serum worked as he expected.

Chapter 15

After sleeping for a few hours, I felt a little better physically, but I was still wrecked mentally. I spent the next several hours pacing around my cell like a trapped animal while worrying about the results of the latest serum. When lunch was shoved by the usual means through the stupid supernormally created hole in the door, I ate it mechanically, barely tasting the chicken pot pie, while I brooded about Kevin and Anna's fate if — when — Isaac ordered my execution. He wouldn't need either one of them for leverage if I was gone.

Fear-inspired nervous energy drove me to run through some shadow boxing drills Uncle Dan had taught me in what felt like the distant past. I couldn't believe it had only been six days since I'd been training in the warehouse with my family. I missed them, even Uncle Dan a little bit. His outbursts seemed so tame compared to the anguish Isaac put me through. At least I knew Uncle Dan wasn't evil, though I wasn't quite able to forgive him for attacking me when he found out I'd been filmed running super-fast.

I was running through a series of balance exercises designed to improve focus when Zander opened the door to my cell. "Hey." He stood there, framed by the gray walls, his blue eyes watching me with the same thoughtful expression he usually wore when talking to me.

I deliberately finished the pose before saying, "What do you want?"

"Isaac is pretty psyched about your results in the last flashback," Zander said as he came further into my cell. "He has decreed you should get a special treat." His tone was flat, but I thought I caught a hint of derision. Was it directed at me or at Isaac?

I automatically went into a steady, balanced stance, full of trepidation at whatever Isaac might consider a treat. Zander caught my fear. "It's not a trick, I promise. You're not going to be hurt." He stood up and held out his hand. "Come on." He kept his hand out, waiting for me.

I hesitated — as nice as it would be to get out my cell for something other than a revisionist flashback or one of Wesley's lessons, I knew nothing truly good waited for me out there.

Zander sighed, "Okay, the nice part of it is you'll get to see Kevin."

Kevin! No one had told me anything about him for days even though I'd asked several times. I felt a reluctant smile tug at the corners of my mouth. Zander was right; the chance to see Kevin was a treat.

I took Zander by the hand, aware it had been too long since I'd been touched by another person without coercion. His skin was rough and very warm in mine.

"What's the not so nice part?" I asked.

Zander led me from my cell, letting go when we got the stairs so I could go in front of him. "Black Gaea has returned from her mission." At my curious look, he said, "Isaac sent her out on a special mission for something to help with Scorched Earth. And she's on her way back with the package."

"The package?" I repeated.

"You'll see." Zander's expression was closed off, so I didn't push for more information.

There were guards at the doors, but no one stopped us as Zander directed me outside. I breathed in the fresh air. Even though I'd been outside recently, I still missed the breeze. I didn't think the outdoor settings in the various flashbacks counted. I tipped my face to the sun, feeling the wind ruffle my hair. Ignoring the curious stares of people scattered around the square, I followed Zander.

"Where is Kevin?" I had no idea where he'd been while I was undergoing flashbacks and blood draws. "Where are we going?"

Instead of answering my question, Zander kept going until we were past the square of main buildings and walking towards a set of long, low buildings tucked away near a large hill in the distance. I saw other people heading in the same direction, but we were well away from anyone.

We were alone for several minutes when Zander spoke up. "You and Kevin need to take your normal and get out."

"Huh?" I said hoarsely, astonished by his words. I swallowed and managed to say, "What, how? Um, why now?" Then I felt stupid for asking why now when I knew the answer to that question already. He was only confirming my fears about Isaac's plan for me.

Zander continued to scan the area, I assumed to make sure we were alone. "I'm trying to figure out the how, but since I'm guessing you won't leave without your friend, Anna, that makes it harder." He gave me a querying look, sighing a bit at my emphatic nod. "As to the why, you know that if this serum works, Isaac plans to execute you."

I shuddered at hearing my fears confirmed so bluntly, but I nodded wordlessly. I noticed he'd said Anna's name. He was the first Asher to do so.

"I'm not going to let that happen, because..." He grimaced. "Well, I have my reasons."

"No." I stopped walking, crossing my arms and scowling at him. "I need to know why. Why would you help us escape? In fact, why are you being nice to me at all?" I felt fear and anger swirling through the emotional dullness in my head. "You're not some ploy to convince me Mountain of Ash isn't all bad, are you? Maybe show me the softer side of the big evil?" I didn't add my chief dread: *Are you trying to trick me into believing you'll help me escape?*

Zander gaped at me for a moment, finally closing his mouth with a slight grin. "Softer side?"

"Whatever. My point is you're the bad guy, and I don't know if I can trust you."

Zander looked down at his feet, no longer grinning as he kicked at the dirt. "Remember how Logan and I had to join Mountain of Ash when our parents did?" When I nodded my head, he shoved his hands in the pockets of his tan jacket. "It's not like I had a choice, but it seemed okay here, at first. They took care of us, trained us, and stuff." He started walking slowly so I could easily keep up. "Before we joined, when we were little, my family tried to integrate with the normals."

I murmured with surprise. Mixing with normals was unusual. My family was considered eccentric at best because, not only did we spend time with normals, but we often married them.

Zander slanted his gaze at me. "Yeah, well, my mom and your aunt were roommates in college. A normal college." Aunt Kate had gone to Stanford, but I hadn't thought much about it. Mom had also gone to college, where she'd met Dad.

A couple of runners sped past us heading in the direction of the hillside. One shouted at us, "Hurry up. She's almost here."

Zander acknowledged the shout with a wave at me, clearly blaming our unhurried pace on me. For once, I was okay with walking at a slow pace.

Zander slowed down even more because we were about halfway to the line of buildings, and I sensed he didn't want to take this conversation around other ears. "Anyway, we lived in San Francisco back then. We saw your aunt and her family a lot. Your cousins are pretty cool."

I tried to remember if Zoe or Lange had ever mentioned Zander or his family, but I didn't think they had.

"What happened? Why did you leave and come here?" I added silently, *Why did your parents swing so far to the other side?*

"Well, as I said, we mingled."

"Did someone, a normal, find out about your abilities?"

He shrugged, "Nah, not so simple. It was a bunch of things all leading up to one big thing. Logan got bullied a lot. Even aside from abilities, he and I look weird." He waved a hand over his face, I guess to point out his ice blue eyes that contrasted with his dark skin. I decided now wasn't the time to tell him I thought his appearance was striking. "So, there were a lot of jokes about being mixed race, that kind of thing. I could ignore it, but Logan got in a lot of fights. Which made it worse, especially since, to normals, he's freakishly strong. So, there were a lot of steroid jokes." He sighed while I winced, remembering Mindy Careen's rumors about steroids causing my own freakish strength. "He got into a bad fight with one kid. A few days later, a bunch of them trapped him in the school showers and, well, even supernormals, especially untrained ones, can have the crap beaten out of them by normals if there are enough of them. Mom and Dad took him out of school after that. I'm not sure what they had planned..." He trailed off.

"But that's not why you left San Francisco?" I asked.

"No, no it wasn't." He seemed loath to continue, chewing on his lower lip before blowing out a breath. "Not long after that, when Mom and Dad were out of town, at the research center in Colorado, we got to stay with friends in the neighborhood, normals." He said the rest in a rush, "That Saturday we went to the movies with them. And there was a guy who brought in a bunch of guns. He shot up the place, killed the father of our friends, wounded both kids. A lot of other people died." He gave me a bleak look. "Logan and I did our best to shield people. We even tried to get to the guy, but it was before we had our significant abilities. And since we'd never been trained to use our abilities that way, we weren't very good at fighting. Not like your family."

I vaguely remembered the theater shooting several years ago when I was six. It was a copycat incident where the shooter was trying to impress another gunman who'd gone to prison for a similar attack. "Weren't you both really young?"

Zander's next words shocked me. "Your mom stopped the shooter. She was in town with your dad for something, I don't know what. She saw the police around the movie theater and just charged in. She was amazing. I can't describe what she did to stop the guy, but the cops never knew she did it. She saw us and stayed with us until our parents came back." He gave me a sympathetic look. "I was sorry when I heard she died. I owe her for saving those people, for doing what I didn't know how to do." He looked at the ground, kicking at the dirt.

I kept silent, not sure what to say over the lump in my throat. Pride at Mom's bravery fought with sadness at losing her; the memory felt as fresh as if it had happened yesterday. I recognized that the raw feeling of loss was brought on by the recent flashback, but it still hurt. I realized I was rubbing my hand over my heart and quickly dropped it to my side. I didn't want to seem vulnerable.

"So, my parents freaked out, decided all normals were bad, and brought us here." He waved a hand around the scenery. "And then, a few years ago, they went out on a mission and never came back. Isaac said they're true martyrs to the cause." Zander said in a flat, expressionless voice.

"Zander." For a moment, it didn't matter that he was on the side of evil holding me prisoner. He looked so sad that I only felt sympathy for his loss. "I'm so sorry."

He shrugged, "Yeah, at least I've got Logan and these guys." He waved a hand around to indicate the ranch.

I watched him thoughtfully as we continued towards the low line of buildings, a suspicion blooming in the back of my mind. I replayed my interactions with Zander over the past few days. In every meeting he'd been, well, the best word I could think of was approachable. In fact, if I'd met him anywhere other than at Mountain of Ash's lair I would consider him a friend in the making. I closed my eyes at the sudden threat of tears, overwhelmed with the hope that Zander wasn't a true believer in the mission of Mountain of Ash. Was there a chance he might really be honest about helping me?

I cleared my throat a few times, then managed to say, without revealing my emotions, "So you're helping us as a way of repaying my mom?" I kept my eyes on the ground as we picked our way through a rocky partition.

Silence met my question, and I risked a glance at him. He was watching me with a pensive expression. When he saw my look, he gave a lopsided smile. "Yeah, it's a way of repaying the debt." He hesitated, sighing a bit as he rubbed the back of his neck, lowering his voice to a soft whisper. "Well, and I don't like what they're doing to you." He spoke quickly. "It's not right, how they're torturing you. I don't know what Isaac makes you see, but I can't stomach watching." He turned to me with a tormented expression, the same one he'd been wearing behind Isaac's back earlier in the lab. "I've tried to reconcile your treatment and Mountain of Ash's mission against normals with what happened to Logan and in the movie theater, the shooting, you know? And, I don't think I belong—"

"Hey, Zander!" Logan shouted from the line of building, "Hurry your ass up. I'm tired of babysitting."

The frustration on Zander's face mirrored my own as he turned abruptly away to answer his brother. What had he been about to say?

In the time it had taken us to walk to our destination, a crowd of people had gathered between the hillside and the low buildings. I saw several Ashers I recognized from the hangar. Most were looking at the sky. I looked up but didn't see anything of interest. Just clouds and birds.

I forgot my churning thoughts when I saw Logan was standing in front of Kevin. My cousin looked dirty and exhausted but still managed to grin at me. I gave a hoarse shout and ran to hug him.

Kevin wrapped his arms around me tightly until I grunted, his cuffs pressing into my back. "Ollie, it's good to see you." He held me by the shoulders, peering into my face, brow furrowed at what he saw there. I fought against a surge of emotion that clogged my throat with unshed tears. I refused to cry in front of Logan. I found I minded less about showing emotion in front of Zander. Kevin put his arm around my shoulders. "Come on."

When Logan started to protest, Zander said, "Hey, let them have a little space. It's not like they can go anywhere. We're in the middle of the ranch, and everybody else is here too." Logan grumbled but stayed put while Zander said to us, "Stay where we can see you." And he winked at me with the eye Logan couldn't see. "Black Gaea is due in about ten minutes or so."

Kevin gave me a strange look as he guided me over to the corner of one of farthest buildings where we could still see the crowd, but they couldn't hear us. Unless they used their supernormal ability. With that thought in mind, I whispered, "How are you?"

Kevin dropped his arm from my shoulder and rubbed his forehead. "Okay, I guess. They mainly have me working on labor projects." He rolled his shoulders, wincing. "Which sucks without abilities."

"Yeah." I found myself envying him. At least he got out of his cell for non-torture related activities. "Have you seen Anna? They let me see her once."

Kevin nodded. "I saw her this morning."

My heart leapt at the news Anna was still unharmed.

"What about you?" Kevin asked. "You look, um, kind of rough."

I touched my cheek. Was there evidence of the mental torture on my face? "Ah, well, they want my blood for a serum. So, they keep taking it."

"What?" Kevin stared me in shock.

"Yeah, it's both gross and awful." I flexed my bruised and sore arm. It hadn't had a chance to heal since the twin doctors seemed to favor taking blood from the same spot. "Not to mention scary."

"Why do they want to make a serum?" Kevin paced around in an angry loop.

"Isaac has some crazy idea it can be used to make significant abilities stronger." I sighed at his incredulous stare. "Yeah, yeah, I know. Ridiculous, absurd, blah, bah, blah."

Kevin leaned in, peering at me. "I'm guessing they haven't been successful, so they need to take more." He squinted, tilting his head, "But you're not telling me something. Just taking your blood wouldn't make you look so," He gripped my shoulder gently, "beaten down, like you've been sucker punched."

I swallowed hard. "They—Isaac, Wesley, Black Gaea— they think it's best to get my blood while I'm," I held up my hands, palms out like I was shooting fire, "using my abilities. Like it'll make it super-charged, or something."

"And how do they take your blood while you're using your power? I assume you're uncuffed?" Kevin looked a envious as he poked a finger at his cuffs.

"Sort of." I said the rest in rush. "I don't know how they get me there, but I wake up strapped to a chair, and they cuff me immediately."

"Wake up from what?" Kevin latched onto the uncomfortable detail I'd breezed over.

"Um," I was reluctant to say the words aloud, "Isaac, well he, gets into my head, and he replays some things that happened in the past. But he changes them just enough to make me upset, enough to fire up." I stopped. Just talking about the flashbacks made me think harder about them and how Isaac had corrupted those memories. I clenched my fists.

Kevin raised an eyebrow, "Keep going. Which memories?"

I sighed, "The bank robbery, Emma and the bridge." I met his eyes with difficulty. "The fight with the cockroach cluster. Mom's death."

Kevin touched his cheek where he still bore the scars from the cockroach cluster attack. "Ollie, that blows." He hugged me, muttering, "Those bastards."

"Yeah, and the worst thing is, I think it may have worked this last time. Isaac and the doctors were pretty excited."

Kevin didn't answer for a moment; he was very still while continuing to hug me. Finally, he spoke softly into my ear, "Ollie, when I let go, turn around slowly but don't react." His voice was filled with quiet elation.

"What?" I asked, confused by the change in topic.

"Just trust me." Kevin let go and I turned around.

I was glad he'd warned me not to react, though I couldn't quite suppress the gasp of air I let out.

An eyeball hung in the air behind the long, windowless building.

Chapter 16

The eyeball hung in the air under the eaves of the low building. It hung unblinking, because there was no eyelid or even the rest of a body. Just a freaking eyeball. I stared at it while I assumed it stared back at me.

"Kevin…" My mouth opened and closed a few times before I found the words. "Um, can you tell me if I'm seeing what I'm seeing?" I knew I was babbling, but even in the supernormal world I was sure a random floating eyeball was bizarre.

With his back to where most of the Ashers still milled around talking excitedly and looking at the sky, Kevin grinned at me, all despair gone from his face. "I know that eyeball."

"Huh?"

"Come on, let's get closer." He nudged me into movement until we were a few feet from the building. I glanced around, expecting Logan and Zander to march over at any minute demanding to know what we were doing, but Zander was just talking animatedly to Logan.

Kevin leaned forward, speaking quietly with his lips facing the eyeball. I stared at it too, noticing the iris was a warm caramel brown. Kevin spoke softly but made sure every word was enunciated carefully. "Hey, Laurel. It's good to see you."

I pressed my lips together to suppress a snort of hysterical laughter. Kevin kicked my ankle as he kept talking. "If there is a rescue planned, you need to know that we won't leave without Ollie's friend Anna. Okay?"

We both jumped when the eyeball vanished without a sound.

"Kev, what—who was that?" I rubbed my eyes.

Before he could answer, the eyeball was back. And it wasn't alone. A coffee colored hand crab-walked through the dirt towards us. I involuntarily stepped back, thinking of Thing from *The Addams Family*. Kevin crouched down as if he was tying his shoelace. The hand did a sort of fist bump with Kevin's hand. I saw the rolled-up paper between the middle and ring fingers as Kevin grabbed it. He faced the eyeball and mouthed 'thanks' as the disconcerting hand-eye coordination team vanished.

We moved away from the building as casually as possible, watching the Ashers for any signs they were coming our way. My hands were shaking with nervous excitement as Kevin carefully unrolled the slip of paper while keeping it hidden in the palm of his hand.

"What's it say?" I asked impatiently.

Kevin spoke very quietly, "They know where we are but can't figure out how to get to us." He raised his eyes to mine, struggling not to grin too much. "It's from Aunt Kate."

I jumped when Logan shouted, "They're coming!"

I spoke quickly, "Kevin, who was that?" I was still dumbfounded by the sight of a bodiless eyeball and hand.

Kevin smirked which made my heart lighter even as I scowled at him. He rolled the paper into a tiny ball as he said, "Laurel Hathaway. She can split off body parts." He glanced back at Logan, who was watching us with a glare. "Transporting them is new, but I bet she had help."

"Excuse me? That's a thing? Being able to just," I waved a hand as if to show it was firmly attached. "How does that even work? I mean, the body part is…" I trailed off, unable to express how disturbing it was.

"How do we do anything? You shoot fire out of your fingers, dude." Kevin finished rolling up the paper and stuck it in his mouth. He swallowed. "Anyway, disjointers, that's what her skill set is called. They're kind of reclusive." He gave me a thoughtful look, "Maybe they creep people out, I don't know. They look, well, unusual, even when all their parts are together. Dad told me once disjointers remind him of those old marionette dolls."

"How do you know Laurel?"

Kevin shrugged. "When Aunt Kate was on the Council, we went to Colorado a few times and I met her there. Her dad had some high position in the government, and they lived there. She's pretty cool, but we lost touch."

"How were you so sure it was her?"

Kevin looked puzzled. "I don't know, I guess I recognized her eyeball?" He smiled. "She used spy on Zoe, and it really pissed her off."

My sentiments were with Zoe. Not only was being spied on not cool, but if it was by an eyeball, then it was just weird.

Logan started walking towards us with Zander trailing behind.

"So, what are we going to do about escaping?" My energy was charged up, knowing that my family was nearby. If only we could figure out how to get out of here. I rubbed my wrist where the cuffs were chaffing my skin. We really needed to get these ability blockers off, but I couldn't think of a way to piss off Black Gaea again. We also needed to figure out how to break Anna out of her cell. And I was certain there was no way out of here without our powers. There were too many Mountain of Ash followers between us and escape.

Logan marched up. "Come on, I don't want to miss this."

We followed Logan and Zander towards the hillside where the excitement was palpable among the Ashers. For the first time, I wondered what Black Gaea was bringing back from her mission. Given that it was something for the big event, it was probably a weapon of some kind. And, because everyone kept looking at the sky, I guessed it was a plane—maybe a fighter plane or something. I couldn't figure out why they would need another plane, though. Not when there were supernormals at the ranch who were transporters.

Movement caught my eye, and I saw Isaac walking through the crowd with Wesley, Emma, and Ben trailing him. At that moment, someone shouted, "There they are!"

My heart caught in my throat at the sight of five objects flying towards us. As they came closer, I realized I was watching dragons circling down, coming closer to the ground with each sweep of their wings. All five beasts were jet black and as large as city buses. As they wheeled and turned in the sky above, I caught glimpses of diamond-faceted eyes reflecting the sunlight.

Black Gaea rode on the back of the largest dragon, and four more riders sat on the other dragons.

"Wow," I breathed, awed by the dragons' deadly beauty. "Why didn't anyone tell me dragons really existed?"

Kevin answered, "There aren't many left, and they are all kept in sanctuaries. There's one in the U.S., and I think the others are in South America and Africa." He winced a little at my stare. "Lange's seen them and told me." He was referring to Lange's job at the bestiary in Death Valley.

"Are they tame? I mean, how are Black Gaea and rest riding them?"

Logan snorted. "Tame? Not in a million years." He pointed to the neck of one of the dragons. "Black Gaea managed to collar them."

I squinted, seeing black metal studded collars with reins attached around each dragon's neck. Black Gaea had looped he reins in hand and waved at us with her other.

"That's all it took, reins and collar?" Kevin asked with surprise.

"No," Logan said impatiently, his eyes following the dragons as they descended towards a field nearby. "The collars are inhibitors." He glanced over to see our puzzled looks. "If the dragon doesn't do what we want, they feel pain."

"Why would you want to hurt them? They were fine in their sanctuary!" Kevin shouted.

"How else are we going to use them?" Logan shouted back.

"You could have left them alone." I snapped out the words heedlessly. "Them and all the other monsters you keep here."

Kevin gave me an alarmed look at the news there were more monsters at Mountain of Ash's lair.

"They're tools, meant for us to use, like everything else in the world." Logan clenched his hand in a fist, and I stepped back. I was afraid that if he punched me it would hurt me as much it would a normal.

"Is there a problem here?" Isaac's question cut through the argument.

Zander surprised me by stepping forward. "No sir, just a healthy debate." He gave me a shushing look. "We'll take these two back to their cells now."

Isaac merely nodded, dismissing us as he turned back to watch as the five dragons landed in the field. Their flapping wings blew dirt and grass in air for a moment before the dragons settled down. Black Gaea and the other riders slid off and greeted the Ashers who surrounded the beasts. I could tell the dragons were chafing at their captivity. The smallest dragon craned its head up at the sky and bunched its back legs as if it was about take flight. It opened its mouth and let out a blast of energy that shook the air. Its rider, a small man with black dreadlocks, pressed a device on his wrist, and the dragon keened in pain before huddling on the ground. The other dragons let out soft warbles of distress, but none of them fought.

Zander gave me a gentle push. "Come on. Let's go"

I wanted to argue, to stay and help the dragons even though I wasn't sure what form that help would take, but I knew it would be pointless at best and dangerous at worst.

I looked at Zander. Could I really trust him?

This time, all four of us walked back to the main quad of buildings, with Logan at Kevin's side and Zander at mine.

When we got to the quad, I expected Logan to hustle Kevin off somewhere, but they followed Zander and me into the building where my cell awaited. As we all went down the stairs, I noticed Zander was scanning the stairwell. I tensed; was he about to help us escape? He saw my look and gave a brief shake of his head.

We reached the second level down from the main floor, Logan shoved open the door, pushing Kevin ahead of him. My cousin gave me half grin before the door closed.

"His cell is on this level?" I murmured to Zander, who nodded.

I started to speak again, but he caught my arm and squeezed gently. I interpreted his caution as meaning he wanted me to stay quiet for now.

My cell felt even more confining after being outside in the fresh air. Zander paused in the doorway, looking around before looking directly at me and mouthing, 'I'll be back soon.' Out loud, he said, "Rest up."

I nodded and as the door swung shut, sat on the hard, cold bed, and rested my head in my hands. My foot jiggled with nervous excitement, knowing that my family was nearby, but my stomach was twisted into knots as I mentally listed all the obstacles between us.

Fact: Kevin and I were bound by manacles, cutting off our power.

Fact: I didn't know how to rescue Anna.

Fact: The cavalry was outside the gates, but I had no idea how far or in which direction.

Fact: Mountain of Ash now had *dragons* in addition to their fighters.

Scariest fact: Any minute, Isaac or his minions could show up to haul me off to my execution.

This fact kept distracting me from planning, thinking, or focusing on escape. I wondered how they would do it. Would it be a public execution with all of Mountain of Ash watching? Or would it be done in a quiet lab with no one there but my executioners? I'd put money on a public execution since Isaac seemed to really enjoy grandstanding and he really didn't like the Brighthalls. Any chance to eliminate one of us and get a show out of it fit his persona.

Clenching my fists, I fought the urge to curl up into a fear ball in a corner. If anyone came to take me to my death, I vowed to fight as hard as I could. It mattered to me that I was willing to fight and not give in to despair. Even if it was a pointless struggle.

My head ached, and my stomach rumbled. Signs I was hungry. Despite the other discomforts of my prison, I'd never been hungry. Each meal had come at regular intervals and had been hearty enough to keep me full for hours. I watched the door, expecting the slot to appear so my dinner would slide into the cell.

The door remained tauntingly solid. *Okay, maybe I'm hungry early. After all, I got some exercise today.* I pushed back the panic threatening to consume me.

What felt like hours later, I stopped watching the door, expecting food to arrive. I knew I wasn't getting fed. And I knew it meant the latest serum had worked.

I guessed there wasn't going to be a last meal for the condemned.

Chapter 17

I shot to my feet at the sound of the lock turning in the cell door. I may not have had my powers or any weapons, but I wasn't going to let them take me easily. To quote the mothers of Sparta—with my shield or on it. One way or another, I was getting out of there.

The door opened to reveal Zander. I only slightly relaxed my stance. Despite his promises of help, I wasn't ready to give him all my faith.

He didn't speak, his eyes scanning me, noting my defensive posture. With his finger to his lips, requesting silence, he stood back enough to make space for me to exit the cell. Zander's stealthy behavior intrigued me enough to make me decide to follow him, so I didn't hesitate, leaving the cell that had been my resting place in that awful time. I was still on the watch for him to flip sides, but, since any escape plan relied on me not being in a cell, I figured this was progress.

As he passed me, I saw he held a small black case the size of large textbook. He shook his head at my inquiring look.

I followed him up the stairs to Kevin's level, where Zander opened my cousin's cell. I heard Kevin let out a startled exclamation. I peered around the edge of the door, waving for Kevin to be quiet. He looked from me to Zander with a querying expression but followed us.

Zander led us to down a level below my cell. He paused in an isolated hallway.

"Alright," Zander spoke softly and quickly, eyes scanning the area. "Bad news, the serum works now." I shivered at his confirmation of my fears. "Yeah, Isaac and Wesley gave it to a couple of the weakest firestarters, and now they're almost as strong as I am. They're all at the hangar seeing what they can do. I pretended to be annoyed by their strength and stomped off."

He scowled, leading me to think he wasn't completely faking it. I understood how he felt. "Good news: I can get you and Kevin the tools to take off the cuffs." Kevin started to speak, but Zander stopped him with a burst of flame from his pointer finger. "Then we get your friend."

"Why are you helping us?" Kevin hissed out before Zander could stop him again.

Zander lowered his gaze to the floor. "Does it matter?"

I tilted my head thoughtfully, watching Zander's expression when Kevin sputtered out in an unconscious echo of me earlier: "Yeah, it does."

I answered for Zander. "Mom helped him a long time ago." Zander shifted his eyes to meet mine as I said, "That's the only reason, right?"

Zander twisted his mouth into a grimace as if he was trying to force out the right words. He leaned forward and said softly, "Not the only reason." He cast a look around before saying very quickly, "Iwannagowithyou." He took a deep breath as if a weight had been lifted and repeated more intelligibly, "I want to go with you."

"What?" Kevin snorted. "Seriously?"

I didn't say anything since Zander had just confirmed my suspicions.

"Wait," Kevin said, holding up a hand. "You want to leave Mountain of Ash?" Zander nodded, his blue eyes shifting between me and Kevin. "I assume you've been thinking about this for a while? Isn't Isaac a mind reader?"

Zander gave Kevin a 'duh' look as I felt a chill down my spine. I faced the way we'd come, fully expecting guards to come charging towards us.

Kevin explained, "Doesn't he know what you're thinking?"

Zander's mouth twisted in a devilish grin. "Oh, I've gotten really good at shielding." He straightened his shoulders, lifting his chin proudly. "Isaac can only read your mind if he's looking at you, and if he focuses on it. It's not like he's always in your head, right? But he gets very angry if he thinks you're shielding more than basic thoughts."

"I remember Ben telling me that a few days ago." I'd forgotten about that part of my conversation with Ben. I'd gotten the impression Ben was little bit smug that his ability was stronger than Isaac's. Though, based on my experience, Isaac wielded his power with greater skill compared to Ben. I recoiled at the memory of Isaac's mind touching mine. "Wait, he was never in the room during my flashbacks."

"His ability works through windows." Zander said. "Kind of like a line of sight thing."

"Oh."

Kevin still looked skeptical, "Are you sure about his range?"

"Yes, I've been testing it for a year now." Zander assured us. "I know he'll skim through people's minds at random. He calls it culling the herd." Zander grimaced at our reactions. "Yeah, it can be awful. Whenever he wasn't in a room, I'd let myself think whatever I wanted, but when Isaac's in the room I only think about training, food, or sleep." He rubbed his hands on his thighs. "It was scary at first, but I've gotten better at it. It's like I have layers of shields, and I can tuck different thoughts behind each one." He paused before adding, "I knew I needed to keep secrets—before Mom and Dad died, they were talking about leaving. I think Isaac found out. And I think he had them killed on their last mission."

I gasped in sympathy. "Zander, I'm so sorry."

"Yeah, well, I hate Isaac as much as you do, but I didn't know how to leave or where to go."

"What about your brother?" Kevin asked.

Zander shook his head as his gaze turned bleak. "Nope, he's all in. 'Go Ashers' for him." Kevin opened his mouth, but Zander said urgently, "Look, we don't have a lot of time to waste. The twins have your normal—your friend—in Lab A right now. She's not locked up, so it's relatively easier to get to her." He looked at me. "When Isaac knew the serum worked, he gave Peter and Paul the go ahead to take Anna for whatever experiments they want."

Fear washed over me, and I clenched my fists. "Where is she?"

"You knew they were taking her down here." Kevin came up behind us to stand beside me.

"Yes." Zander sighed at our glares. "Look, do you want to argue with me, or do you want to save your friend and get your asses out of here?"

"Okay, what's your grand plan?" Kevin asked stiffly, crossing his arms.

"Come on, let's get rid of the cuffs first." Zander strode forward, adding, "Look pissed." He glanced back at me. "Yeah, that'll do." He seemed to grin as he faced forward again.

Kevin and I exchanged a look before following Zander to the door of the lab, where he pushed it open. The guard standing inside held up a hand. "What's your business?"

Zander took me and Kevin by our arms and shoved us forward. "Isaac wants one last test of their blood." He shrugged. "Something about the long-term effects of wearing the cuffs or whatever. You know how he is."

The guard nodded. "Okay. The doctors have that normal down the hall. Want me to tell them?"

Zander pushed us forward. "I know. I can tell them myself." He didn't stop pushing us until we were down the stairs. We stopped at the bottom and listened. The hallway was quiet and lined with sturdy doors.

I looked up and down. "Which way?"

"Come on." Zander stepped down the hallway towards the second-to-last door on the left. We followed him in, and I stopped, my heart pounding at the sight of an array of tools neatly lined up on the table. Kevin made an 'ah' sound in his throat.

"Who's first?" Zander headed for the table. He looked back at us. "Hurry up. The guard might decide to call the docs."

I nudged Kevin. "You first. It's been longer for you."

Kevin didn't waste time arguing; he practically ran over to Zander. Zander picked up the cuff removal tool and touched Kevin's cuffs one at a time. The cuffs opened with a *snick*. Kevin bounced away from the table, landing across the room. He spread his arms wide, grinning, eyes lit up with joy. He said a quiet, fervent, "Oh hell, yes!"

I didn't want to wait any longer, holding out my arms, wrists upturned. "Now me."

When my cuffs dropped off, I sighed with relief. Even though it had only been a day since I'd been cuffless, this time it felt so much better because Isaac and his minions weren't standing there. Which reminded me...

"Kevin, don't forget to shield."

"Yeah, thanks. I am." The reminder of our still-perilous situation sobered him slightly, but he still looked more like the Kevin I remembered from before Hugh's murder. He was examining the cuffs. "We should take these with us just in case." He tucked them in his pocket.

"Yeah, Aunt Kate will want to see them." I shoved my cuffs into the pocket of my filthy pants. "Come on," I said. "Where's Anna?" I asked as I headed for the door.

Zander opened it. "This way."

I led the way in the direction Zander pointed. Kevin flanked me. Zander followed, keeping an eye out behind us.

I stared at the door, thinking, *Why be subtle?* I raised my foot and kicked in the door. Inside the twin doctors stood on either side of Anna, who was gagged and strapped to a table. Peter held a set of clamps around Ann's thigh. Her hands gripped the edge of the table so hard that the her hands were quivering with the strain. She strained against the gag, trying to scream through the leather.

The twins looked annoyed by the invasion, but I smiled tightly at them and tilted my head. "Hello, Peter and Paul. I regret to inform you Anna has another engagement right now and won't be participating in any more of your tests." I raised my arms, slowly letting flames outline my body. "Any arguments?"

The twins shared a look before charging at us. Paul leapt over the table in a single bound while Peter executed an impressive parkour move off the counter. I stumbled back when Paul punched me. I hadn't expected the twins to fight so fiercely. I'd assumed they spent all of their time in the lab and hadn't trained in combat. Kevin was also surprised by the quick assault.

Luckily, Zander clearly expected the twins to fight well because he didn't hesitate to respond to the attack with his own. He didn't flame up, choosing to fight with his fists. I switched to ice, forming ice balls that I threw at Paul, hitting him in the shoulder and leg. He yelled as I managed to grab him and force him to his knees.

In the meantime, Zander punched Peter in the face, knocking him sprawling to the floor.

"Hold them down while I look for something to tie them up with." Kevin started opening drawers.

"No, I thought ahead." Zander used his chin to point at the black case he'd dropped when the fighting started. "Open that."

Kevin unzipped the case, revealing several filled syringes. He raised an eyebrow at Zander, who said, "It'll knock them out. Toss me one."

Kevin threw a syringe at Zander, who caught it and plunged the needle into Peter's neck. The doctor slumped to the floor.

Kevin gave me the other syringe, and I stuck it in Paul. As Paul joined his brother on the floor, I said, "This is what they used on me to take me to the lab?"

"Yeah." Zander shoved Peter into a corner that was out of sight from the doorway. I did the same with Paul, feeling a vicious satisfaction at their slack, unconscious faces.

Working carefully to avoid hurting Anna any more that she was, Kevin pulled off the gag.

Anna said, "Oh my god, I'm so happy to see you guys."

I melted through the metal clamps holding her to the table. Once Anna was freed, she slid to the floor, gripping the table as her legs buckled under her.

"Oh, Anna," I caught her with one arm, "what did they do to you?"

She gave a shaky cough. "I don't know, but the muscles in my leg feel like I've run a thousand miles."

Kevin laid a hand on her shoulder. "I can carry her." He didn't wait for an answer before he picked up Anna. "Come on, let's get out of here."

Zander pulled out another syringe from his little bag. "For the guard."

"Why didn't you knock him out earlier?" Kevin asked, his eyes narrow. I could tell he still didn't completely trust Zander.

Zander seemed to be aware of Kevin's suspicions, but he simply said, "In case anyone came into the medical area after us. I thought it would be a big red flag if they found the entrance unguarded or the guard passed out."

Kevin made a face, conceding the point, as we followed Zander back down the hall. When we reached the door, Kevin stepped out of the way, protecting Anna.

Zander gripped the syringe. I shoved open the door and Zander darted through, swiftly knocking out the guard.

Blowing out my breath, I headed for the door leading to the stairwell. "How much longer do you think they'll be at the hanger?"

"I'm not sure, but we'd better hurry. I don't want to test our abilities against the newly enhanced firestarters." Zander lead us up the stairs to the exit.

As if his words were a curse, we stepped outside to find Wesley standing in front of a line of guards, all holding weapons.

Chapter 18

Wesley looked sorrowful. "Olivia, Kevin, I really hoped it wouldn't come to this." He lifted a hand. "I voted to not eliminate you two, but I suppose it's best." Wesley sighed. "And Zander, your parents would be ashamed."

Zander growled, "Shut up."

I went cold at Wesley's casual attitude about killing us. Deciding there was no point in trying to negotiate, I coated the air between us and the Ashers with a wall of fire. Through the flame and heat, I saw the looming shadows of the fighters trying to rush the wall.

I heard Wesley shouting orders for firestarters to come put out the fire and even saw some enterprising person throwing a bucket of water at the wall. I effortlessly swept flame over the small gap created by the water.

Kevin wrapped his arms around Anna. "I'll take care of Anna. You two keep them away from us." He lifted her up.

"Okay." I formed two balls of ice, reasoning it was safer for me to fight with ice than fire. I was less likely to lose control and kill someone with ice.

Zander said, "This way." He mirrored my ice with flame.

Anna mumbled, "Guys, I—" before passing out.

I resisted the desire to grab her from Kevin and make sure she was okay. "We have go *now*."

My wall of fire sputtered, and I realized at least one firestarter had arrived and was pulling the flames into their body. Zander muttered "Trent" by way of explanation.

Kevin tighten his grip on Anna. "Let's go."

We charged away from the massing Ashers through a narrow passage between two of the buildings. I looked over my shoulder at my wavering fire one last time before we turned the corner to head for the hills behind the Victorian house.

Zander and I ran while Kevin bounced ahead, glancing back occasionally to watch for directions. For a moment, I hoped we'd outrun any followers, until Kevin bounced to the top of a hill. He stumbled, almost dropping Anna, as he fell to his knees.

I dashed up and froze, gaping down at what looked like the entire assembly of Mountain of Ash glaring up at us from a little valley. I recognized the same orderly formations they'd used the second time I went to the hanger.

Isaac, Black Gaea, and Wesley stood in front of the Ashers. Wesley and Black Gaea flanked Isaac, mirroring his stance — legs braced wide, hands clasped behind their backs, and expressions grim. In a line behind the leaders stood Emma and Ben along with Logan and a few others who I assumed had an elevated status given their proximity to the trifecta of evil.

I automatically looked for the dragons and the other monsters, but I didn't see any.

I tightened my mental shields when I saw Ben, his gaze intent on me, but he just stared at me with a puzzled expression. Emma stood on the other side of Ben, grinning viciously though her sword was still in its scabbard.

"Kind of overkill, don't you think?" Kevin tried to sound calm, but his voice shook. He managed to get to his feet with Anna leaning on him. I was only slightly relieved to see she was conscious. It might be better if she didn't have to endure whatever was about to happen.

Zander ran up beside me. "Well, hell." He ran a hand over his face to wipe away sweat.

"Where're the dragons?" Kevin asked as his gaze darted around the gathering. Anna gulped at the mention of dragons, her eyes going wide.

Zander gave a half grin. "We got lucky there. The dragons and the worst of the monsters were moved to the staging location last night."

I wanted to ask about the staging location, but now wasn't the time.

Isaac cupped his hands over his mouth and called up to us, "Brighthalls, nice try, but as you can see, we have the advantage. I'll give you one chance to give up." His gaze skimmed us, resting briefly on Zander. When Zander didn't change his defensive stance, Isaac frowned. He shifted his eyes to meet mine, and I forced myself to deliberately stare back. I could feel him trying to get inside my mind, but I felt a flash of elation as I mentally swatted his attempt away.

Isaac's only reaction to my rebuff was to tighten his lips before he spoke. "Okay, the hard way it is."

Black Gaea gave fierce grin, raising her hands up to the sky, spreading her fingers wide. Sparks of lightning flickered between her fingers. Wesley gave a careless twist of his hands and several rocks floated up behind him, stopping just above his shoulders.

Isaac looked at Wesley, then Black Gaea, before shouting, "Ashers, Attack!"

Trent and several others I recognized as firestarters surged forward. They weren't alone as more Ashers converged, charging our way.

I didn't take my eyes off the approaching attackers. "Kev, take Anna and get out of here. Just keep heading in the direction we've been going, and you should get to an outer fence."

Zander added, "I don't know where your family is waiting, but it's probably northwest of here. There's small town in that direction."

I shifted into fighting stance, raising my hands, mentally working through the possibility of using my disintegration skills to fend off assailants without killing anyone. The first wave of attackers was almost on us, wielding fire, swords, and maces. The line of firestarters spread out, mingling with the rest of the Ashers.

"Shit, Ollie." Kevin expressed his anger succinctly.

"Get going, Kevin. We don't have much time. Zander and I will block them." I side-eyed Zander. "How do you feel about fighting against your compatriots? And your brother?"

In answer, Zander swept a stream of fire in front of the closest line of attackers. They staggered back to avoid the flames. I heard calls for firestarters to hurry up.

"Go!" I snapped at Kevin and Anna. "We'll catch up."

"Ollie, no." Anna stretched out a hand in distress.

Kevin was too well-trained by Uncle Dan to argue my logic. He knew it was imperative to get Anna out of the way, both for her safety and to prevent her from being used as leverage anymore. He had a better chance of escaping using his bouncing ability to cover distances.

And I was the better fighter.

Kevin grabbed a protesting Anna and bounced away. I silently sent them good wishes as I faced the horde converging on us.

I aimed a line of fire at the hillside, using my disintegration ability to dissolve the earth into a wide gully. I saw several Ashers fall into the hole, but I didn't wait as I ran in the opposite direction as Kevin and Anna..

Zander followed, occasionally twisting around to lob balls of fire behind him.

Shouts told me we were being followed, but I didn't stop until arrows and fireballs started whizzing by me. I made a sheet of ice across my back to act as a shield.

Zander and I ran, weaving around each other, attacking the Ashers as if we'd trained together. Even in the middle of the battle, I was thrilled to be fighting beside such a good warrior.

"Where are we going?" I shouted at Zander, hoping he had a plan. Normally, I'd try to decide on a strategy, but I knew he was more familiar with the terrain.

Zander winced as a fireball flew past him at close range. "There's a—"

"Gah!" The shaft of an arrow cut across my thigh, startling me with sharp pain. I stumbled and fell. I rolled over, my training allowing me to get to my feet quickly, though I swayed as my leg tried to buckle under me. I blinked as my vision dimmed, then cleared some. I glanced down at my bleeding leg, guessing the arrow had been laced with a drug designed to knock me out. I counted myself lucky it had only sliced me instead of burying its head in my flesh. Still, the drug had weakened me. I drew several deep breaths, trying to clear my head, but the delay had been enough for the first wave of attackers to reach me.

I dodged punches and kicks as best I could, but the crowd surrounded me, and I was hit from all sides. Fear or the drug weighed down my limbs, and I gasped when

Emma stepped into the circle, her sword free of its scabbard. The others backed off, giving her space.

I tried to focus on my cousin, but I was momentarily distracted by the sight of Zander being restrained by several people behind Emma.

"Olivia," Emma spoke, and my attention snapped back to her. "You are guilty of violating your agreement to work with us." She raised her sword. "And since we have a viable serum from your blood, we don't really need you anymore. Isaac is allowing me be the one to eliminate you." She smiled coldly.

Eliminate me? My body, already fighting the effects of the drug, went weak. I hadn't expected them to kill me, not really. Which was stupid of me. I knew better than to hope for a reprieve. I knew that look in Emma's eyes; she was determined to follow this course. She didn't look at all regretful at the duty of killing her once favorite cousin, just focused on the chore.

Emma darted forward, slashing at me. I jumped back, staggering into a couple of burly women. One of them grabbed my arm roughly, and I felt a knife slice into my shoulder. She shoved me back into the center of the circle, and I barely avoided falling into my cousin. More shakiness flooded my body. I knew I'd gotten another hit of the drug they were using to weaken me. My vision dimmed as I sucked in air through my nose, trying to clear my head as much as possible.

Emma came at me again as a new wave of dizziness had me staggering. I called fire to my hands, but the flames flickered feebly. I tried ice but got slush dripping from between my fingers.

Emma sliced her sword through the air, stopping with the sharp edge against my neck. I managed to stay upright and as still as I could while the world seemed to dim around me. I wasn't going to give her the satisfaction of crying or begging. Knowing it was pointless, I looked for any sign of compassion in her expression, but there was none. I heard Ben shouting but couldn't hear the words over the pounding of blood in my head. All I could focus on was the cold edge of the sword and Emma's eyes.

She drew her lips back in a horrible grin. "Any last words?"

Chapter 19

Just above Emma's head, an eyeball popped into existence. I jerked, the blade from Emma's sword nicking my skin. I recognized Laurel's eye as it spun 360 degrees, taking in the scene. With one last glance in my direction, the eyeball blinked away.

Even though my mouth was dry, either from the drugs or fear, I croaked out, "Bite me."

Emma swung back the sword. "As you wish."

Emboldened by the sight of Laurel's eyeball, I ducked out of reach of Emma's sword. She grunted as she came after me. My condition was deteriorating, so I didn't make it very far before falling to my knees. Looking up, I raised an arm to deflect the sword as Emma sliced it through the air toward me.

The strike never landed; instead, my burly cousin Lange came out of nowhere and punched Emma in the face. I gaped at Lange as he snatched Emma's sword from the ground. He reached his hand down, I grasped it, and he pulled me to standing.

"What...? Where did you come from?" I poked at him to make sure he was real.

"We're rescuing you!" He grinned, and over his shoulder I saw the circle of Ashers had turned into a battleground with supernormals fighting each other. "Or helping you finish escaping, I guess."

"Oh good." I wobbled on my feet as the drug coursed through my system.

"Come on. I'll take you to Uncle Alex." Lange picked me up and ran while I blinked and wondered where the hell everyone fighting against the Ashers had come from so suddenly. The drug made my thoughts fuzzy, but I finally figured out that the cavalry had come in the form of my family and what looked like most of the Council's army.

Emma howled, and over Lange's shoulder I saw her surge to her feet. For a moment, the scene stuttered, and Emma appeared to have covered half the distance to us in a heartbeat. She'd used her ability to stop time around her so she could move quickly.

I wanted to fight her, but I was coherent enough to know I needed to get the drug out of my body before I could. "Lange, she's catching up."

Lange glanced behind him, grunted, then turned and ran faster, dashing through the crowd like a battering ram.

Emma's snarling face was lost in the mass of battling supernormals.

Lange ducked under a stream of water issuing from the hands of a woman I recognized as Carol, the water weaver who'd tortured Anna. She was trying to defend herself from an icer dressed in a Council military uniform. The icer froze Carol's water and used it to whack her on the head, knocking her out. I almost cheered and wished Anna could have seen it.

We reached the outskirts of the fighting, and Lange gently lowered me to the ground. I struggled to sit up, but Uncle Alex appeared, crouching down beside me. I saw fighting all around us, but we were in a guarded circle for the moment.

Lange said, "They drugged her. She's all woozy." He glanced behind him at the melee. "I got there just as Emma was attacking her. I think Emma was about to kill her." He looked sick.

"Okay, get back in there," Uncle Alex told Lange as he took my hand. "I'll take care of Olivia." He put a hand on my forehead like a parent taking a child's temperature. His hands were cool and comforting.

The fuzziness in my head receded until I was able to think more clearly. Uncle Alex shivered, momentarily dazed as his ability worked to quickly clear out the drug he'd pulled into his body. "Whew, that's a nasty concoction they hit you with." He smiled at me, pulling me into a tight hug. "It's good to see you." His voice shook, and he cleared his throat.

"What, I mean—how did you find us?" The confusion brought on by being drugged was gone, but I was still astonished by their sudden appearance on the battlefield.

Uncle Alex pulled me to my feet. "Aunt Kate will explain, but right now we need to get you out of here." He drew his sword from the scabbard strapped across his back.

"Wait, where are Kevin and Anna?" I turned in a circle frantically looking for them. "Did you find them?" I couldn't believe I'd almost forgotten about my cousin and best friend.

Uncle Alex nodded. "We evacuated Anna, and Kevin is fighting." He pointed into the brawl, where I saw Kevin leap up into the air and come down with a nice round kick at an unseen opponent.

I slumped with relief. Anna was safe. A knot in my stomach loosened. Then I remembered. "Uncle Alex, their leader, he's a mind reader and controller like Ben. And Ben, he joined them." I fought back tears that threatened to come now that I was back with my family.

Uncle Alex regarded me compassionately. "Okay, let's get out of this, and we can deal with what comes."

"Olivia!" Zander came staggering up, bleeding from a cut on his arm.

Uncle Alex caught his arm, holding him back while giving me a sharp look, "Olivia, who is this?"

"Zander, meet my Uncle Alex." I said with a sweep of my arm. "Zander helped us escape."

"Zander?" Uncle Alex peered at his face. "You look familiar. Zander Jones? Son of Winnie and Jacob Jones?"

Zander nodded, his eyes wide at being recognized.

"Son, we've been looking for your family for the past seven years." Uncle Alex gripped both of Zander's arm, smiling. "Where's the rest of your family?"

Zander looked stunned as he shook his head. "Just me, well, just me that wants to leave." He turned to face the fight, scanning the melee. "My brother is a believer. And Mom and Dad are dead."

My uncle said somberly, "Now isn't the time. We'll talk after we get you out of here." He seemed to believe Zander, and I relaxed. Uncle Alex's empathic ability didn't allow him to read minds, but it made him a solid judge of people's intentions.

In this brief interlude, the fight had gotten closer, and the guards around us were fidgeting, obviously eager to get back into the battle. I bounced on the balls on my feet, ready to dive back in now that my head was clear. I scanned the crowd, determined to find Emma and pick up where we'd left off in our fight, but I couldn't see her in the commotion that spread over the valley.

Lange fought two Ashers at once, punching a fist in each man's face at the same time. They both fell, knocked out. Lange turned, diving back into the fight.

Uncle Alex said, "This way." He led Zander and me along the edges of the battle, dodging though the combatants, only fighting if necessary.

Uncle Alex seemed to have a specific destination in mind. A remote part of my mind was surprised to discover that my peaceful uncle was a ferocious fighter. Maybe his experience healing people helped him know exactly how to knock out someone in the most efficient way possible. He never wasted a move or picked a fight.

I followed his example. I enjoyed the kicks and punches I got in but refrained from using my fire because I was afraid I might default to disintegration-level heat. I lobbed a lot of ice balls though, taking a vicious joy in knocking out several Ashers.

Kevin bounced in, carrying a mace he'd acquired from somewhere. "Ollie!" I just grinned back at him. "Anna's safe."

"I know. Thank you." I started to ask him where he'd gotten the mace, but a rock fell from the sky. Kevin instantly hit it with the mace, shattering it into a million stones.

We turned to see Wesley running at us. His usually tidy appearance was marred by gore and grime, and his hair stuck up in all directions. Several large stones whirled around him. As he came at us, the rocks flew directly at our faces. Zander and I each hit one with a fireball, and Kevin smashed another with his mace.

Wesley shrieked, his voice shrill. "You're ruining everything!" He called up dozens of stones. Some from the recently shattered rocks shot at us from the ground. They didn't hurt much, mainly annoying me as I diverted some power to layer a shield of ice over my skin.

Zander held out a palm, outlined with fire. "Wesley—" He didn't get to finish before Wesley sent rocks flying at Zander's face.

Uncle Alex reared up from behind Wesley, slamming the Asher with his fist. Wesley staggered but recovered quickly. He tried to use stones to attack, but Uncle Alex fought too closely for the hits to be effective. Wesley was a tough fighter, but it was clear he was more used to depending on his power to fight from afar. Uncle Alex slashed and cut until Wesley was on his knees, with Uncle Alex's sword tip at his chest. Kevin and I stood behind him while Zander watched from one side.

"Yield." My uncle looked more angry than I'd ever seen him. "Yield, and we'll show you mercy."

I was shocked when Wesley sneered, leaning back. I reached for him, expecting him to run, but instead he hurled himself onto Uncle Alex's sword.

"Holy hell," Kevin breathed, staring at the gory tip of the sword jutting from Wesley's back. Blood gushed down the back of Wesley's twitching body.

Uncle Alex pulled out his sword, looking as surprised as the rest of us that the man had sacrificed himself rather than be caught.

Several Ashers screamed in horror at the sight of one of their leaders cut down, and we were suddenly the focus of several attacks at once. I fought, using mostly my ice, finding it very effective. If I aimed at someone's head, I was usually able to knock them out. I saw Kevin bounce into the thick of a crowd, swinging his mace, while Zander kicked and punched his way towards me.

Someone caught my arm, ducking out of the way of the ice ball I lobbed in response. Uncle Alex said, "We need to get to the edge. I'm supposed to be taking you to safety." He glanced around. "The Council army has this well in hand." Kevin and Zander stood behind him.

I fumed at being dragged out of the fight, but my uncle didn't give me a chance to argue. He ran, only fighting when necessary. Kevin bounced ahead, and Zander and I followed behind my uncle.

I halted when Zander shouted, "Logan, wait!" as his brother ran by carrying a blood-covered sword. My stomach clenched at the sight.

Logan raised the sword, glaring at his brother with contempt. "Traitor. Get out of my way before I kill you."

Zander lit up, fire outlining his body. I did the same, flanking him, ready to help him. Logan slashed at Zander, who gasped as the sword sliced his arm. The flames around him wavered as Zander covered the wound with one hand, eyes wide with surprise. "I can't believe you, Logan. You know they're evil."

Logan feinted, snarling, "Normals are the evil ones. You know what they did to me when we were kids."

"No more evil than we are," Zanders shouted in exasperation, holding up his blood-soaked hand. The blood burned away when he called a fireball to his palm.

I stayed back, keeping others away—this was a fight between the brothers. Logan fought with the sword, aiming to maim Zander with every strike, but Zander dodged most of the attempts. He threw fireballs in his brother's direction, clearly trying to hold him back while he yelled, "Logan, come with me. We've got a chance to get out of here and see what it's like on the outside."

Logan just fought harder until Zander aimed a fireball at his sword. Logan yelped as the flame melted the metal. I knew Zander was like me, holding back, not taking his flame to the hottest level for fear of disintegrating someone. Throwing regular fireballs was dangerous enough.

Logan tossed away the hilt of the sword, balling up his fists. "Screw you."

Zander raised his own fists, fire dying out as he prepared to meet his brother on equal footing.

A tremor went through Logan's body, and he dropped his fists while stepping out of range of Zander's swing. He lifted his head as if he'd heard a sound. For a moment, I thought he was giving up, agreeing to come with his brother, but he simply glared at Zander, "To be continued."

"What?" Zander stared after Logan as he ran up the hill. He turned to me. "What happened? Why did he run?"

I looked around the valley. "All of the Ashers are running away. Did we win?" I'd lost track of the main battle while Zander and Logan fought. Now I saw most of the fighting had stopped as blank-eyed Ashers all ran in the same direction.

I grabbed Zander's arm. "Come on. We need to catch up to my uncle."

I pointed to where Uncle Alex stood at the top of the hill with several folks around him. They were looking at whatever lay on the other side.

We ran up to join them. I stopped dead when I saw what lay below.

Isaac was surrounded by a growing ring of Ashers, all flooding in from the battle.

I checked my mental shields instinctively. "Uncle Alex! That guy, Isaac, he's the mind reader."

Uncle Alex called back, "Yeah, Kevin told us." I blew out a breath in relief.

It hurt to see Ben standing beside Isaac. He looked odd, eyes down downcast, and shoulders slumped. It was like he wasn't paying attention to the battle at all.

I didn't see Black Gaea anywhere, but I picked out Emma behind Ben. Logan joined the crowd near the edge.

Isaac raised his eyes to glare at those of us standing on the hill above his Ashers. I braced for him to launch an attack using his mind control. Uncle Alex and the other adults had the same idea, lifting their various weapons or calling their defensive powers.

Isaac merely smiled at our preparations while the Ashers shifted, but the attack never came. Instead, the Ashers began disappearing in large groups. I saw them forming groups of twenty or more, holding hands with an Asher at the center. Shouts came up from around me as the people watching realized they were getting away.

"My God, I've never seen a teleporter move so many people at once," a man shouted from behind me.

I felt my chest tighten. Were these teleporters who'd been powered up using the serum from my blood?

"They're getting away!"

"Stop them!"

"Head for the main compound. See if they're going there!"

I heard orders to attack, and the army surged down the hill while the crowd of the Ashers blinked out of sight group by group. Within moments, some of the teleporters reappeared, grabbing and disappearing with more people.

While his people kept evaporating, Isaac pushed Ben at one of teleporters. Caught off balance, the woman wrapped her arms around Ben and vanished. I swallowed back an unexpected wave of grief.

In a few minutes, only a handful of Mountain of Ash people were left. A man came up to Isaac and put a hand on his shoulder. Before he winked out, Isaac sneered, hate in his eyes, "Until next time."

For a moment we stood in stunned silence, then — BOOM! —the ground shuddered underneath me. I swayed but stayed on my feet, appreciating my basic package abilities like I'd never done before I'd been cut off from them. Around me, people staggered and shouted.

"What was that?" Uncle Alex asked.

I turned around to look back in the direction we'd run from during our escape. I wasn't very surprised to see a large plume of smoke billowing into the sky.

I pointed. "There, that's where the main house, dorms, and labs are." I let my arm drop. "Or were, I suspect."

Chapter 20

When Uncle Alex, Kevin, Zander, and I crested the hill near the compound, I stopped in amazement at the sight of the burning, smoking hole that used to be Mountain of Ash's lair. There was nothing left of three of the four buildings but debris blowing past us. Fires smoldered here and there in the hollows, and the smell of smoke permeated the air.

The fourth building was still standing, but one side of it teetered over the gaping hole left by the destruction of the other three.

Aunt Kate stood near the hillside, watching supernormals wearing Council uniforms swarm around the ruins. I blew out a relieved breath when I saw Anna sitting on a crate beside her. Anna's face broke into a huge smile when she saw us.

"Aunt Kate!" I called out. "Anna!" I left the guys behind to rush over, hugging my aunt hard. Tears I'd been holding back for days threatened to burst out, but I managed to keep it to a few sniffles.

"Oh Olivia, we were so worried." Aunt Kate stroked my hair before holding me by my shoulders. I was startled to see unshed tears in her eyes, but she quickly blinked them away and smiled at me. She looked me up and down, her gaze lingering on my unhealed wrists which still showed signs of chafing from the cuffs. I shoved my hands behind my back. I didn't want the wounds healed by Uncle Alex. I wanted to keep them as a reminder that Mountain of Ash needed to be destroyed.

Kevin threw his arms around her. "Hey, Auntie."

She hugged him as well. "You scared the crap out of us. I'm not sure if I'm angry or happy to see you." She sighed and pushed her hair off her forehead. "And if either of you say anything about how we wouldn't have found Mountain of Ash's compound without you, I'll put you on warehouse clean up duty until you graduate from college." She gave us both a stern look.

I exchanged a guilty glance with Kevin. I'd been about to make that exact point. He grinned back, clearly thinking the same thing.

I gazed over the ruins, trying to calculate which building had housed the cells. I thought it might the building that was still standing.

And, with a twist in my stomach, I wondered where the monster library was or had been. I turned to Zander, who was staring down at the mess with a look of regret. "The monsters, the ones that didn't get moved, where were they held?"

Zander grimaced, pointing to the biggest hole, where there was nothing left. "There. I know Isaac wanted to be sure they could be completely obliterated if necessary."

I understood what he meant. It looked like the explosion had originated from under that building. I rubbed my hands on my face, feeling a mix of emotions. Glad the creatures weren't going to swarm out and attack us but sorry they'd died in such a horrible way.

Kevin said, "Well, I guess it worked." He sighed. "I really hate this place." Anna nodded emphatically.

Uncle Alex said, "They held monsters here?" He looked troubled.

"Yes," I told him, "they called it the monster library." I hesitated before deciding he needed to know. "And there were these two women, Nancy and Paisley, who were the keepers, I guess. They have the same ability as you but they are... different."

I searched for a tactful way to explain the awful way they perverted their ability, but Uncle Alex was already nodding. "I know Nancy, and I've heard of Paisley." He ran a hand through his hair with a tired sigh. "I know how they use their ability. It's repulsive. I guess I shouldn't be surprised they aligned with Mountain of Ash."

I said to Zander, "Do you think they made it out?"

He shrugged. "I would bet on it, but I don't know if they would have taken the monsters to the staging location or somewhere else."

Aunt Kate's eyes were wide. "Okay, you clearly have a lot of news for us."

"Just a bit," Kevin said with a slight smile.

Through the haze, I could see people milling around the ruins in groups of two and three. I recognized a few official-looking people from the Complex in Colorado who were taking photos.

Two women levitated above the remains of the buildings, calling down to a group of people who were clustered together outside a tent.

The floating woman on the left shouted, "Looks like three buildings are a total loss, but the fourth has some of the structure intact."

"I suggest sending in some of the firestarters to see if they can find anything," the other woman responded.

"Are we sure there's no chance of explosions?" The first woman asked as she propelled herself higher above the scene.

A quick discussion between folks on the ground resulted in a man yelling back, "No, Henry says it's all clear, should be safe enough to send someone heat-resistant inside."

It crossed my mind to offer, but, since I was sure the building that remained was the prison/lab, my entire being cringed at the idea of willingly going inside. I didn't have to, though, because two men ran up to the group and listened carefully before turning and dashing into what was left of the building.

"Is Zoe here?" I looked around for my cousin.

Aunt Kate winced. "No, she's at home, probably seething and thinking of ways to get back at us for leaving her there with Dan."

"I'll bet she is." Kevin grimaced.

"Uncle Dan is back?" After everything I'd been through in the past week, my uncle flipping out at me felt like it happened to someone else.

"Yes." Aunt Kate regarded me for a moment, "He came back to help us. I'll let him talk to you if you want to speak with him, but I can say he feels terrible about what he did."

My mind swirled with emotions over the news Uncle Dan had returned from his exile at the family mountain house. I was still angry and scared over his attack on me, but mixed in with those feelings was a smear of sorrow — he'd lost his sister, his daughter, and his wife because of Mountain of Ash. I wasn't sure I could ever forgive his actions towards me, though. However, now wasn't the time to dwell on my curmudgeonly uncle. I forced myself to set aside my feelings until we'd dealt with Mountain of Ash, so I only said, "Let's get through this first."

Aunt Kate's gaze settled on Zander, and she looked astonished for a moment before saying, "Oh my god, are you Zander Jones? Son of Winnie and Jacob Jones?" She unconsciously echoed Uncle Alex's greeting.

Zander gave her a tentative smile, clearly unsure of her reaction. "Yes, I am."

Aunt Kate looked around. "Are your parents here? We lost track of them so long ago." She hesitated, then asked carefully, "I guessing your presence here must mean they joined Mountain of Ash?"

"Yes, they brought us here several years ago." Zander's voice shook a little. Uncle Alex rested his arm around Zander's shoulders.

"I see." Aunt Kate looked distressed, twisting her hands together before stopping herself. "Did they go with Isaac?"

Zander dropped his gaze, shaking his head. "No, they never came back from a mission last year."

"Oh, I'm sorry," Aunt Kate said quietly. She held out her hand to Zander, squeezing his when he accepted it. "You look so much like your father when he was your age." She smiled at him, but her eyes were sad. "With your mother's touch, of course." I assumed she referred to his ice blue eyes.

Uncle Alex spoke gently, "Kate, we can talk to Zander later." He said, "Zander, why don't you stay with me for now while Kate takes Olivia and Kevin for a short debriefing." He glanced at a tent set up several yards way where official-looking people entered and exited.

Zander smiled, with a tinge of bitterness. "Sure."

"Hey, you should know that he helped us escape!" I blurted out with Kevin vehemently agreeing with me. "Why can't he come with us?"

"Understood, but Zander has been here a long time, and we need to be sure of some facts." Uncle Alex said to Zander, "I'm sorry, but if you work with us it will go a long way towards helping us understand what happened to your family."

I started to defend Zander again, but he said, "It's okay. I get it."

I hesitated, then gave him a quick hug, "Thank you for helping us escape." I frowned at my aunt and uncle, saying pointedly, "We couldn't have done it without you."

Aunt Kate said, "Come on. We need to meet with the others to decide on a course of action." She gestured to me and Kevin. "Alex will take care of your friend Anna while you two accompany me. We could use your insight."

Uncle Alex was already holding Anna's hand with his eyes closed. Anna gave me a shaky smile. She sighed softly as the gashes on her arms slowly healed. I gripped her shoulder tightly. "I'll see you when we're done. Okay?"

"Sure." Anna looked around at the flying women and the other supernormal activity. "I'm a little overwhelmed." When she looked at me, I realized she was trying hide her fear.

"Hey, stay with Uncle Alex, he'll take care of you." I looked at the 'rents. "Hopefully we'll leave soon." I felt Anna's shoulder relax marginally when both adults nodded.

She leaned her cheek against the top of my hand, closing her eyes. "Okay."

Uncle Alex's gaze went to my chafed wrists, "Can I heal those for you?"

I circled my fingers around my wrist, "You know what, I think I'll let them heal on their own. I need a reminder of..." I stopped because I couldn't put into words exactly what I needed to be reminded of, but I knew I wanted to resist Uncle Alex's healing which would leave my skin scar free. "I'm okay."

He cocked his head thoughtfully but didn't argue.

Kevin and I followed Aunt Kate to the tent swarming with people wearing Council guard uniforms. Before we entered, Kevin waved to a woman sitting near the folded-back opening. He grabbed my hand. "Come meet Laurel. Well, the rest of her, I guess." He laughed, then snorted with a slightly hysterical edge. "I'm sorry." He directed his apology to the woman. "I'm a little wrung out."

"It's okay, I've heard worse." The woman took Kevin's hand affectionately, her short-sleeved t-shirt and shorts exposing her legs and arms. She looked like she was in her late twenties with pale skin and white blonde hair tied back in a tight ponytail.

Kevin had warned me that disjointers looked odd. Now that I was face-to-face with one, I agreed. For some reason, I'd expected to see seams all over her body, showing where she could split off body parts. Instead, she was the very definition of loose-limbed. At her elbows, wrists, knees, and ankles, her skin was indented and slack. When she let her hand drop after touching Kevin, her arm swung at the elbow in an odd angle, as if her body didn't have to follow the rules of joint movement.

She faced me directly, giving me a smile. I managed to hold back a squeak of surprise when I saw her right eyelid drooped over an empty socket and her left eyeball jiggling in its opening.

"Hi." I tried to act as if I talked to disjointers every day. "Thanks for helping us." I found myself enunciating every word like we had when Kevin addressed her eye. I bit the inside of my lower lip to keep from laughing. All the adrenaline from recovering my abilities and fighting was fading. I was so tired that I was hitting the boundary of uncontrollable laughter.

Laurel nodded, and I wondered if she could detach her head. I decided probably not, because her neck didn't have the distinctive indent or looseness of her arm and leg joints. I was glad. A floating eye was freaky enough; I wasn't ready for a floating head.

Laurel's voice was wispy, as if she didn't use it often. "I'm glad I could help. That place looked awful." She tilted her chin up, opening the eyelid of her empty eye socket as her loose eyeball floated in front of her face, shifted until it lined up with its opening, then slipped in with a tiny slurping sound.

I realized I was staring with my mouth open. Laurel brushed a hand over her face awkwardly, looking down at the ground. I closed my mouth and said, "Sorry, this is new to me." I sounded like an idiot.

To my relief, Kevin saved me from further foolish statements. "Laurel, are you coming back to Portland with us?"

"Not sure yet." She pulled the tent opening wider, waving us inside. "But I think we're about to find out."

Aunt Kate stood beside a large monitor talking to man who I recognized as Smitty, the scientist she often working with on various projects. He'd come out last week to examine Kevin after he'd been attacked by the cockroach cluster. They looked like they were consulting over a tablet, a comfortingly normal sight. Laurel strode over to Aunt Kate and Smitty, already telling them what her right eyeball had seen.

My attention was diverted to the group near a large map of the United States. Several uniformed men and woman listened as a short Asian man wearing an impressive collection of medals spoke with emphatic gestures. As his hands moved through the air, he flipped one hand over, letting an intricate ice sculpture of a face form. He held it up, and I recognized Isaac's features.

"That's General Stone," Kevin commented from my side. "Close your mouth. You look like a fish."

"But... did you see what he just did?" I stood on my toes, trying to get a better look at the frozen version of Isaac. It was an improvement over the real thing since the ice gave Isaac's features an otherworldly appearance.

At my movement General Stone looked up, his gaze focused on me, "Olivia Brighthall, Kevin Brighthall. Come here."

"Oh no," Kevin muttered. I agreed; getting called out by a general felt a lot like getting called to the principal's office.

Aunt Kate marched over with great purpose, saying sternly, "Wally, I must be present for any questioning. They're both minors."

He acknowledged her statement, still watching us intently. "I'm glad we were able to find you." His gaze swept the room before returning to mine. "Where is your friend, Anna McLeod?"

"Ah, she's with Uncle Alex. He's healing her. Sir." I added awkwardly, unsure how to address the general. I doubted calling him Wally was acceptable.

General Stone nodded. "Good, I'm glad she's getting the help she needs." One of the uniformed women handed him a sheet of paper, which he glanced at before asking her to give it to another woman. "I would like to question you personally, if your aunt will allow it." To my surprise, his serious face relaxed into a mischievous smile at my aunt. "She doesn't trust me. She still thinks I'm the same guy who used to prank her when we were kids in San Francisco."

Aunt Kate crossed her arms. "Wally."

"Kate." He gestured toward the table where several chairs were clustered near the map. "I will be gentle with your family. I haven't frozen anyone in ice in years."

He winked at me, giving me the courage to say, "It was amazing, what you just did." I pointed to the frozen image of Isaac melting on the table. "I've never imagined using my ice abilities for something like that, sir."

General Stone held out his hand, letting an ice ball form. I watched, breathless as it became a cat. He handed it to me, saying, "Your fire ability has been well-trained by your family, but your ice ability has been neglected. After things settle down, I suggest you spend some time with the McEveety family in Texas. They are very adept, and you'll learn a great deal."

I turned the beautiful ice figure over in my hands, admiring the detail in the cat's face. "Thank you, sir."

"Are you and your cousin able to talk about your experience here?" He gestured for us to sit. Aunt Kate sat across from us so she could watch our faces.

I nodded while Kevin said, "Yes, sir."

"Good." General Stone waved to a woman, who joined us with a nod at Aunt Kate. "My wife, Sibyl, will assist." He folded his hands on the table. "Now, let's find out what you know so we can stop Isaac Milton and Mountain of Ash before they can do more harm."

Chapter 21

General Stone took us through our experience several times, stopping for details while his wife took notes. I learned that Kevin had spent most of the time in his cell or on a work detail, forced to do construction work. He didn't see the terrible triad much, though he did see Emma several times.

When my turn came, I took several deep breaths, explaining our first escape attempt, how Anna was tortured, and, finally, that Isaac wanted my blood to create a serum. "And I think he did it." I flushed with shame. "I tried to make it unusable, but he, well, he, you know he's a mind reader, right?" I stuttered over the next details: "He forced me to relive a bunch of stuff—scenes in my head, but he made them worse." I took a shuddering breath, the tears I'd held back for days finally falling. "I'm sorry. I tried so hard for so many days to stop it."

I buried my face in my hands, sobbing over my failure and over the fact I was crying in front of everyone. I felt Kevin put an arm around my shoulders. "Ollie, I didn't know it was so bad."

Arms enclosed around me, and I heard Aunt Kate murmur in my ear. "Ollie, you did well. You have nothing to worry about. I'm so proud of you."

I leaned into her, comforted by her embrace. It wasn't as good as having my mother or father, but I felt better. I gave a few last sniffles and lifted my head, remembering. "They had a countdown clock. I'm pretty sure it was counting down to their big plan, Scorched Earth. I saw it about a day ago, and it was down to five days."

General Stone watched, his expression kind. "Olivia, you did well to hold out as long as you did." I must have looked puzzled as to how he knew. "We were able to hack their system once we came onsite. We didn't get everything before the explosion, but we got enough. Peter and Paul Haung made copious recordings and notes of their experiments," His voice turned cold, "We have more than enough to condemn the Twins for many, many crimes."

I sat up, "You caught them?"

"We did, along with several other Mountain of Ash members."

"Where are they?" Kevin asked.

"Already on their way to Colorado. We didn't want to risk Isaac recovering any assets."

I sat back, examining my feelings. I decided I was relieved not to see the twins. It was Isaac and Emma who I really wanted to find.

"What happens now, sir?" Kevin asked.

"Now you go back to Portland." He stood up and we followed. "Kate, your family can head back soon. Use the smallest plane. I think we'll come to Portland before going back to base. You have good resources, and I may have more questions for your niece and nephew. I'd also like to talk to Anna McLeod. I suspect she'll have a unique perspective."

With that announcement, we were clearly dismissed, as several more uniformed people who'd waited in the back moved forward to talk to the general.

Obviously affected by our story, Aunt Kate drew me close while reaching out for Kevin, "Olivia, Kevin, I'm so sorry you went through this experience."

Kevin shrugged uncomfortably. "It's okay."

She shook her head but let us go. "Give me about thirty minutes to get ready to head out. Kevin, go find your father and Anna."

I stood in the middle of the tent, looking around me. Lange caught my eye and beckoned me over to the group he was huddled with around a table.

As we neared Lange, my steps slowed with shock. My bulky cousin sat with Six. After leaving Six in a coma a week ago when her sister, Three, was killed, I didn't expect to see her up and about anytime soon. I'd assumed all of the Octad sisters were still in a coma.

Six looked very different from a week ago. Instead of the Octad standard dress of gray tunic and pants, she wore jeans and a dark green Henley under a jean jacket that I recognized from one of Zoe's outfits. She smiled at me as I approached. "Olivia! I'm so happy to see you."

I took her outstretched hands in mine, noting the use of "I" instead of "we", the way the Octad usually referred to themselves. "Hey, I'm glad to see you too. I'm so sorry about Three. How are you doing?"

"Thank you." Six lost her smile and let go of my hands. "I'm okay. I came out the coma first."

"Is the link between you and your sisters still broken?" I blurted out before I realized it was probably a delicate question. "I hope it's not hard to talk about."

Six shook her head, "No, our connection wasn't permanently broken, thank goodness." She wove her fingers together with a wry smile. "But it's not the same." For a moment her pupils dilated in what I recognized as accessing the hive mind she shared with her sisters before returning to normal size. "You see, we're still able to talk to each other, and we can still access our archives, but it's different because I, each of us, can choose to join mentally with each other. Before Three died, it was compulsory and, well, it felt right, you know?" she said. "Though when I spent time training with your family, I started to enjoy my own time. I learned a lot from your family about hunting and training." We shared a smile at the memory of her first hunt, where she caught the mole-like creature in Colonel Summers Park.

Six sat down leaving room for me to sit next her. "I think that helped me when we lost Three. Already having a little bit of separate identity." She faced me. "When I came out the coma first, I was able to find my sisters in their heads. And I helped them adjust some."

"Are they okay, your sisters?"

"Yes." Six paused. "Well, not completely, of course. But we will manage."

"What was Three's birth name?" I suddenly wanted very much to think of Three as a separate person.

"Harriet." Six answered.

"Harriet," I repeated softly, thinking of all the people who'd been hurt or killed because of Isaac's mania to remake the world.

"We'll mourn her as a group when we've caught her killers." Six cleared her throat. "I heard that Ben defected."

I cleared my own throat. "Yeah." I tilted my head to look at her thoughtfully. "You don't sound surprised."

She shrugged. "I heard Isaac is a mind reader." She fluttered a hand in Aunt Kate's direction to indicate how she knew. "I figured Ben would be drawn in by the idea of someone like him. It would be very tempting, even understandable."

I didn't want to think about Ben, though the memory of his curiously blank face as the Ashers were fleeing troubled me.

Kevin and Anna came in, angling towards me. I searched Anna's face, relieved to see she looked better, though the shadows of her experience remained in her eyes. I greeted them. "Hey, where's Zander?"

"General Stone sent someone out to question him. They're all pretty curious about what happened to his family." Kevin answered, before giving Six a smile. "Six, it's good to see you. I'm sorry about Three."

Six nodded in acknowledgement.

"How did Aunt Kate know about Isaac, about where to find us?" I asked the question that had been brewing in my mind ever since we'd seen Laurel's eye floating in midair.

"It was Mom's idea," Lange said. He shoved his hands in his pockets. "Mom tracked down Nick Carradine. Remember him?"

I did remember Nick Carradine, the homeless, mentally-shattered supernormal with the ability to accurately track monsters. Even before I'd rejoined the Brighthalls, I'd noticed him on street corners occasionally, clad in worn jeans and a light blue jacket, his arm half raised, jabbing his pointer finger in different directions like a broken compass with his white hair sticking out like dandelion fluff. At the time, I simply thought he was one of the unfortunate mentally ill homeless folks dotting Portland's landscape. I came to find out he was a valuable resource for the Brighthalls. Aunt Kate often sought him out to help find monsters, and in return the 'rents made sure he was fed and as safe as he could be. Whatever incident had caused his breakdown left him with an intense, pathological fear of being indoors. He could barely speak except to provide directions to find whatever monster was on his radar.

"Why?" I asked. "Can he track the Mountain of Ash members?" Had their deeds somehow made them monsters by Nick's definition? Or had he been able to track the monsters held in the monster library? I decided the ranch was probably too far off Nick's range, or else he would have led us to the monsters earlier.

Lange shook his head, "Nope, but he tracked down another monster who knew Isaac Milton, another one he'd sent to distract us."

Kevin opened his mount in a silent 'O' of understanding. "And it just told you guys where Mountain of Ash and Isaac were hiding?"

Lange and Six exchanged a look. "Not really, not at first." Lange met my puzzled gaze, "We held it in the containment facility. Then Uncle Dan had the idea to ask Godfrey if he would help."

I remembered Godfrey had been shipped off to one of the sanctuaries. "Wait a minute. Uncle Dan thought it would be worthwhile to talk to a monster? To ask for help?" My voice squeaked with astonishment that my uncle, out of all of my family, was the one willing to seek assistance from something he deemed an animal.

Six smiled. "Yes, it was quite the conversation, but Godfrey eventually agreed to tell us where the ranch was." She gave a wry laugh. "He had some conditions, but I think the main reason he did it is out of anger that Isaac tricked him. Apparently, the mind control that Isaac uses wears off after a day or two, so Godfrey was very angry at his situation."

Lange ran both hands through his hair, then held them out in a shrug. "I know, it's weird to work with a monster, right?" He touted the usual line supernormals took on what they called monsters, but he looked uncomfortable when I pushed back.

"Is he? A monster, I mean? Godfrey was able to hold a conversation, tell you guys where to the find us." I snapped out the words.

Lange looked like he wanted to argue, but he kept his mouth shut when Aunt Kate strode over, followed by Smitty.

"Olivia, Kevin," Aunt Kate spoke briskly as I realized Kevin had joined me while I was talking to Six, "you remember Smitty?"

My cousin and I nodded. Smitty smiled at us. "I'm heading back to Colorado, but I wanted to say hello."

Kevin asked. "Aren't you going after Mountain of Ash?"

"Do you have any idea where they went?" Smitty asked sharply. "We can't trace them, and the members we caught won't tell us. Yet."

"No." Kevin looked chastened while I wondered who else they'd captured other than the Twins.

Smitty nodded like he'd expected Kevin's answer. "We're leaving a small force here to see if anything can be salvaged from the wreckage." He waved a hand in the direction of the ruins.

I was glad we were heading back to Portland, though I felt a twist in my gut over seeing Dad. I hadn't even talked to him before I left. The only communication I left him with was a note for him to find. I could only imagine what he'd thought when I didn't come home. I twisted my hands together before asking my aunt, "Does Dad know where I was? Does he know you found me?"

"Yes." She gave me a hard look. "I think he's planned a fairly long lecture for you when you get home." Her expression softened. "I let him know we found you safe. He'll be waiting for us in the parking lot at the warehouse —" she cast a look in Anna's direction, " —with your friend's parents." Then she added, "And Dan is at the warehouse, but I can ask him to leave before we get back."

I felt a flash of gratitude that Aunt Kate would ask me if I didn't want to see my uncle. I hesitated while trying to decide if I wanted to tell Uncle Dan about Emma. And I wanted to find out if he remembered Isaac. I looked at Kevin for his reaction as I said, "I think we need to talk to him about Emma and Mountain of Ash."

Kevin nodded.

"Okay, I'll ask him to stay," Aunt Kate answered. "Come on, the plane is ready for us."

I followed her, thinking it was going to be an interesting reunion at the warehouse.

Chapter 22

When Zoe picked us up at the airport, she gave me a fierce hug. "You scared me."

"I know. I was scared too." I held onto my cousin, my only female one since I'd decided Emma was no longer part of my family.

Kevin said, "Hey Zoe," and she reached out an arm to pull him into a group hug.

Anna stood smiling at us but also looking left out. When Zoe released us from her embrace, she turned to Anna. "Hey, I'm really glad you're okay."

Anna nodded, "Thanks."

Uncle Alex nudged us along. "We need to get back to the warehouse before everyone else does."

General Stone and his team were about an hour or so behind us with Zander and Six. I suspected at least part of the delay was to give the Brighthalls a chance for a brief family reunion before we were pulled into planning how to track down Mountain of Ash.

As we drove through Portland, I looked around, feeling out of sync with the city. Everything looked familiar but different than I remembered. I felt like I'd been gone much longer than a week. During that time, it seemed like all the flowers in Portland had decided to bloom, or maybe the bright sunlit colors simply contrasted with the dull gray, bright white, and bland tans that encompassed the color scheme at the ranch. I rolled down the windows of the van, enjoying the city smells with my restored super sensing abilities—food scents wafting from restaurants, sweat from a passing cyclist, even the smell of a guy smoking a pipe.

When we pulled up to the warehouse, I experienced the same sense of disorientation. I knew intellectually it had only been a week since I'd seen the place, but so much had happened that it was jarring to return. The version of me who stood here a week ago seemed so naïve.

Well, there was one tangible difference between now and then. Anna's parents stood in the parking lot, her mother pacing back and forth while her father shaded his eyes for a better look as we drove up. Mr. McLeod called out to his wife, who ran to his side and grabbed his hand. My heart flipped when I saw Dad leaning against his SUV, arms crossed. I couldn't see his expression under the baseball hat shadowing his face.

Anna peered at her parents, nervously rubbing her hands together as if washing them. "Oh no. What do I tell them?"

Aunt Kate spoke up. "We have a cover story for you. We've been telling them you went camping with Olivia and Kevin and got lost."

Anna frowned, while I laughed despite the serious situation. When Aunt Kate gave me a perplexed look, I explained my amusement, "Anna hates camping and almost always finds a way to get out of family camping trips."

Aunt Kate said, "Yes, they did mention that fact." She looked irritated.

I gave her a sharp look, realizing what it meant for us to be missing for a week, "Did they call the police?" I wondered how much Jack knew about our disappearance. He was in the police intern program and, as of right before we went missing, he knew about my heritage.

My aunt looked uncomfortable. "We told Anna's family we'd gotten the authorities involved, that there were search parties tracking you in the wilderness." She tapped a finger on her always-in-hand phone. "We managed the data, so they'd know we were close but not to what." She gave Anna an earnest look. "We didn't want them to worry while we did everything we could to find you. And, as you can see, we did find you."

"You lied to them." Anna and I spoke at the same time.

"We couldn't tell them the truth because we had to protect—" Aunt Kate began but Zoe parked the van and Anna's parents rushed the door before she could finish.

Anna jumped out and hugged her mother tightly while her father wrapped his arms around both. Anna and her parents were all crying and talking at once.

"Ollie," Dad hugged me, "I'm glad you're home." He held me at arm's length by the shoulders. "But you can't do that again, just go off without telling me. Leaving a note was a crappy thing to do." He looked so tired that my heart twisted with sorrow over causing him to worry.

"I know. I'm sorry, Dad."

He sighed, taking off his hat, running a hand through his hair. I was surprised to see glints of gray mixed in with the brown as he pulled on his cap again. Had they been there before I made him worry so much?

Uncle Dan spoke from behind me, "Hello, Olivia. It's good to see you."

I turned and nodded carefully, noncommittally. Now wasn't the time to go into everything between us.

Kevin didn't seem to feel the same reticence I felt. He put his hands on his hips, "Uncle Dan." Then he faltered before saying, "Emma stayed with them, she's, well, she really has gone dark side."

Uncle Dan didn't explode in anger, he just looked very sad as he answered, "I know, I, um, spent some time thinking and reflecting over the last week." He swallowed. "And I've got a lot to answer for."

His words reminded of what Isaac had said about Uncle Dan ruining his life.

"Now isn't the time to get into this," Aunt Kate said, "We need to —"

Aunt Kate didn't get to finish because Anna's mother focused everyone's attention on her when she said loudly, "Anna, why did you go camping without telling us?" Her bewildered expression made my stomach clench at the lies the 'rents had told them.

Anna hesitated, giving me a long look before turning to Aunt Kate. "I can't do this." She waved her hand at her parents. "I can't lie to my own parents."

Mr. McLeod said, "What do you mean, lie?" while Mrs. McLeod scrutinized Aunt Kate closely, eyebrows drawn together.

Anna put her hands on her hips and faced her parents. "I wasn't camping. I went to help these guys —" she pointed at me and Kevin, "— find a friend of theirs who went missing because he was captured while helping them find some bad guys." She gave me an apologetic look before adding, "We were in a fight and got taken by the bad guys. Oh, and by the way, the Brighthalls and Olivia — " she flapped a hand to include me and my family, " — all have superpowers, and so do the bad guys." She gave everyone a defiant glare as if to say, 'so there.'

Her parents gaped at her, my family stared at her, but I couldn't help grinning at her bravery. I was proud of her for revealing our secret even though I didn't know what would happen to her. With that thought in mind, I stepped to her side, unsure what I would do if anyone tried to hurt her, but ready to help her no matter what anyone did.

Anna's mother found her voice, saying patiently, "Anna, honey, clearly you've had a rough time and need to come home with us right now. I'll make an appointment with Dr. Dinna, so you can work through your trauma."

"Mom, I don't need to go to a therapist." Anna twisted the ends of her dirty, tangled hair between her fingers. "Well, maybe I do, but not because you think I'm making up a story." She faced me. "Ollie, show them, please?"

Uncle Dan started to speak, but I made my choice quickly. If Isaac was going to try to kill off normals, they needed to know about us so they could be involved in defending against the Ashers in whatever way they could. I could start with Anna's parents, right here and now.

I held up my hand, letting flames flow from my open palm, up my arm and all over my body. I watched Anna's parents for a moment before letting the fire outlining my body die out. They wore identical expressions of shock.

Aunt Kate gave a great sigh and walked to the door leading into the warehouse. She paused, head lowered in thought before pushing the door open. "Everyone, inside. It's foolish to have this ... conversation out in the parking lot." When Uncle Dan and Uncle Alex started to argue that normals weren't allowed into the warehouse, she just said, "*Everyone*—now."

Dad glanced at me, then at the open door, before practically running inside as if he was afraid Aunt Kate would change her mind. I knew he'd always felt left out of Mom's life and, subsequently, my life because he couldn't go into the warehouse. We'd argued about it just last week, and I'd had to use my ability to keep him from trying to come inside. I hoped this moment would help us get over the lingering damage to our father-daughter relationship from that incident.

Anna gently nudged her parents. "Come on. This is important." They followed her, still speechless.

Once inside, Aunt Kate directed the group to the classroom area, set up with the familiar couches and chairs.

When I walked past Uncle Dan, he said, "Olivia," in a warning voice.

I kept walking, saying firmly, "No, this is the right thing to do. They deserve to know what's coming; it's their world too."

His lips tightened, but he stepped back to let me pass.

I sat next to Anna. Kevin sat on her other side, winking at me with what I took to be approval of my actions. Dad sat next to Uncle Alex, avidly staring around the huge space. He tilted his head to peer into the rafters at the ropes and platforms we used for balance and precision drills. I wondered if he was imagining Mom training here, like I sometimes did. He looked at the sparring area, and I thought I saw unshed tears in his eyes. He took one shuddering breath.

Anna's parents hesitated until Lange kindly suggested they sit on the couch next to ours. He sat in a chair nearby with Zoe standing beside him, shifting restlessly from foot to foot.

Aunt Kate walked to the front of the classroom, turned, and surveyed the group before her. She shook her head, gave me a wry smile, then directed her gaze at a remote control laying on the table beside her. I grinned when the remote control lifted without visible means of support and floated to her outstretched hand.

Mrs. McLeod opened her mouth, closed it. She squeezed her eyes shut, took a deep breath, and opened them. Mr. McLeod leaned over and reached for Anna's hand, giving her an inquiring look. She nodded vigorously. "See? They all have powers, like I said."

Aunt Kate set the remote down, "Okay, as Anna stated, and Olivia and I have shown, there are people in the world with abilities."

Mrs. McLeod spoke up, "What do you mean abilities?" Then she held up her hand as if to scrub her question out the air. "You know what, we'll get back to that later." She looked pissed. "You lied to us about where our daughter was all this time. You made us think you were looking for her, that the authorities were looking for her." She stood up, furious. "You sent us on searches in the woods. You told us you were looking in other parts of the woods." She jabbed an accusing finger at the 'rents. "You had no idea what Anna was going through, where she was. But you knew more than we did, and you chose what not tell us." Mrs. McLeod took a shuddering breath. "If she never came home to us, what lies would you have told us? Would we have ever known the truth?"

Her accusations reverberated around the room like shockwaves. I waited for Uncle Dan to explode with anger, or for Uncle Alex to start soothing everyone, or for Aunt Kate to explain in her logical manner. But the 'rents looked at each other, seeming to be at a loss to explain their motivations in the face of Anna's mother's righteous anger.

Aunt Kate gave my dad a pleading look. "Sam, can you lend your unique perspective here?"

Dad leaned back in his seat, crossing his arms behind his head, "You know what, Kate, nope. I'm on their side in this argument."

Anna's mother whipped her body around to face Dad. "Sam, you knew?"

Dad dropped his relaxed pose, hunching forward with a remorseful expression. "Yes, Sara. I'm sorry for not telling you." He straightened, eyes on Aunt Kate's. "But I'm done with hiding. Kate, Alex, Dan, she's right. You knew where the kids were two days ago. You should have told Sara and Jim."

Aunt Kate glanced at the monster containment room. I wondered if the monster Uncle Dan had caught was still in there, locked up.

We all jumped when Aunt Kate's phone played the first notes to Bon Jovi's "Living on a Prayer". She glanced at it. "Okay, the others will be here in a few minutes." She looked at Anna's parents, "We'll have to continue this conversation later. You need to leave. Can we all agree to keep your knowledge on the down low for now?"

"I'm not leaving." Anna gripped the edges of the couch as if she could hold on tightly enough to prevent any of us from dragging her out of the warehouse. I, for one, wasn't going to try. In fact, I wrapped my hand around hers to help her hold on more firmly.

"Then we're not either," Mr. McLeod tugged his wife's hand, and she sat down beside him. Both wore the same stubborn expression as Anna.

Dad grinned as he also settled in, clearly planning to stay as well.

The 'rents shared a frustrated look before Uncle Alex shrugged. "Okay, fine. Just stay out of the way."

Zoe's phone pinged. She glanced at it and rolled her eyes with a bark of laugh. "So, hey, Jack's outside."

"You talk to Jack?" I had no idea she knew Jack other than meeting him once or twice with me.

She shrugged. "When you guys were missing, he got worried and tracked me down. I remembered you'd told him about us at the Hawthorne Theater. I was there after all. He was pretty freaked out that you were missing and wanted to help." Zoe pulled out her phone. "I told him they were going after you. I owe him an update, but I wanted to see you first." She looked at Aunt Kate. "I say let him in. After all, everyone else is here."

Uncle Dan said, "Why not? Let in the world." He said it sarcastically, but Zoe grinned and ran to the door, shoving it open, and calling out, "Come on in, Jack."

I heard a muffled response, and Jack followed her in, neck craned as he peered around, taking in the scene. When he saw me, he ran up and hugged me tightly. "Olivia, hey."

"Hey, Jack," I said, surprised at the lump forming in my throat at the sound of his voice.

"Are you okay? Are you hurt?" He took a breath. "Hey, Anna. Hey, Kevin."

I hugged him back, then stepped back as he hugged Anna. She gripped his arms. "Jack, I'm so glad we both know about Olivia's other world." She pulled him down to sit beside her.

Another voice spoke up, "I've always wanted to see what was inside." Harold smiled when everyone stared at him. "Jack brought me. He knew I was worried about you kids. Hi, Alex." He greeted my uncle, who he knew from running a surreptitious clinic for the homeless.

"How do you know each other?" My worlds were not only colliding but also melding together.

"I was there when you first met Harold." Jack reminded me of the day six months ago I'd inadvertently exposed my abilities to Jack for a second time to retrieve Harold's money from another homeless man.

Jack and I shared a look; I wondered if he was thinking about how much had changed since that day, like I was.

Aunt Kate waved Harold into the seating area, "Okay, okay, everyone's here." She sounded resigned. "Here's the synopsis so you're all caught up. Yes, there are people with supernormal abilities. Superpowers, as you would call them. We've existed as long as you have. There aren't a lot of us because a couple of hundred years ago most of us were killed by another supernormal with the power to read and control minds." She ticked off facts on her fingers. "Now we're threatened by another supernormal with the same abilities." She paused, closing her eyes as if in pain. "By two supernormals with the same ability."

A ripple of sighs went through the room as we remembered Ben.

Aunt Kate kept talking quickly, "We hid from normals—what we call you—for many reasons, mostly because we don't want to solve all of your problems with our powers." She made a face at Anna's snort, but didn't argue with her. "Okay, now, I need everyone to stay quiet. The Council and some of our military force are on the way here to discuss how to subdue Isaac and Ben, the supernormals I mentioned, along with stopping Mountain of Ash, their terrorist group. This is our highest priority right now because they are threatening to do something big in less than a week. And we'd like to stop him, if you don't mind."

With that, she marched over to her desk. Uncle Alex moved over to Anna's parents, talking to them, asking if they needed anything.

After giving everyone a fulminating look, Uncle Dan followed his sister. I realized he hadn't said much since we entered the warehouse. He'd mainly glared around as events unfolded. I figured we should be glad he was determined to be on good behavior for the moment.

Aunt Kate called me over, "Oliva, Kevin, what can you tell us about Isaac Milton?" She looked at the picture of him on her screen. "He looks a little bit familiar, but, even though I've heard his name before, I can't really place the face." She was clearly ready to turn her focus back to the bigger issue.

Kevin shrugged. "I never got to see much of him or anyone in charge. They mainly had me on work detail, like I told General Stone."

"He told me he knew you, all of you." I blurted out the words I'd been holding back since I'd first seen Uncle Alex on the hillside. "He said he went to camp when he was twelve. Uncle Dan and the rest of you were there." I looked directly at Uncle Dan. "You were in the same cabin or team, something like that. He said you ruined his life, but you also gave him purpose." I shook my head, lifting my hands in a 'who knows' gesture. "I don't know what he meant. He's kinda pompous."

Uncle Dan rubbed his chin, looking perplexed, "I don't remember anyone named Isaac at Camp Tera." He frowned thoughtfully. "Kate, Alex, ring any bells?"

Aunt Kate shook her head, "When you were twelve, hmmm, I think that was the year I only stayed a week before leaving to intern at the tech center in Colorado."

"I think that was my first year at camp." Uncle Alex stared off in the distance for a moment. "I didn't see you much, you were doing your own thing." Then he laughed a little. "That was the year you and a couple of others campers snuck out, right?"

Uncle Dan glowered at his brother. "Not funny. It was a serious mistake and ..." His voice trailed off for a moment as his eyes widened and his mouth went slack with shock. He stared into the distance for a moment before saying, "Oh no."

"Oh no, what?" I prompted him, sure we were near understanding Isaac's connection to my family.

He blinked, focusing on me. "I snuck out with three friends." Embarrassment flashed across his face. "We'd heard there was a cool comic book store in the town nearby. We were bored of camp. It was our last year, and we'd done all the stuff there was to do. We were just going to buy some comics, get in and out without anyone seeing us. But one of the guys, Tommy Jacobson, got into an argument with a normal who cut in line. He, Tommy, started a fight and almost punched the guy, but we stopped him. We managed to sneak back into camp without being caught, but later on I heard that the guy in town had been killed. I confronted Tommy about it in front of a camp counselor. No one could prove it was Tommy, but he got kicked out anyway."

Uncle Dan paused, frowning. Aunt Kate looked thoughtful. "I remember Tommy. He idolized you." She smiled a little. "He followed you around. I think you kind of liked having a fan." Her expression turned serious. "What does Tommy Jacobson have to do with any of this? How does he connect to Isaac Milton?"

"Because Tommy Jacobson is Isaac Milton." Wanda Jones spoke from the doorway of the warehouse.

Jolted by the announcement, I stared at Council Leader Jones for a moment before realizing the entire supernormal Council stood behind her. Seeing all seven leaders of our highest governing body in one place underscored the seriousness of the situation.

Echoing my thoughts, Zoe muttered, "Holy shit."

Chapter 23

"Tommy Jacobson is Isaac Milton." Uncle Dan repeated Council Leader Jones's statement. He didn't look surprised by the news. "It makes sense."

"Yes." Council Leader Jones marched into the room with the Council following. She paused when she noticed my father and the McLeods clustered with Jack and Harold. I shifted, ready to defend the normals, but she merely turned away as if not ready to deal with the incursion.

As she approached Aunt Kate's work area, she asked, "With your permission, Kate, may we start setting up? General Stone is not far behind us."

"Of course," Aunt Kate answered. "Your team can use the southeast section." As Council Leader Jones turned to direct her people over to the open area near the laser tag room, my aunt grimaced at my uncles. Uncle Alex sort of smiled while Uncle Dan shifted on his feet, taking a step after them like he wanted to go defend his territory.

Jones glanced at two of her team, who turned to greet the rest of the people streaming in through our doors. For several minutes, it seemed like the doors to the warehouse never stopped opening and closing. General Stone and his entourage came through the door with great purpose, carrying all kinds of equipment—monitors, computers, and other tools. The general greeted us briefly before joining the crew setting up the command center.

A few minutes later, Six, followed by several identical women, came in together. Six didn't speak, at least not aloud, as she guided her sisters over to greet us.

It was a bit disorienting to be regarded by seven matching faces. The similarities ended there. The women no longer wore matching outfits in different shades of gray. Most of them were dressed in neutral tones, almost camouflage-like clothing.

I addressed the rest of the sisters. "I'm sorry about Three. How are you all doing?"

"Thank you." Six looked at her sisters. "We're okay."

The nearest sister frowned at Six. "Speak for yourself, Gabriele," then she winced, giving me a wry look. "We'll," She corrected herself deliberately, "*I'll*, never get used to calling a sister by name instead of by birth order." She sighed and ran her hands through her hair as if settling her mind. The sister next to her stood slumped, staring at the floor.

Six grinned, "Olivia, meet Five, or, since we're trying to think of each other by our birth names, Elizabeth."

Elizabeth shook my hand. "I'm glad to you see you and the others safe." She turned to Six, continuing to speak out loud, probably as a courtesy to me. "Gabriele, we're here to help with communications. As soon as General Stone has an idea of where he wants us to go, he'll use transporters to take each of us there." Her gaze flicked to her dejected sister next to her. "Well, most of us."

I was pretty sure the slumped sister was One because her lips were pressed together like they'd been back in the research facility in Colorado when they were testing Ben's abilities. When I'd met One at the Council's seat in Colorado, she was clearly the leader of the hive mind, but now she looked to be the most shattered of the seven sisters. Her gaze was unfocused, as if she was searching inside herself for the once strong connection of the hive mind. She was the only one still wearing the gray tunic and pants that had been the women's standard outfit.

When she raised her eyes to meet mine, I forced myself not to wince at her devastated eyes. She looked so lost, so lonely, that I wanted to hug her and tell all would be okay. I reached out a hand, but she twisted away. Five said softly, taking her sister's arm, "Hey Sofia, let's get you settled somewhere comfortable." The rest of the sisters gave me varying versions of critical glares before following Five.

I looked wordlessly at Six, who blew out her breath. "Sofia hasn't recovered much." She looked after her sisters. "I don't know if it has anything to do with being the firstborn. Maybe our link was strongest in her mind? We brought her with us because we thought it might help her to be with her sisters." She rubbed her eyes tiredly before adding. "I don't know if it's helping. When any of us touch her mind, it's like stepping into a chaotic mess."

"Wow." I felt awkward and wished I knew how to help Six's sister.

During our conversation, General Stone's team had been whizzing in and out of the warehouse, bringing in equipment. From where I stood, the command center appeared to be completely set up. I saw different displays across several monitors—some showing maps with red markers scattered in various locations and showing diverse images, including some of members of Mountain of Ash.

Zander entered, looked around, and saw me. He came over slowly, as if he wasn't sure how he'd be greeted, but I smiled at him to welcome him.

Clearly irritated by the pause in the larger conversation, Uncle Dan spoke impatiently. "Wanda? Will you explain how Tommy Jacobson became Isaac Milton?"

"Dan, I can't believe you haven't put the pieces together yet." She ignored his huff of annoyance. "Okay, where to begin." She thought for a moment. "Does anyone remember Henry Milton?"

The 'rents exchanged looks in puzzled silence before Aunt Kate said thoughtfully, "Yes, wasn't he the guy Dad caught trying to steal land from a rancher, a normal? I was a baby, but I read something about it later. Henry Milton killed several hikers over a few months and buried them on the man's land." She looked repulsed. "Then he told the police it was the normal who was killing and burying the hikers. They arrested the normal. Dad figured out what Henry Milton was doing and turned him in. Somehow Dad got the normal exonerated. Wait, I think I can find a picture of Henry Milton." She bent over her phone, murmuring into it, then swiped the image onto the large screen.

I stared at the mugshot-style photo of an angry man with disheveled hair falling over his face. His mouth was twisted into a bitter pout. The man in the photo shared the same intense glare as Isaac, but unlike Isaac, Henry Milton's crazy showed on the surface. He looked like the stereotype of a wacked-out religious cult leader.

"Wow, I'd hate to run into *him* in dark alley," Kevin muttered. "Is he still alive?"

"Yes." Council Leader Jones answered as she took a seat, indicating we should join her. "We've doubled his restraints and added guards in case Isaac tries to break him out." She gazed at the photo for a moment. "I remember his arrest. I had just joined the army. He ranted about how he'd been denied the land that was his right as a superior being. He kept shouting about how he had big plans for that land, to make his stand in taking over the world for supernormals. How he was going to raze the earth and start anew."

A shock ran through me, and I murmured, "Like Scorched Earth."

Council Leader Jones met my eyes and nodded. "Exactly. When we first heard Emma Brighthall use that phrase, we started to wonder about a connection between Mountain of Ash and Henry Milton."

"How is Tommy Jacobson, or Isaac Milton, whatever you call him, connected to Henry Milton?" Uncle Dan looked like he'd guessed the answer but needed to know for sure.

"We know that a woman, a supernormal, named Helen Jacobson was Henry Milton's girlfriend around the time he was using his transporter ability to kidnap, murder hikers, and hide their bodies to frame the normal for murder. We could never determine if she knew what he was doing. We do know she had a son by Henry Milton that he didn't know about. After his arrest, she'd moved back in with her parents and found out she was pregnant. She died not long after giving birth, so Thomas Isaac Jacobson was raised by his grandparents." She sighed and ran a hand over her short hair. "As best we can tell, he was ignorant of his father's deeds until he was twelve."

Uncle Dan looked sick. "I couldn't prove he killed that guy, but I had a feeling he may have."

"We haven't put all the pieces together yet, but we know he returned to his grandparents' home after camp." Council Leader Jones paused as Aunt Kate called up a photo of Isaac Milton and put it side by side with his father. "His grandparents died in an accident about a year later."

"When he was thirteen?" I blurted out, putting that piece together at least. "When his significant power manifested, right?"

Council Leader Jones nodded. "Given what we're learning about Isaac Milton, we now suspect he had something to do with their deaths." She sighed. "It's likely they knew who his father was but never told him. Once his mind reading ability manifested, there was nothing they could hide from him. We lost track of him until about ten years ago."

"How long have you known about Isaac Milton?" I recognized Aunt Kate's tone—it was the one she used when she was mad about something but trying to gather information objectively before she decided how angry she should be about it.

Council Leader Jones grimaced. "That he was the leader of Mountain of Ash? About five years. That he is a mind reader? A few days." She frowned. "There are many details we still don't know for sure, but we're working to gather them. They may give us clue to where Isaac Milton took the rest of Mountain of Ash after they fled the ranch today."

"How did you first hear his name?" I asked.

Council Leader Jones gave me a kind look. "When he took credit for a series of attacks on normals. They were designed to look like acts of nature, but we discovered they were caused by Eva Maralah, the individual you know as Black Gaea. During the investigation that led to her capture, we kept hearing the name Isaac Milton. But until now, we haven't been able to identify him with any certainty."

She sighed, looking tired, lines showing on her brown face. For the first time, I realized she was about twenty years older than Dad and the 'rents. Her powerful presence made her seem ageless, but recent events clearly weighed heavy on her shoulders.

Uncle Dan asked, "How do you know about the connection to Henry Milton?"

"The name was a clue, but he could have been an admirer for all we knew, taking the name as a homage to Henry Milton. The man did have a few followers." Council Leader Jones stood up and called out to a lanky white guy bustling around what looked like a centrifuge. He darted over, moving so fast he almost appeared to teleport. "Jeffery, tell the Brighthalls what you discovered."

Jeffery was a dapper dresser, his fitted suit set off with a polka dotted bow tie. As he spoke, his movements were controlled and precise. "I admit to having a suspicion about Isaac Milton's origins, which is why I ran the DNA test from the blood we collected when one of our heavies punched Isaac." In contrast to his small size, his voice boomed out, easily heard by the entire room. "Once I had the results, I sent them to Emily back at the lab in Colorado, and she confirmed that it's a strong likelihood Isaac is Henry Milton's son." He dusted his hands off, grinning around at us. "All neat and tidy."

I rolled my eyes, saying quietly to Kevin, "Neat and tidy. I'd hate to see what he thinks is messy."

"Thank you, Jeffery," Council Leader Jones dismissed the man.

"Any idea how much it will matter to him that Wesley Thornton is dead?" Uncle Alex asked. I was surprised to learn Wesley's last name. And surprised Uncle Alex knew it. He caught me watching. "I asked Wally if he knew the man's last name." He looked regretful. "I thought I should know it."

"Is Black Gaea with Isaac?" Kevin asked.

"We're fairly certain she is. And we don't know what the impact of losing Wesley Thornton will be." Council Leader Jones started to say more, but I was suddenly so tired of listening to speculation and theories.

"What are you going to do about Isaac and his followers?" I demanded.

Uncle Alex murmured soothingly, "Olivia," but I ignored him, staring fiercely at Council Leader Jones.

She acknowledged my question with a nod. "Young lady, that is why we're all here, to find answers to your question." Her gaze shifted to Zander who stood beside me, quietly taking in the conversation. We both jumped when she said, "Zander Jones."

Zander stared at her, clearly shocked that she knew his name. She didn't give him a chance to answer. "I was sorry to hear about your parents' deaths. I don't know if you are aware that your father was my nephew." Zander's eyes widened, and his lips parted as if to speak, but she kept talking. "Your parents cut off their entire family when they disappeared. Your grandfather, my brother, is still alive. I know he'll be happy to see you. We tried to find you several times over the past years, but I see why we were unable to locate you." She looked at him with regret.

"You're my great-aunt?" Zander's eyes were wide, and his voice shook a little. "I didn't think I had any family left. Well, except for —" He paused, then added, "Logan, I guess."

"We'll do our best to extract your brother. However, we could use your insight. You know a great deal about Mountain of Ash..."

"Yes, I'll help. I hate them for what they did to me, to my brother. They killed my parents, I know it." Zander said fiercely, clenching his hands by his sides.

"I'm so sorry."

Zander spoke in a rush. "I'll tell you what I know about their plans. I don't know where they are now, but I think I know where they'll be in five days." He looked uncertain, "Assuming Isaac sticks to his schedule."

"Come with me," Council Leader Jones said as she stood up, "I'll introduce you to General Stone."

Zander made a face indicating his amazement at the turn of events as he followed his great-aunt. I couldn't help smiling back, I was happy to learn he still had family.

They headed over to where General Stone's people had set up a command center while we'd been talking to the Octad and to Council Leader Jones. They were using some of Aunt Kate's equipment—white boards, monitors, and tables—along with other equipment I didn't recognize.

I started to follow, then clamped my hands over my ears as someone yelled. *ASHERS!*

The words vibrated through my skull, reducing all other sounds to background noise. I stumbled, dropping my hands as I fell to my hands and knees on the floor, overwhelmed. I managed to lift my head; no one else was reacting to the shouting and I realized in was all in my head.

The voice sounded like Ben's.

"Olivia, what's wrong!" Dad was at my side, wrapping his arm around me, supporting my body.

ASHERS, LISTEN!

I tried to speak but I couldn't form a thought over the voice yelling in my head. Ben's intrusion in my mind was stronger than I'd ever felt from him and there was an echoing quality to it that I didn't remember from the past. It sounded like he was on a speaker phone.

I only had a moment to worry if he'd also been enhanced by my blood before the next onslaught.

ASHERS, WATCH AND LEARN HOW THE WORLD OF NORMALS ENDS!

My stomach twisted with fear as I realized the voice in my head sounded like Isaac and Ben together. Had they combined abilities to get past my mental shields?

The warehouse faded around me. For a moment I thought I was being transported but since I still felt the cold floor of the warehouse under my knees, I guessed I was getting pulled into a vision. I dimly heard Dad calling my name next to me.

The double-toned voice echoed through my head again, reverberating so loudly in my skull that I shut my eyes in agony.

ASHERS, THIS IS YOUR CALL TO ACTION!

Chapter 24

My eyes were glued shut in horror as the Empire State Building in New York City flashed into my mind's eye. I felt like I was watching a movie scene—the street view of the iconic landmark in front of me, intact, until I saw the building crumbling from the top. My throat tightened as of thin streams of flames hit the building, igniting fires so hot the concrete and steel burned to ash like dried leaves. In seconds the building disintegrated, ash billowing after the panicked mass of people running away from the destruction.

The scene switched to show Washington, DC where there was nothing left of the White House but a pile of smoking ashes. Dragons wheeled in the sky over the Mall while hundreds of people ran away in terror.

SEE HOW THEIR PUNY, PITIFUL BUILDINGS CRUMBLE BEFORE OUR MIGHT! Isaac/Ben bellowed in my mind.

I felt like my body was floating while my brain seemed to tighten as I strained to process what was happening. The speed and scope of the destruction could only mean it was caused by supernormal disintegrators. Only they could demolish a building so thoroughly that no debris was left.

I tried to open my eyes, but more scenes slammed into my head. The London Eye turned into a rolling ball of fire, flying, spinning over the Thames, finally smashing into the Houses of Parliament Building. Water from the Thames exploded, washing over the rubble and bodies floated in the river as the water receded.

"No, no," I chanted, unsure if it was in my head or aloud until I felt a hand on my shoulder. I could barely hear Kevin ask, "Ollie, what's going on? What's happening to you?" Dad was yelling for Uncle Alex.

I couldn't force my eyes to open but I gasped out. "Scorched Earth has begun! The Empire State building, The White House are gone."

Kevin's hand spasmed, gripping me more tightly for a moment before letting go, "Where? What do you see?" His voice shook, "Is Isaac in your head?"

I could only nod as more images blasted into my mind. The Pyramids of Giza shattered into millions of pieces, bombarding the streets of Cairo with a deluge of rocks. The city was reduced to rubble in minutes with bodies pounded into pulp under falling stones.

Normals didn't have a chance against the power Isaac and his Ashers commanded. I clenched my hand on my arm where the needle marks once marred my skin before Uncle Alex healed me. I wasn't sure we had the power to stop Isaac's forces, not if he was using the serum from my blood. He probably had too many super-super-powered people on his side.

ASHERS, REJOICE! AS WE SHOW OUR DOMINANCE OVER NORMALS, MORE OF OUR KIND WILL BE FREE TO STOP PRETENDING THEY CARE ABOUT THE WEAKLINGS!

A crowd of people stood on a hillside above Paris. As one they raised their hands, flames shooting out, arching over the city. My breath stuck in my chest. There were more disintegrators than I'd seen at the ranch. And, as the city of Paris crumbled to ash under the onslaught of fire, more joined the attack.

Buenos Aires was mobbed by supernormals, some shooting at buildings with fire or energy blasts while others drove herds of monsters through the streets, slaughtering anyone in their path. I saw an Anone hugging a sobbing woman in a parody of comfort as its neck mouth slowly opened to engulf her head. A herd of tiny rustlings, the beautiful lizard butterflies, swarmed over person after person, leaving behind only skeleton fragments.

More scenes flooded my mind, coming so quickly I had trouble keeping them separate. Cities disintegrating, airplanes burning in midair, monsters chasing children through a field — normals fleeing, dying, unable to fight back against the overwhelming supernormal force of Mountain of Ash.

"We have to stop them!" I shouted, wrenching my eyes open to see General Stone crouched in front of me with my family watching anxiously behind him.

He caught my hands in his, saying, "Olivia, there are no attacks being reported. The White House is still standing, so is the Empire State Building."

"But I'm seeing so much destruction." I protested.

"Isaac could be trying scare you?" He asked, looking unconvinced but his question even as he said the words.

"Why would he—" I was yanked back into Isaac/Ben's vision.

ASHERS! SEE WHAT OUR TRUE POWER WILL BE AS WE REMAKE THE WORLD AS IT SHOULD BE!

An island with a large city sprawling across it began heaving and bucking. Buildings toppled over each other, roads cracked, and sinkholes breached in the earth. For a moment all was still until the earth erupted in jets of lava and ash shooting into the air and covering the island surface. The city disappeared into the ocean as a huge volcano burst out of the sea.

Though my throat wanted to close in horror, I forced out a description of what I saw, trying not to choke on the words. In the back of my mind, the part that was not overwhelmed by the shouting in my head, I wondered why I was seeing all the devastation if it wasn't real. Was it a preview of coming attractions? A trailer for Isaac's Scorched Earth plan? Why would he show me?

The scene shifted to one I knew from a trip with Dad, Yellowstone National Park, easy to recognize by the geysers. I didn't need the ring of supernormals standing around Old Faithful to know what was coming. I'd read articles about the super volcano under the park, and my voice shook as I told my audience what I saw. None of the supernormals looked familiar until I noticed Black Gaea. She grinned fiercely as the others focused their gazes on the ground. In slow motion the earth rippled, churning under their feet. Transporters, obviously enhanced, appeared and disappeared taking the earthmovers with them. Black Gaea was the last go, her eyes gleaming in the fiery eruption. In a scene straight out of apocalyptic horror movie, a torrent of ash and fire filled the air, blocking out the sun and sky.

I knew then that what I saw wasn't real because I was sure I should have felt tremors from the super volcano erupt under my feet. The knowledge didn't stop me from feeling terror down to my bones.

General Stone called out orders. Aunt Kate talked to someone about putting up perimeter guards near the larger landmarks.

Uncle Alex's voice seeped into my ears, "Ollie, I'm here. Take my hand."

I reached out, holding on tightly to my uncle. He couldn't stop the mental invasion using his empathic ability, but I felt him soothing the headache caused by the clamor in my mind.

The view changed to show smoke and ash from the Yellowstone eruption swirling across the US.

I shivered as the images from the super volcano subsided. I started to draw a breath of relief, but Isaac/Ben's voice echoed through my head as the sight of the city of Portland swept across my mind.

ASHERS, THERE IS BUT ONE HURDLE BEFORE WE CAN EXPECT OTHERS TO JOIN US.

"He's coming to Portland," I said, my fear so strong that my voice came out flat. A babble of voices spread out around me, but I focused on what Isaac/Ben were saying.

WE MUST SHOW OUR STRENGTH BY DEFEATING THE COUNCIL AND THEIR SYCOPHANTS, THE BRIGHTHALLS.

I could barely hear over the voices in my head and the commotion in the warehouse as everyone reacted to the news that Isaac and his followers were coming.

ASHERS, UNITE!

In an echo of the visions of Emma's misdeeds Ben had sent me only a week ago, I saw an image of the Steel Bridge. From the angle I decided I was seeing the bridge from west side of the river, maybe from somewhere in the park that ran along the Willamette River.

I opened my mouth to tell everyone, anyone, that Mountain of Ash was in Portland, but Isaac/Ben's next word struck me speechless.

OLIVIA BRIGHTHALL! WITNESS THE DESTRUCTION OF PORTLAND AND YOUR FAMILY.

Chapter 25

I couldn't speak. I couldn't breathe. I was locked in my head, forced to watch as words and images pounded into me.

But I had enough self-awareness to wonder why Isaac/Ben were only now talking to me when I'd seen Mountain of Ash's plan laid out over the past few minutes. Then I caught the faintest murmur, like a word hum, under the next mental onslaught.

OLIVIA, WITNESS AS PORTLAND'S DESTRUCTION BEGINS.

Was it really Ben saying these things, or was Isaac forcing his voice through Ben's greater range? If I focused hard enough, I thought I heard an echo under the voices, but I couldn't quite decide if I was imagining it.

Then, very quietly, I heard the words. *Ollie, stop him. I'm not strong enough.* It was Ben's voice, alone.

My mind reeled. Had Ben somehow looped me into Isaac's rally call to the Ashers? Could Ben be trying to warn us? I tried not to hope too much as I huddled on the floor.

The Steel Bridge loomed in my mind. I guessed I was watching the scene from a viewpoint behind Ben's eyes. I shuddered as he turned his head to show me the people standing beside him. I recognized the firestarter Trent, the icky enhancer Joshua, and Emma.

And Isaac. He stared at Ben with intensity while holding Ben's hand in a strange parody of intimacy.

OLIVIA, SEE WHAT YOU HAVE BROUGHT UPON PORTLAND.

I fought to separate my thoughts from the voice in my head.

AND SO IT BEGINS

Isaac *had* to be speaking through Ben. Ben would never be this pompous.

Joshua smirked, his flabby lips twisting cruelly as he looked directly at Ben while clasping the shoulder of Trent.

"No, No!" I managed to cry out, but I couldn't manage more than fragmented shouts, and there was no way Ben or Isaac could hear me. Outside of my head, I felt someone shaking me by the shoulders, shouting my name, but I couldn't focus enough to form an answer.

I watched in horror as Trent raised his fist, aiming it at the Steel Bridge. Ben afforded me a slow scan of the targeted bridge. It was a beautiful Saturday afternoon, the sunlight bright and welcoming. Cars drove across in both directions, sharing the bridge with joggers, walkers, and cyclists who crowded the sidewalks lining upper and lower parts of the bridge. The Blue Line Max train rumbled down the center lane.

Small craft boats left trails of waves along the river below the bridge while dragon boat teams paddled near the edge of the river.

Did Ben or Isaac know the Steel Bridge was my favorite bridge? Ben might know, especially since it's where he and I had met. I liked how the middle of the bridge lifted like a lid being pulled up for ships to pass under it. There was a time I thought the coolest job would be to live in the big machinery house controlling the bridge lift. Now I frantically hoped no one occupied the little house.

I gasped as if punched in the gut as Trent opened his fist, sending a thick stream of fire to the west side of the bridge where the edge of the bridge met the riverbank. In the spaces between my agonizing breaths, the metal dissolved into an ash so fine it looked like that part of the bridge had never existed. Destabilized by the gaping hole, both ends of the bridge twisted, tremors running along the edges.

My vision didn't include sound except for Ben's voice, so I couldn't hear the shrieks of the people falling off into the water.

Trent closed his hand into a fist, extinguishing the fire coming from his hand, but as quickly as he stopped, he started again. This time he made a slow sweeping motion, inexorably destroying the remnants of the Steel Bridge and anyone left on it.

The dying didn't have time to scream, but the living more than made up for it. Walkers, runner, and cyclists tangled together, desperate to escape from the crumbling edges. On the roads leading up to the bridge, cars crashed into each other, some drivers frozen in horror while others jumped out and joined the frantically running fray. A large truck slammed into a line of cars, sending the front vehicle into Trent's line of fire; the car fell, fading into ash before it hit the river.

A Red Line Max train hurtled into the line of fire, dissolving in slow motion. I wondered if the occupants had time to understand they rode directly into death.

As if from far away, I heard shouting around me, as everyone else in warehouse became aware of the destruction outside.

Sunlight flaring against my closed eyes pulled me back into my body enough so I could force my eyes open. The large warehouse doors had been opened, letting in sunlight and distant screams. My eyes watered against the bright light, tears rolling down my cheeks. The people running in and out of the doors were wavy shadows in the brightness. The sound of roaring from the city sounded like the shouts of a distant football game.

I tried to stand up, but I was shaking too hard as Ben's voice turned colder, sounding more like Isaac. *OBSERVE HOW WEAK AND DEFENSELESS NORMALS ARE.* He laughed with satisfaction as the Steel Bridge was destroyed, the last remains holding their original form in ash for a moment before blowing away. *THEY DON'T DESERVE THIS WORLD. LISTEN TO THEM SCREAM.*

And, horribly, Ben thrust sound and scent into my head.

I could smell smoke and fire through the open doors. I could hear the screams in stereo from outside the warehouse and from Ben's sending. The floor under me throbbed from running feet. I felt like I was being battered by sensory overload. I gasped in deep, sobbing breaths.

Trent, Joshua, and the rest of the Ashers turned, facing the Burnside Bridge. Without speaking, Trent and Joshua joined forces again. With a horrible shock, I realized it must be Saturday because crowds of people swarmed around the shopping stalls and food carts set up for Saturday Market under the west side of the Burnside Bridge. Trent aimed his powerful fire at the supports holding the bridge. The supports turned to ash, and the bridge crumbled, falling in chunks, crushing the stalls and shoppers below. People ran in all directions from the market. People running in the direction of the Steel Bridge collided with folks fleeing that damage.

The Mountain of Ash people ignored the fleeing normals rushing past them. I caught a glimpse of a terrified man trying to hold onto his bicycle while running through the crowd. I saw a woman clutching her little boy in her arms as her husband picked them up, staggering into a run. Several teenagers darted through the throng while trying to film the confusion around them with their phones.

Trent continued destroying the old bridge.

WE ARE THE TRUE INHERITORS, Isaac pontificated through Ben.

Anger surged through me. I was furious at Ben, at Isaac, at Emma, at all of Mountain of Ash, I was tired of them deferring blame for their horrible actions. I was sick of feeling like a victim. I ground my teeth together, feeling them creak as I fought an internal battle to take back my mind. I tried to build a mental shield, but it was hard to do with Ben and Isaac so firmly in my mind. I pounded my fist on the ground as if that could drive out the mental invasion. I gasped out, "Get out of my head, stop it, get out, get out."

Aunt Kate was suddenly by my side, grabbing my hand and crouching down until she was sitting shoulder to shoulder with Dad. "Olivia, where are they attacking from? Come back to us so you can fight."

Somehow, I managed to pull out of the mind screw long enough to lift my head, breathing in deep gasps. "On the west of the river, on the Waterfront Park between the Burnside and Steel Bridges, near the Saturday Market." I winced as I mentioned the bridges. The Burnside was almost gone, disappearing before my mental eyes. "Ben and Isaac. Emma. Others."

As I finished speaking, I saw the Burnside Bridge was gone. Through Ben's eyes, I saw emergency personnel converging on the Ashers. I swallowed down nausea when Isaac pulled Ben along by the hand. They started running with the rest of the group clustered around them. The group tore through the massed police force as if the normals were paper, killing indiscriminately. I shuddered as Joshua ripped off the arms of a police officer, using the limbs to bludgeon another police officer in his way.

I had no doubt Isaac and his band of horribles were heading for the Morrison Bridge, the next one after the Burnside.

I gasped out for the benefit of Aunt Kate and anyone else who was listening. "The Morrison."

I squeezed my eyes shut as I forced myself to focus on building my mental block against Ben and Isaac's invasion. I had to get them out of my head so I could join the fight against the Ashers. I tried screaming back at Ben, but the sending didn't work in two directions. I shrieked in anguish as Trent blasted through a crowded homeless camp clustered between two buildings.

Bit by bit, I managed to slowly push out their minds from mine as I imagined my shield getting higher and thicker. With a mental snap, his voice was finally gone. I fell face down on the cold floor before pushing myself up.

All alone in my head, I rubbed my hands over my face, realizing my cheeks were wet with tears. I got to my feet, shaken to the core at what I'd witnessed through Ben's mind.

I was surrounded by Aunt Kate, Kevin, Anna, and Dad.

Behind them, people were running around in an ordered chaos, grabbing weapons and darting through the open doors. I saw supernormals take to the air or dash off with inhuman speed. There were normals standing across the street, gaping as my people displayed their abilities with no regard for secrecy. Zoe and Lange ran out of the opening together, disappearing as they both kicked into their super-fast running speed.

I gasped out, my voice hoarse from screaming, "We have to stop them. They're heading for the Morrison Bridge next."

Aunt Kate acknowledged my statement with a sharp nod as she got to her feet, calling for Uncle Dan while walking quickly over to General Stone.

Kevin said, "You need Dad."

"No, I'm fine. I'll feel better when we stop them." I stood up.

"Got it." Kevin followed my dash to our lockers, where I pulled out my sword, sighing with a kind of relief when my hand closed over the hilt. Kevin looked pleased to have his sword in hand as well.

General Stone was shouting orders, and I heard enough to know the army was heading for the Morrison and the Hawthorne bridges.

Uncle Dan strode over to a huge door I'd never seen open. He pressed his thumb on a keypad, and the door rattled open, revealing rows and rows of weapons— swords, maces, whips, and dozens of other armaments.

"Did you know that was there?" I asked Kevin in astonishment.

"No, but damn." Kevin shook his head, impressed by the number of weapons hidden away.

The ground shook under us, reminding me that I didn't care where everyone else was going. I knew exactly

LeeAnn McLennan

where Isaac, Ben, and Emma were headed. I could see their destination as clearly as if it had been embedded in my mind.

Together, Kevin and I headed for the door when Anna stepped in front of me, forcing me to stop. She glared at me, arms crossed. "I want to help." Her parents came up to stand behind her, looking confused but determined. She glanced at them. "We want to help."

Jack and Harold were in deep discussion behind them. I saw Harold peer out the door, gesturing frantically towards the water. Jack nodded. He glanced up, saw me watching. He waved and followed Harold. Once outside, they separated, running in opposite directions. I wondered where they were going but I didn't have time to worry about it.

Kevin protested but I said, "Okay, you're right. It's everyone's fight now." I tapped my fingers on the hilt of my sword, considering the best way for them to help. "Can you get people away from the waterfront? Mr. McLeod, I know you know the mayor. Can you get in contact with him, and get them to focus on getting people out of the way so we — " I waved my hand at the supernormals, "— can fight Mountain of Ash?" I glanced to where Zander and Captain May had been standing but only saw Captain May. "That's Captain May; he should be able to help you."

Mr. McLeod blew out a breath. "Yes, I can do that." He touched his wife's shoulder, "Come on. Let's give the mayor a call."

Anna still waited, her hands on her hips. I asked her, "Can you catch up with Jack? Where did he go?" I realized she held a phone in her hand. "Go help him if he needs it."

She gave me a sharp nod. "I think he's helping Harold — there are several homeless camps close to the bridges." She dashed away, calling for Jack.

"Hey!" Zander ran up from behind us. "I'm coming with you." He held the sword he'd found in the battle at Mountain of Ash's ranch.

Kevin and I exchanged a look. I asked him and Zander, "You ready?"

"Let's go," Kevin answered.

Chapter 26

We ran outside into smoke-filled air. The commotion, which had sounded loud from inside the warehouse, was deafening outside it. The streets were clogged with people running away from the river. I started to cross the street then stopped, sticking out an arm to prevent Kevin from getting hit as two cars crashed into each other. The drivers got out and yelled at other briefly until a loud boom sounded from across the river. The drivers froze like startled deer before darting off down the street without a backward glance at their cars.

Another bang shook the air. "What's going on?" I shouted at folks running from the river. The noise didn't sound like the Morrison Bridge was being destroyed yet. The boom came again, reminding me of bombs going off.

A woman shrieked, "There's some kind of creature, and it's throwing balls of light or... I don't know, but you should run!" She took her own advice and fled.

A group of three cyclists pedaled towards us, their gazes rapt on something in the air. I turned and saw several flying supernormals take off from in front of the open warehouse doors.

The flying V of supernormals zoomed past above my head, aiming for the river, the sunlight glinting off their swords. Figures blurred around me as runners dashed at top speed into the warehouse, grabbing weapons that appeared from Uncle Dan's cache, and charging back outside.

The three of us rushed through the crowd, working hard to avoid hitting anyone in the frightened masses. None of us bothered with a glamour, since there wasn't any point in hiding when what seemed like every other supernormal in the country was charging towards the river.

"Olivia!"

I stumbled, gritting my teeth when I recognized that annoying voice.

"What?" I turned to face Mindy Careen, once my biggest nemesis in a time that felt like ages ago. Now she looked frightened, her usually perfect hair and clothes grimy and disarrayed. She supported her friend Donna, who was bleeding from her head.

"Oh man." I crouched down and looked at Donna's wound; it looked bad. "Can you make it over there, to that building?" I pointed back to the warehouse. "Tell Alex Brighthall I sent you. He'll help Donna."

Mindy managed to nod. "What the hell, Olivia?" I bristled, expecting her to start in on me, but she said, "You have powers?" Her eyes lifted to watch three flyers zip over us on their way to the river.

Impatient to get to the waterfront, I said, "Yes. Now get your friend to my uncle."

Mindy swallowed and nodded, supporting Donna as they aimed for the warehouse.

We ran down the Eastside Esplanade, in the direction of the Hawthorne Bridge. I stumbled to a stop at the sight of a whirlwind of dirt and debris blocking the path under the bridge. Before I could assess what was happening, Jack called out from where he, Harold, and Anna stood with several unkempt men and women. Some clutched backpacks or blankets bundled into makeshift bags. Harold was bandaging a women's arm while Jack seemed to be trying to get the little crowd organized enough to move.

"Are you okay?" I caught Anna's hand with the vague thought I could keep her safe if the whirlwind got closer.

"Well, I—" she began, but a man cradling a dog in his arms interrupted.

"That woman! She just started waving her arms in a spinning motion, like." His eyes were wide above his messy beard.

I peered at the whirlwind. "It must be Black Gaea or someone like her." My heart started pounding. I was ready to stop the weather-controlling menace.

Kevin said in a placating tone, "It's okay. We'll get you to safety."

"But, but, she's not black!" The man insisted, pulled his little dog into a tighter embrace. The dog snuggled into the man.

"I know, I know it's just what they call her," I said, frantically thinking of where they might be safe.

"Who?" Another man shoved his way forward, his eyes dark with suspicion and fear. "We've just called her Maude for three years. She never said anything about any Black Gaea."

"What?" I focused on the man.

Harold finished his first aid and saw us. "Olivia, Kevin, I know that woman in there." He pointed to the whirlwind. "She's been on the streets for several years, but she never did anything like this." He looked at the little group of people clustered around him. "These folks were a part of the same community. They've been camping under the bridge. They say when the attacks started, and Maude saw a woman create a funnel cloud, Maude started laughing and then, well, this happened."

"She blew away my stuff," the dog owner said mournfully, "all except Bobo." I assumed Bobo was the dog.

"What are we going to do?" Kevin asked, his brow furrowed.

"I, ah." I fought against the urge to keep running for the Morrison Bridge, certain that Isaac and his group would already be there.

As if in answer to my impatience, a cry came from within the whirlwind, and the dirt and debris collapsed around the prone body of a small woman.

"Maude!" Several of the homeless folks surged towards her then stopped in confusion. The dog owner looked at Harold. "Is it safe?"

Harold looked at me with his eyebrow raised. I ran over to Maude, stepping through the remnants of her storm. She was still breathing. "If I had to guess, I'd say the effort of using abilities at that intensity while untrained drained her. She'll probably be unconscious for a while." I stood up, deciding. "Take her to the warehouse. Uncle Alex or another healer can help her."

Harold came to my side. "I wonder if there are others like her?"

I met his inquiring gaze. "I have feeling she's far from the only one."

He looked so worried that I gave him a hug. "Get her and these folks to the warehouse. Kevin, Zander, and I are going help stop the Ashers before anyone else gets hurt."

Harold nodded and picked up Maude gently.

I faced Jack and Anna, reaching out to grip each of my oldest friends by their arms. "Be careful." I started to say more but couldn't find the words to tell them how much they meant to me.

Anna threw her arms around me, murmuring, "You, too".

Jack gave me a short nod before raising his hand in farewell.

As they headed back to the warehouse, the rest of us continued running under the now open path under the bridge, past where the statue of Vera used to sit before Emma blew it up last year.

The Morrison Bridge loomed before us, still intact.

Boom!

A flash of light brightened the sky above us. My steps slowed when I saw the source of the blast. "Is that a dragon?" I asked weakly.

Zander squinted at the sky where a dragon, almost as big as the Morrison Bridge, wheeled in the air above us.. As I gaped at it, its mouth opened, and a bolt of energy shot out, blowing a large riverboat into splinters.

"Yep. Now we know where at least one of them is," Kevin said weakly.

I followed the guys, trying to ignore the fact we were running in the direction of a dragon. We weren't the only ones. Kevin shouted and pointed to where supernormals were charging up the ramp of the Morrison Bridge.

When we came up the ramp, I saw the east side of the bridge was filled with supernormals on our side standing still. The Morrison was a wide bridge with ramps for cars converging in different directions leading from I-5 and from the cross-town streets as well as pedestrian walkways. The roadway looked like scene out of a post-apocalyptic movie, with abandoned cars scattered about, but I didn't see any normals. It appeared they'd all managed to flee in time.

LeeAnn McLennan

"What's going on?" I pushed through the crowd, searching for someone in charge, but I froze when I saw what everyone was looking at.

Directly across from me, on the west side of the bridge, stood what must be every member of Mountain of Ash. At least a couple hundred supernormals, twice the number I'd seen at the ranch, filled the wide pavement. Eerily, no one was displaying any obvious powers; they simply stood in orderly formations.

Mixed in among the supernormals were monsters from the ranch. I saw the Anone crouched down between Nancy and Paisley, who each held the end of chain leading back to the collar around the creature's neck.

It was hard to tell from all the noisy chaos around me, but I thought the Ashers were standing in silence.

The dragon flew overhead, the air from its wings sending gusts of winds over the crowd. The sunlight flashed off the spikes on its collar as the Asher riding it yanked the reins back, forcing the monster to arch its neck.

Portland police, fire personnel, and other emergency teams swarmed around the edge of bridge behind the Mountain of Ash force, but they weren't attacking. News helicopters hovered overhead, and police boats churned through the river.

Among all the activity, the Ashers stood waiting, but for what?

I didn't need to scan the horde for my torturers. Isaac stood front and center, looking back at us. Black Gaea had arrived at some point; she stood beside Isaac, mirroring his posture with her arms clasped behind her back like him.

I couldn't find Ben at first, but I was shocked when I finally saw him. He slumped against a concrete barrier, head drooping. But as I watched, he straightened, as if on strings like a puppet, stepping over to stand beside Isaac. I squinted, my supernormal vision homing in on his blank expression.

"They started appearing a few minutes ago," Aunt Kate spoke softly, stepping to my side. "The teams from the other cities that were under attack are saying that the attacks have stopped. I suspect they're all coming here." She assessed the crowd facing us for a moment. "Clearly the fact they could move so many people, so quickly, means they've upgraded the abilities of their transporters. As you saw at the ranch, of course."

"With my blood?" I managed to ask over the lump in my throat.

"Maybe," she answered, "or they're using their amplifiers." She gripped my shoulder. "If they are using your blood, it's not your fault. You need to let go of any guilt."

I swallowed, nodding, thinking, Yeah, right. I said aloud, "Why are we just standing here?" I looked around; there were at least a hundred supernormals standing around me. We were less militant looking, less organized, which worried me, but everyone looked determined to stop Mountain of Ash.

"Well, two reasons." Aunt Kate looked at a message on her phone as she answered. "Much of our fighting force was headed for other cities; now they're changing direction to come here. But we don't have amplified transporters, so it's taking longer."

"What's the second reason?"

"We hope to stall long enough to give the police time to get people to safety. There are too many people who will get hurt if we start fighting now."

I scanned the surroundings. The police were gesturing for people to move away from the waterfront, but many people weren't cooperating, clearly fascinated by the scene unfolding before them.

While Aunt Kate was speaking, Uncle Dan arrived, carrying the biggest broadsword I'd ever seen as he strode through the crowd with great purpose while narrowing his eyes to look across the river. He looked like he was in his element.

The crowd around me was growing louder and larger as more supernormals arrived.

Uncle Dan brushed past me and Aunt Kate, barely acknowledging us in his march to the front of the crowd. I exchanged a look with my aunt, then she followed her brother. Kevin, Zander, and I pushed after them.

When we arrived at the front of the crowd, I saw Zoe and Lange by the railing near General Stone. I wondered how he'd arrived ahead of me, Kevin, and Zander, but my focus was mostly on the waiting Ashers.

Zoe ran her whip through her fingers as she glowered at the scene. Lange stood calmly; only the flexing of his muscles giving away his tension.

When General Stone saw Uncle Dan, he frowned, reaching out to put a hand on his arm. "Dan, don't pick more of fight than we already have here."

Uncle Dan stepped away, General Stone's hand sliding off his arm. "Wally, with respect, we're already in the shit." He swept his arm around to indicate the scene. "We need to take decisive action now."

I found myself agreeing with my short-tempered uncle. Mountain of Ash wasn't going to stop unless we stopped them. I bounced on my heels, ready to end this now.

Suddenly, Isaac's voice boomed out. I was shocked at the strength of his voice, but then I realized he was speaking aloud as well as broadcasting mentally. Most of the people around me were holding their heads in agony, but I could only hear him aloud. I was puzzled, because just a few minutes ago Ben had been able to break through my shields easily with Isaac. Why couldn't Isaac get through my shields now? Then I saw that Ben wasn't standing near Isaac any more. He was on the other side of Emma, who looked furious for some reason.

"Stand down, and you'll be given a quick, painless death. Join us and reap the rewards of our new society," Isaac called out, spreading his arms wide as if to welcome us. "Accept our inevitable victory. Let go of your inhibitions and free your powers." He paused. "This is a one-time offer."

The Mountain of Ash members all shouted in unison, "Ashers united!" Their chant rolled over the river. I saw the edges of the river were lined with even more people gawking, pointing, and holding up phones. I wanted to shout for them to run as far away as they could.

Uncle Dan muttered a curse and jumped up on a concrete block. "Tommy Jacobson!"

The noise level dropped so quickly I thought I'd gone momentarily deaf. I kept my gaze fixed on Isaac. His broad smile disappeared, his eyes narrowed, and his lips drew back in snarl. "Daniel Brighthall. So, you know who I am. Or rather, who I was."

"I know you weren't always a self-righteous egomaniac." Uncle Dan stood on the concrete block, his stance relaxed, and his sword strapped to his back. Having trained with him, I recognized the signs he was prepared to fight.

Isaac didn't respond, at least not verbally. A line of Ashers carrying crossbows rose up in the air from the crowd behind him. I braced to duck as the flying strike team released their crossbows in unison, the bolts zipping through the air. Before I could react, three women leapt forward from the crowd behind me, each one sweeping an arm and sending the arrows flying harmlessly into the river or clattering onto the pavement.

Black Gaea shouted, raising her arms, bringing a fierce wind whistling down the river. I grabbed Zander and Aunt Kate, and we held on, bracing each other as the wind raged around us. Uncle Dan jumped down from the concrete block so he wouldn't be sweep away.

After a moment, the wind died down. I looked up. Black Gaea swayed on her feet, falling onto the concrete, her body shaking. One of the Ashers near her bent over her, pulling her up and carrying her to the back of the crowd. Isaac looked annoyed.

"Pulling that much wind had to take a lot of effort," Aunt Kate commented as she smoothed her hair. "It'll take her a few minutes to recover."

Fear rippled through me when I saw several of the firestarters form a line near the middle of the bridge. As one, they aimed lines of the fire at the middle of the bridge.

At the same time, General Stone commanded his forces to attack. A wave of runners and flyers surged past me, brandishing swords, maces, and other weapons. As the attackers neared the firestarters, several of the Asher firestarters aimed tongues of flames at them.

"No!" I shouted, running forward with an outstretched hand, already pulling fire into my body. As I did, several of the flyers swooped in and lifted the fighters over the Ashers' firestarters. I could see fighting through the haze of smoke and ash filling the air while I kept my attention on the Asher firestarters.

I'd never pulled in fire from another firestarter's flame and I was astonished to feel heat; usually, when I pulled in my own fire I didn't feel heat at all. I stumbled back, still trying to stop the attacks, but I felt my bones burning. I faltered, my hands dropping to my sides.

"Olivia!" Zander put a hand on my back to steady me. I blinked away sweat to see he reached out with his other hand, pulling fire from the air like I had been. His help gave me the willingness to stand up and keep working to extinguish the flames before they hit the pavement.

Ashers came charging around the edges of the bridge, aiming at Zander and me, clearly trying to stop us from extinguishing their firestarters' flames. I was too drained to jump when Zoe ran past me, brandishing her whip as she fought to keep the Ashers from reaching us. Uncle Dan fought on the other side Zander, his fists moving so fast they blurred. Kevin and Lange spread out on either side of Zander and me, each holding their swords ready to defend us.

Shouts came from behind me, and I saw shadows loom as more of our firestarters ran to help, all of us trying to stop the disintegration of the bridge. But most of them staggered back within minutes, flushed and sweaty. A few even passed out, and I saw others dragging them away from the line of fire.

Clearly, Zander and I were the strongest, but even we couldn't keep up with the enhanced firestarters. My body felt like it was about to explode from all the heat I was taking in, and I knew I had to stop or risk death.

"Zander!" I shouted, my voice rough from my dry mouth. "Can you keep up?"

He just shook his head. His hands were trembling, and he finally let them fall to his sides.

I wanted to keep going, but against my will my arms wilted. I staggered to lean on Zander, who wrapped an arm around my shoulder, leaning on me as much as I rested on him. My fingers smarted. I held up one hand to see my fingernails were smoking. As I watched, one nail fell off, drifting to ground.

My body was so engorged with heat I was sure heat waves were coming off my flesh. Zander's face was flushed, and his short hair clung damply to his forehead.

Zoe and Uncle Dan managed to drive the Ashers back past the line of firestarters. I saw Zoe glance down with a startled expression as the bridge started to shake under our feet. With triumphant shouts the Mountain of Ash firestarters abruptly stopped shooting fire at the concrete and as one sprinted back to the west side of the bridge.

The middle of the bridge crumbled under Zoe and Uncle Dan's feet, dissolving into ashes. I took two stumbling steps as the pavement shuddered under my feet. I felt it slide away as I fell. I hit the water with a splash. I gasped with shock as the cold water steamed on my skin. Zander landed with a splash, shouting incoherently at Kevin, who fell into him. Lange bobbed up on the other side of me. Yelling echoed all around us as others fell into the chilly water.

Ashes and chunks of bridge rained down around us. Frantic to find Zoe and my uncle, I started swimming against the strong current towards the other end of the bridge, hoping to find them in the water, but Lange grabbed my arm.

"It's not safe! We need to get away from the bridge!" he shouted.

"But — " I protested, trying to pull away from his extra strong grip, ducking instinctively when a metal-studded concrete block landed nearby, sloshing water over us.

When we surfaced, Lange said, spitting out water, "I know, but we're no good to them if we're crushed." Clearly deciding not to argue with me anymore, he started swimming to the middle of the river between the bridges, pulling me in his wake. Zander and Kevin were ahead of us, Zander treading water as Kevin waved anxiously for us to hurry.

With a deep groaning sound, the remainder of the bridge toppled into the water. We fought to keep from getting pulled under and managed to make it to Kevin.

In the relative safety of calming waters, I faced the direction of the shattered bridge. Most of the bridge was gone, leaving only jagged edges on each shore. I didn't see as many heads bobbing in the water as when I'd first landed. I telescoped my vision, scanning for Zoe and Uncle Dan as best I could in the rolling waves. For a heart stopping moment, I thought I saw Zoe's dark hair on the other side of the jutting remnants of the bridge, near the west shore. I winced, ducking underwater at the sound of screeching from above. When I surfaced, I saw the dragon fending off several flyers armed with morning stars and maces. From my angle, it was difficult to tell who was winning.

When I tried to catch sight of the dark haired swimmer again, they weren't anywhere to be seen.

On the west shore, the fight between Ashers and the rest of the supernormals still raged. I could see some of the firestarters in the fray, shooting firebombs. Throughout the melee, supernormals used their powers in a frenzy of attacks and counter attacks.

On the east shore, there was a smaller fight going on, but it was harder to make out the details because there were more buildings in the way. I hoped Aunt Kate was okay.

Kevin called out, "I'm going try to find—" when suddenly the water started swirling around us, threatening to pull me under. I spat water out of my mouth, but it filled up again. Choking and gasping, I tried to keep my head above the water, but it was difficult as the whirlpool sped up, pulling me under. Through the churning water, I thought I saw a row of men and women standing on the Hawthorne Bridge, their hands extended over the water. Lange shouted something unintelligible as he was pulled under the surface. Through a film of water, I saw Kevin grabbing at Zander as he flailed frantically, trying to keep his head above water.

I gurgled, gasping, trying to keep water from filling my mouth as I struggled against the whirlpool.

With a shocking abruptness, there was no water around me, and I hung suspended in air for a moment before falling through empty space. Other bodies fell around me, yelling as we plunged down.

My fall ended when I splashed several inches into thick mud that smelled like a dirty fish tank. I choked and coughed, struggling to stand up in the deep sludge. My feet made sucking sounds in the muck.

I looked up. "Holy shit!" I was standing in the riverbed of the Willamette.

"Yeah, smells like shit, too." Lange squelched over with Zander following. Both were covered in stinking mud. Lange stood several feet away, staring up the walls of water framing the exposed the riverbed. Each wall pulsed against the force holding the water in place. The water was high enough that I couldn't see the Hawthorne Bridge or whatever was left of the Morrison Bridge. Either side of the river was exposed, revealing moss stained concrete no one had seen in years. Decades of debris littered the bottom of the river—rusty oil drums, a wide variety of skeletons, sunken row boats, old shopping carts, and many other objects, most too waterlogged to identify.

I didn't see Kevin. I spun around in a panic, relieved when I saw him bouncing down from the river bank. He was already mud-coated, so I figured he'd fallen with the rest of us but had gone up to the shore. He bounced over to us, leaving big splashes in the mud. "You okay? We need to get moving before the water is released."

"What happened?" I tried to brush off some of the mud on my face.

Kevin answered while waving everyone else over to where I saw people using their abilities to jump or fly out of the riverbed on the east side. Some helped those whose ability didn't allow them to get out on their own. "Their water weaver sent a whirlpool. Ours countered by getting the water out of the way." He glanced worriedly at the pulsating walls of water. "For now, anyway, but I don't know how long they can hold back the water."

I cringed at the idea of being under all that water when it fell. I had a better chance of survival than a normal, but it would still hurt like hell.

"Come on," Kevin turned to the east side.

"No." I grabbed his arm. "We have to stop Isaac. We have to get to the west side now!"

"Olivia," Zoe protested.

"She's right," Zander stated. He didn't wait for anyone else; he began making his way through the sludge. I followed.

Kevin nodded. "Yeah, come on, Zoe. You've never backed down from a good fight before. Don't start now."

Zoe uncoiled her whip from its clasp on her belt, flicking it to shake off the mud. As she marched towards the west bank and the waiting army of enemies, she shrugged, "Sure. Let's be heroes."

Chapter 27

We were about a hundred yards from the shore when I felt a splash of water on my neck. I looked up as Kevin said, "Oh no." I followed the direction of his stare, afraid we were under attack, but he was looking at the wall of water obscuring the Hawthorne Bridge. At first, I didn't see what alarmed him, but then I realized the water was slowly descending towards us. I whipped around to look at the wall of water where the Morrison Bridge used to stand; it was also creeping in our direction.

Uncle Dan inhaled sharply, making me jump since I didn't know he'd joined us. He said, "The water weavers must be weakening. We don't have long, Hurry!" He marched off, and somehow he still had his broadsword strapped to his back. My sword was lost somewhere in the mud.

As we all splashed through the muck, fear lent urgency to our steps. The water probably wouldn't kill us, but it would hurt us. And there was always danger of getting knocked unconscious and drowning.

I was sure I'd never be able to be near a fish tank again after being immersed in the revolting smell. Zoe pointed. "There's a ladder along the side, over there."

A shadow passed in front of me, and I felt a gust of air that was strong enough to make me feel like I was walking into a wall. The mud around me rippled, splashing up to my hips. I looked up, my mouth dropping open at the sight of the dragon circling above us. It was so close I could see its diamond-faceted eyes. From my angle, its wings seems to occupy all the space between the riverbanks.

"Crap!" Lange yelled as the rider reined in the dragon so it blocked our way to the ladder and subsequent escape from the looming water. And the east shore was too far way for us to make it in time.

I stared at the dragon, my heart pounding so hard that my blood pounded in my ears. The rider kept yanking on the reins, forcing the dragon's head up, until it let out a blast of energy that went wide because the dragon was fighting the reins. The air around the spiked collar crackled with electricity. I saw the skin under the collar was raw and bleeding.

The dragon was fighting the reins; the dragon seemed to be trying to fly away. It thrashed, trying to shake off the rider. The dragon craned its neck to shriek at the sky.

I had a sudden crazy idea.

"Lange," I yelled over the noise of dragon wings and chaos from the city around us. I figured Lange knew about dragons from his work at the sanctuary.

"What?" He shouted back impatiently. "I'm a little busy here." He was digging in the mud. With a grunt, he pulled out a long metal oar from the ooze with a sucking sound.

"The dragon is collared."

"I know!" He said, shoving his hair out of his face. The others spread out, facing the creature. The rider pulled up, and for a moment the dragon lifted up enough so I got a tantalizing view of the ladder. With beating wings, the monster lowered down again until its back legs were kicking up sludge.

I faltered when I noticed the wall of water was getting closer. "Okay, okay, so what if we got the collar off? Do you think the dragon would leave?"

Lange opened and closed his mouth a few times, hefting the oar easily while gazing up at the dragon. Then he looked over at me with an grin. "I like how you think. How are you planning to get the color off, though?"

Zander spoke up, "I think I could burn it off."

I shook my head. "Too risky. It's already hurting. And it would think it was an attack." I tried to ignore the pit in my stomach. "If I could get up there, I could freeze it off."

Zoe shouted, "Whatever we're going to do, we'd better hurry. I don't know how much longer we have before we're under water."

"Okay." Uncle Dan took charge. "Kevin, you have the best chance of getting Olivia up there. The rest of us will keep it busy." Uncle Dan gave me a fierce grin. "It's a crazy idea, but it's better than anything I can think of."

I nodded back, already regretting my idea as I gazed at the huge black creature looming over me. Kevin wrapped his arms around me. "All right, I'll bounce. I'm going to aim for the back, behind the rider. I'll try to knock him off while you release the collar."

"What's our exit strategy?" I asked, but he'd already leapt. In one great leap, we bounced towards the back of the dragon. We almost made a clean landing, but at the last minute one of the dragon's wings hit Kevin in the leg and we spun around past the rider. I flailed, my hands out, then clutched something and held on tightly. I almost let go when we jerked to a stop, slapping against dragon hide, but I held on. I realized I'd somehow grabbed one of the reins out of the rider's hands, and we dangled against the side of the dragon's leg a couple of stories above the muddy ground.

There was no time to recover because the dragon was still whipping around, and the rider was yelling while reaching for the reins. "Kevin, grab the end!" He took the part of the reins I shoved in his hands. I started to pull up, bracing myself to walk up the dragon with Kevin following. It was hard work and seemed to take forever, trying to stay balanced and keep the rider from yanking the leather out of my hands, but somehow I made it to the collar. I gripped the leather loop where the reins met the collar, feeling the shocks from the collar but somehow insulated from them. I looked down on Kevin, lifting my part of the reins so he would know I was going to let go. He tightened his grip and jumped the rest of the way up to the dragon's broad back, yelling defiantly. The rider was startled and barely reacted as Kevin slammed into him, punching the man so furiously the rider fell off the dragon. Kevin grabbed the other rein. "Olivia, hurry up. I don't know how long I can hold it."

For a moment, I thought about jumping off. After all, we'd gotten the rider off, the dragon could just leave. But I looked at the wounded skin around its throat and knew I couldn't let it leave while in pain. I gripped the loop with one hand, holding out my other hand as I froze the collar, careful not to hit the skin, but my ice wasn't cold enough to crack the leather quickly. Wincing at a particularly rough jerk, I knew I had to hurry. I muttered, "Ok, let's see how good I am." I wrapped my hand around the collar, wincing as the electrical charge prickled my skin. I took a deep breath and used my fire to disintegrate the leather and metal so quickly that I almost fell off when the collar dropped free.

The dragon roared, arching up so suddenly that I lost my grip. I fell into the slime and muck, with Kevin landing nearby. Starting up, the dragon launched itself up with a mighty squelch. It hovered in the air above the west bank, seeming to gaze down on the people running around below it. I struggled to my feet, afraid it was going to attack. Instead, the creature roared again before turning and flying away over the hills to disappear in the distance.

"Come on!" Lange screamed, pulling Kevin up. The water was so close I was sure we only had seconds.

As I scrambled up after Lange, I kept looking at the encroaching water. I could almost feel the effort involved in keeping it from crashing down on us. I didn't have time to scan for whoever was holding up the water, but I sent a silent plea for their strength to hold out for a minute longer.

Zander grabbed me by the arm, urging me onto the ladder where Uncle Dan was waiting for us. Zoe reached the top and pulled me up when I got close.

Uncle Dan was the last to climb up. The minute he reached the top, the walls of water exploded, cascading down, covering the riverbed. I was grateful for the wash of water over me; it cleaned off some of the stinking mud.

We stood on the banks of the river in Tom McCall Park, near the Rose Festival building. I thought the park was deserted until I saw what waited for us.

Naito Parkway, the street running parallel to the river, was filling with hundreds of police, all aiming their guns at Isaac, Emma, and Ben. The police officers' guns wouldn't do anything to the three supernormals, of course, but it was still reassuring to see them, though I worried for their safety when the inevitable fighting started again. Out of the corner of my eye, I saw Trent, Joshua, and Black Gaea coming up behind Zander, my family, and me. Isaac held Ben by one arm. Ben still wore the blank, dazed expression he'd had on bridge. His hands trembled, and he listed to one side.

Where were the rest of the Ashers and the rest of the Council army? I looked in the direction of the remnants of the Morrison. It looked like fierce battles were being fought on both sides of the river. Here, we were in a bubble of calm.

Then Isaac shifted, deliberately exposing the scene behind him while Emma crossed her arms, smirking at me.

Somehow, somewhere, Isaac had captured Anna and Jack, who knelt bound and gagged behind Isaac, Emma, and Ben. They both looked terrified and angry. Anna lifted her head, grimacing defiantly. My heart sunk as I realized the police officers actually had their guns aimed at Anna and Jack. Since my friends were clearly Isaac's captives, I knew the cops were under Isaac's mind control.

Isaac smiled. "Reunions are so nice, aren't they? I was so pleased to hear Anna's thoughts, because of course I'm attuned to her after spending time in her head this week." He ran a hand over Anna's hair, and she shuddered. "And, bonus, another Olivia Brighthall normal." He kicked Jack in the ribs, and Jack grunted in pain. "It's getting to be hazardous, being your friend, isn't it?" Emma laughed out loud, her voice grating on my nerves.

"You need to let them go." I spoke through gritted teeth, flames in my hands.

Isaac raised a hand, dropping one finger. In horrible synchronicity, every police officer stepped forward as one, all while keeping their guns aimed at my friends. I let out an involuntary moan. Zander muttered, "Asshole."

Uncle Dan held his broadsword in one hand, but he didn't attack. I knew what he was thinking. If we attacked, the guns wouldn't hurt us, but Jack and Anna would be cut down in seconds. He regarded his daughter, his lips pressed together tightly. He swallowed, saying roughly, "Emma."

Emma sneered at her father. "What? Am I still not powerful enough for you now, father?" She snorted. "Bet you never thought I could help destroy the world!"

Uncle Dan said, "Oh Emma, I'm sorry for ever letting you think you weren't good enough. You were always wonderful. And I should have told you I was proud of you." Unshed tears glistened in his eyes.

For a moment, Emma faltered, but she drew in a breath. "Too little, too late."

Black Gaea came up, shoving past Uncle Dan. "Move aside. She doesn't want you."

I was surprised when Uncle Dan simply stepped to one side, allowing Trent and Joshua to pass. Isaac smiled as his team assembled around him.

Ben lurched slightly, squeezing his eyes as if he was waking up. He seemed to shiver, and he met my eyes, his own widening as if he was surprised.

Isaac didn't notice Ben's sudden alertness because he was smiling at Black Gaea. "Don't worry, my dear, we'll find that dragon and punish it just as soon as we're done here."

Black Gaea glared at me, muttering, "After suitable punishment here."

Ben was staring at me with a laser like focus, more attentive than he'd been since they appeared on the waterfront. He narrowed his eyes, trying to convey a message, but I didn't understand. He kept looking hard at me, grimacing, then looking away.

Abruptly, I got his meaning. Isaac could only control minds when he was looking at someone. Clearly, he was only able to control the police officers' minds without looking at them because he was tapping into Ben's power to be stronger.

And he was controlling Ben while using Ben's power. It explained Ben's blank expression, why he'd been so out of it for most of the battle. In fact, Ben had been different since that moment in my cell when he'd told me he knew what Isaac's plan was. In that moment, I knew. Isaac must have taken over Ben's mind and been controlling him ever since that night. That was why Ben stopped visiting me, why he'd been so remote.

Even in the middle of the battle, with so much hanging in the balance, I felt relief—Ben had meant what he said that night in my cell. There was a chance Ben could be saved, that he wasn't an all-evil Asher.

I looked back at him, trying to convey my newfound awareness of his condition. I considered dropping my mental shields, but it was too risky with Isaac right there, so I just gave Ben a half smile.

If we took Ben out of the picture, Isaac wouldn't control as many normals.

The only trouble was, I couldn't figure out how to do that without killing Ben.

Chapter 28

The mesmerized police force took slow steps forward in unison. I knew Isaac was toying with us by showing us how much control he had over the normals.

Still held in Isaac's grip, Ben's mouth was set in grim lines of determination. He looked at me and mimed something, but I couldn't tell what he meant.

Ben yanked his arm way from Isaac, kicking out a sweeping leg, making Isaac stumble. Isaac was surprised enough to drop his hold on the normals, who all freaked out in their own ways. Several dropped the guns in their hands and ran screaming. Others reacted by shooting at us. I jumped in front of Anna and Jack. The previously-entranced normals were even more shocked when the bullets hit me and fell to the ground.

Zoe and Lange grabbed Jack and Anna, speeding out of the line of fire before either was hurt. I heard Anna shout something, but she was gone too quickly for me to catch her words.

Black Gaea spun her arms in the air, sending waves of wind at Uncle Dan as he raised his sword and charged towards her. The wind pushed at him, and he skidded back a few steps before using his strength to push closer. He swung his sword at her, and she dropped her arms, letting the wind die out as she dodged the attack.

I screamed at Isaac, trying to shoot fire at the ground around him to distract him, but he was clearly too confident in his own defenses to lose focus even though he stood in a ring of fire. I was aware of Zander fighting Trent, matching his flame with his own. Neither one was getting hurt, but it was enough to keep Trent occupied.

Ben stumbled a few steps away, holding his head, grimacing with pain. He collapsed onto his knees. Uncle Dan drove Black Gaea towards the edge of the waterfront. She dodged, ducking under the sword and darting away.

I saw my chance: Isaac stood alone, no normals, no Ben. I raised my hands, palm out, staring straight at Isaac. He smirked at me. "You won't do it. You forget I've seen inside your head, the guilt you're feeling."

"I don't have to kill you to stop you." I aimed one hand at him and one at the ground around him. Fire issued from my hand pointing at the ground while ice streamed from my other. I froze Isaac while disintegrating the ground beneath him. With all the fire around, I knew the ice would melt quickly, but it held Isaac long enough to drop him into the hole I'd created.

I had the vague idea I could bury Isaac under rubble, but Kevin shouted and ran at the hole, pulling something out of his pocket.

Kevin bounced into the hole, appearing behind Isaac and punching the block of ice surrounding him. I shouted, "What are you — ?" Then I stopped when I saw he was holding a pair of cuffs, and I remembered Kevin grabbing his pair when Zander released us. My cousin grabbed one of Isaac's arms, snapped a cuff on Isaac's wrist, then cuffed the other one.

Isaac started screaming immediately. Rage contorted his features in rictus of hate as he spat at Kevin. "No, no, I can't hear anything! The silence! The silence!" Water from the ice dripped off him as he clutched his head.

Kevin hauled him out of the pit with one hand, letting him fall into a heap on the grass.

Emma shrieked, "Let him go!" Suddenly she was standing in front of Isaac. She'd used her ability to stop time to get closer to Isaac. Emma punched Kevin and snatched Isaac, cradling him in her arms. "No, no." She snarled, yanking at the cuffs, trying to remove them while Isaac moaned in despair.

Black Gaea screeched, sounding remarkably like the dragon. She flung her hands in the air. I gasped, realizing what she was trying to do. "Stop her! She's calling lightning to open the cuffs!" The sky darkened as storm clouds formed.

Before anyone moved stop her, lightning slashed down from sky at Isaac. He was too incoherent to hold up his arms, but Emma grabbed each one, raising his wrists to meet the lightning, heedless of her danger in the path of the lightning.

"No!" Uncle Dan cried out, diving at Emma, knocking her several feet out of the way. He took the entire force of the lightning, stiffening as the powerful surge of electricity jolted his body, flinging him through the air to crash onto the sidewalk.

I drew breath when I saw him lift his head, but he didn't seem to be able to get up. With a yell, I threw balls of ice at Black Gaea as quickly as I could form them, but the electricity haloing around her melted my ice projectiles. Desperately, I tried fireballs, but they only added to the vortex of power swirling around her. Kevin tried to bounce and throw her down, but he couldn't get close enough.

Emma snarled, running for Isaac again as more lightning flashed down. She was still a few feet from Isaac when lightning ripped through her body. She flung out her arms as her body arched in the air. I smelled singed hair and burnt skin as she fell to the ground next to her father.

Black Gaea was unhinged, crying hysterically, as she sent bolts of electricity at Isaac, but he was curled in a ball, unwittingly preventing her from blasting open his cuffs. All that happened was bursts of energy flashed around his body. In between the blasts, I could hear him keening in anguish over his blocked abilities.

Lange spoke from behind me. "Oh my god." He took several steps forward, stopping in frustration when he couldn't get any closer. I saw Zoe with him, her eyes narrowed as she tried to figure out how to get to Uncle Dan.

Uncle Dan managed to raise up, cradling Emma in his arms. When more uncontrolled lightning slashed down, he lifted his head to look at me. The lightning struck Uncle Dan, flashing around him to hit Emma. With a powerful boom, the blast tossed my uncle and my cousin in the air like rag dolls. Uncle Dan still held his daughter in his arms as they landed in the grass. Uncle Dan's neck was twisted at any angle no one could survive, and Emma's eyes were burned out. Her mouth gaped opened, slack and limp.

"No!" Kevin yelled in horror.

I couldn't speak as I stumbled towards their broken bodies, but I couldn't get any closer because Black Gaea cried out, staring at Isaac, "Isaac, let me help you!" Isaac didn't move from his pitiful huddle.

"Black Gaea!" Ben managed to get to his feet, though he was pale and sweaty. He gripped his hands by his sides, stepping towards her. "Stop it! You've lost."

She whirled her head around. "No! Help me save him. You can force your will on these weaklings, make them release him." Her hair whipped across her face as she floated up, riding the winds in the middle of her raging storm.

"No," Ben said, "I was a fool to join Mountain of Ash. You need to stop." He gave me an agonized look before he said, "This has to stop." He straightened, closed his eyes for a moment before opening them to gaze at Black Gaea intently.

Even though he was directing his mind control at Black Gaea, I felt the weight of his ability pressing again my mental shield and took an involuntary step back, echoes of Isaac's mind screws making me edgy.

Black Gaea's face twisted in agony. "Get out of my head. Only Isaac can be in there. He's the only one I give permission to. Get out. Get out!"

"Then stop! I don't want to be doing this to you. Give up, and I'll get out." Ben wore a focused look, but my heart wrenched in my chest when I saw tears rolling down his cheeks.

Ben knew that by using his ability, even to stop someone like Black Gaea, he was once again breaking the law. And we both knew that meant he would go back into prison and probably back into a forced coma. This time forever.

Black Gaea shrieked again, fighting whatever Ben was doing in her head. Her eyes were wide with fear, and she let her hands drop, slumping to the ground, sobbing uncontrollably.

Black Gaea's storm faded away, until all that was left was the smell of lighting-charged air. Ben moaned, wrapping his arms around his chest like he was trying to keep himself from falling apart.

The fight was over, and everything seemed to pause as if the world was asking, "Now what?"

Chapter 29

I was breathless, only able to stare around for a moment.

Zander had knocked out Trent and was standing near his prone body. At some point, General Stone had arrived with a dozen or so military personnel who were already setting makeshift barriers to keep out onlookers.

General Stone strode over to look into Isaac's eye as guards hauled the leader of Mountain of Ash up from where he crouched on the grass. Isaac was still moaning nonstop, his gaze turned inward. Guards also cuffed Black Gaea.

General Stone lifted his voice so that it resounded across the waterfront. "Thomas Isaac Jacobson Milton, I arrest you and charge you with crimes against humanity." The general swept a hand around the scene, indicating everyone—the Brighthalls, his army, and the normals watching from behind the barriers and lining the Hawthorne Bridge. "All of humanity."

Isaac pulled his focus from uselessly searching for his abilities to stare at General Stone with contempt. "Weak, useless normals don't deserve our kindness. They do horrible things to each other and this world." His eyes turned crafty. "Let me go." He held out his wrists, the cuffs gleaming in the bright sun. "And I'll help the Council find the true power in the world."

General Stone didn't bother answering Isaac's offer. "Take him away."

Isaac shouted, "You'll regret this when they, —" his glare took in the normals making it clear who 'they' were, " — crucify you for being different!" He tried to fight the guards who caught his arms. "You're risking everything!" He sputtered for a moment before adding, "I'll find my father in prison and join with him. Together we'll remake the world!"

A woman wove ropes around Isaac and then did the same to Black Gaea, then waved a hand to lift them both up. Guards grasped the ropes and leapt into the air, taking the Mountain of Ash leaders away.

The crowd of normals who hadn't run away watched in stunned astonishment. "They're flying!" Several women pointed at the guards. "Can you believe it?"

"I'm posting this right now!" A group of teenagers held up their phones, then lowered them, mirroring the actions of those around them.

"Did you see the ones who shot fire out of their hands?"

"What about the lady who made the lightning storm, that was crazy!"

I tuned out the astonished babbling of the crowd when General Stone said to me, "Olivia, how are you holding up?" He looked at the grass, where Uncle Dan's and Emma's bodies were sprawled, so still among all the activity.

I started to speak but the words clogged in my throat before I managed to say, "I, um, I don't know. What Uncle Dan did..." I trailed off, unable to find the words to express the sorrow I felt. Fatigue leached through my very bones, but I force myself to stand up straight. "Um, I need to..." I gestured at Kevin, Zoe, and Lange, who were all clustered around Uncle Dan and Emma.

I didn't finish as he nodded. "Of course. My condolences." As he turned away, I saw Anna and Jack running back from wherever Zoe and Lange had taken them. At the same time, Anna's parents had managed to force their way through the onlookers; I saw they were in the company of Portland's mayor who immediately went to speak with General Stone.

Anna's father swept her up in a tight embrace while Anna's mother hugged Jack. They all started talking at once.

I joined my cousins, feeling a sense of unreality as I gazed at my Uncle Dan and Emma, father and daughter reunited in death.

Lange crouched down, carefully closing Uncle Dan's staring eyes, gently smoothing his rumpled shirt, and brushing off ash from Emma's burned hair. Kevin leaned into me, and I put an arm around him. He looked devastated, not bothering to wipe away the tears running down his cheeks and dripping off his chin.

Zoe knelt beside Emma. Her eyes were dry, but her lips were pressed together tightly. She carefully nudged off a leaf that had drifted down onto Emma's cheek. "You idiot. I can't believe you're dead so you can't hear me cuss you out for leaving us." She sighed.

I wasn't sure what I felt. Mostly numb exhaustion, but as I gazed at my uncle's face, I knew I'd miss him for his firm beliefs, and I wished we'd had a chance to resolve our last fight. Now we never would.

As for Emma, it was hard not to hate her for what she'd become. I knew it would take me a long time to figure out if I could forgive her for what she'd done to my family. I rubbed a finger over the wounds on my wrists; they were healing but would leave scars.

The four of us stood in silence until Aunt Kate and Uncle Alex came running over from the direction of the Hawthorne Bridge. Both fell to their knees beside their brother and niece. Uncle Alex took Uncle Dan's hand, concentrating for a moment before gently reaching for his brother's other hand and folding them across Uncle Dan's chest. There was a sense of finality in the gesture, and I realized I'd held on to a tiny hope that Uncle Alex could heal him.

Kevin ran to hug his father, who turned and held on tightly. Zoe went to her mother, murmuring quietly. Lange stood over all of them as if he was on guard.

I felt left out, apart from their grief, so I slipped away. Then I saw Dad was also walking from the direction of the Hawthorne Bridge. A guard stopped him at the barrier, but before I could call out, Dad pointed to me. The guard gave me a long look, then let Dad in.

"Dad!" I ran over. It was so good to see him. He wrapped his arms around me, and I took several shaky breaths.

He stroked my hair and patted my back. "Ollie, I was so scared for you." He released me, holding me by my shoulder while he looked at me with a smile, "but so proud of you at the same time." He let me go, throwing an arm around my shoulder. "I wish there was a manual for how to be the normal parent of a supernormal kid, but I think I'm figuring out it's learning how to balance abject terror with extreme pride." He exhaled, his arm rising and falling with the motion. "Now that I say it aloud, it's probably not all that different from being any other kind of parent."

He gazed around, his eyes stopping when he saw Uncle Dan and Emma. "I was with Kate and Alex when they heard about Dan." His voice trembled, and I suspected he was remembering Mom's death, also at the hand of Isaac and his Ashers. "I'm glad Dan stopped Isaac. I hope it gives him some peace."

"Me too." I noticed Dad didn't comment on Emma's death.

The crowd behind the barrier was growing larger. Several people held up phones and cameras. I could only imagine what was happening on social media right now — it had to be exploding with posts about people with superpowers.

"I should go see if Kate and Alex need anything." Dad's brow furrowed.

"I'll catch up in a minute." My attention was on someone else.

Ben looked lost, surrounded by General Stone's guards. His arms were cuffed behind his back, but otherwise everyone was leaving him alone. I rocked back and forth on my heels a moment before deciding to talk to him.

He looked at me, saying nothing as I approached. I expected to feel him try to get in my mind, so I checked my shields. Then I saw his bindings were of the same metal as the cuffs at Mountain of Ash.

"Thank you for stopping Black Gaea." I tried to keep my tone level. I felt such a mix of emotion surge through my tired body—anger at his betrayal at the ranch, sympathy for his reasons, and gratitude he'd come through for us in the end.

He lowered his head, hunching his shoulders and not meeting my eyes. "I'm sorry, so sorry. I wish I'd never …" His voice was soaked in misery. "I was, ah, it was so exciting to…. And at the time I thought joining Mountain of Ash was a better option than prison and coma." He trailed off. "Well, you know all that."

We were silent. I figured we had parallel lines of thought: he'd sealed his fate by once again saving the Brighthalls.

He lifted his head, finally meeting my stare. "Back at the ranch, I started to doubt Mountain of Ash's intentions, but Isaac read my mind and started controlling me." His expression was grim, his green eyes dark as he confirmed my suspicions about his abrupt change in behavior. "It. Was. Horrible. When he used me to attack you today," Ben paused, breathing hard, his chest rising and falling rapidly. "Well, I couldn't take it anymore."

"I'm sorry." I said it softly. "I think it's going to take a while to forgive you, but what you did here, it helps."

The guards responded to some signal I didn't hear and took Ben's arms, ready to lead him away. Unexpected panic surged through me. Was this the last time I would see him?

"Wait!" When I called out, the guards stopped, and Ben gazed down at me as I put a hand on his shoulder. "I'll tell them you didn't help Isaac with the flashbacks at the ranch, and I'll keep reminding them you helped us here." I squeezed his shoulder before dropping my hand, "Maybe it'll help."

Ben smiled a little. "I'll miss you, Ollie."

I swallowed down unexpected tears as the guards took him away. In the background, Aunt Kate and Uncle Alex were talking to a man and woman as Uncle Dan and Emma's bodies were levitated onto stretchers. The 'rents followed as the stretchers floated away. Dad trailed along behind.

Lange, Kevin, and Zoe saw me and headed in my direction.

"Sorry about your boyfriend." Zander came over from where he'd been guarding Trent, who was also bound and heading for a van.

"He's not my boyfriend, but thanks. I actually don't know what he is to me." I rubbed my face tiredly, knowing I wasn't making a lot of sense. "How are you doing?" Zander looked as exhausted as I felt, and as sad. "Have they found Logan?"

Zander nodded, the shadows in his eyes telling me the news. "He died on the bridge when it fell." He took a deep breath. "I wish I could have talked to him, maybe tried to get him out, but..."

As my cousins reached us, I didn't say I thought Logan had been too entrenched in Mountain of Ash to listen to Zander. Instead I took Zander's hand and said, "Come on, let's see if there's a chance of a meal and a shower in the near future." The dunking in the river had barely touched the grime on my body. And, if possible, I thought I smelled worse than I had at the ranch.

Kevin said, "Yes, and some sleep." He rubbed the back of his neck. "I think we're going to be really busy for the next little while."

I stood shoulder to shoulder with my cousins and Zander as we faced the crowd of normals staring back at us from the barrier. The variety of expressions was fascinating—some people were clearly frightened by the rampant use of superpowers they'd seen over the last hour, while others looked thrilled. Some even waved at us.

Kevin started to wave back, but Zoe caught his arm. "Don't wave, you goofball."

"According to Harry," Lange said, referring to his boyfriend as he glanced at his phone that had somehow made it through the battle intact, "super-powered people and events are trending on Twitter and Instagram. Shocking."

I let the babble of the crowd wash over me.

"Do you think they're good?"

"Well, some of them aren't."

"Yes, but the others stopped them."

"I wonder if you have to be born with power?"

And the repeated refrain: "Have they always been here, living with us?"

Chapter 30

The mid-June sunshine warmed my shoulders as I stood looking out over the Willamette River near what was once the Steel Bridge. For the moment, I ignored the crowded park behind me. Like me, everyone was there for the dedication ceremony, but I wasn't quite ready to join the throng of normals and supernormals filling the wide grassy area now called the Battle of Portland Memorial Park.

I formed a ball of ice between my hands, creating a flower out of the ice. I turned the result from side to side critically. Even though I was getting better at using my ice ability to form shapes, I wasn't up to the level of General Stone's skill. My flower looked like it was a cross between a rose and an acorn. I rolled my eyes at myself, tossing the ice into the river.

The river flowed past me, sunlight glinting off the ripples in the wake of two motorboats. It was hard to believe that four months ago the waters had parted, exposing the bottom of the river. Of course, that wasn't the most amazing reveal that day. Now the world knew for certain that supernormals were real. And the world still reeled from the discovery.

One of the most shared photos from that day was the image of the two walls of water bracketing the empty river bottom with the dragon hovering in the air over downtown Portland. Every time I saw it, I wondered where the dragon had gone. No one had seen it since that day. Most of the other monsters had perished or been recaptured.

Someone on Twitter dubbed the water parting as The Moses Moment. The name stuck, along with the Unveiling or the Harbinger—Unveiling for those who viewed the discovery of supernormals with excitement and Harbinger for those who thought the existence of supernormals was a sign of the end times.

Zander shifted from foot to foot on the walkway next me. I followed his gaze to where two supernormal flyers flew into sight, carrying several girders between them. They soared past us, heading for the staging area for the teams working on rebuilding the Steel, Burnside, and Morrison bridges. The bridge work represented the first official collaboration between normals and supernormals.

I'd been astonished at how quickly the rebuilding in Portland started after the battle, but it probably had a lot to do with the need for bridges to cross the river. The four remaining bridges were clogged with traffic at all hours of the days now.

The Steel Bridge would be completed in a few months. The architects chose a modern design with sweeping curves and beautiful lights lining the walkways, but I still mourned the loss of the old industrial-style bridge.

"Olivia!" I turned around, laughing as Kevin bounced his way through the crowd of people. Normals murmured in alarm or amazement, still getting accustomed to people with abilities in their midst. Kevin was very careful to aim for empty spots, smiling at the people around him. A few guys Kevin and I knew from high school shouted his name, so Kevin bounced over and exchanged high-fives before continuing through the crowd.

I shook my head at him when he landed beside me. "Show off." Zander gave him a friendly shoulder punch.

Kevin grinned, eyes alight, looking like the cheerful imp I remembered from when we first reconnected last fall. "It's nice to be out, you know." He looked over his shoulder at our classmates. "It's easier, mostly."

"Yeah, mostly." I grimaced, thinking of Mindy's reaction when she found out about my abilities. She'd been grateful to Uncle Alex for healing her friend but still resented me. Some of her sourness could be attributed to Jack breaking up with her, but I didn't see how that was my fault.

Zoe and Lange strolled in our direction. Even though they weren't overtly using their abilities, they still looked powerful because they weren't hiding their movements behind a glamour anymore.

"Hey," Zoe greeted me. "How long before the dedication starts?" She gazed at the large structure that had been constructed near the sidewalk leading to the new walkway across the bridge. It was covered by a white cloth. My cousins and I, along with a few others, were going to unveil the memorial during the ceremony.

"I think it starts soon. It looks like the grandstand is on its way." I pointed in the direction of downtown where a platform floated into view from under the Burnside Bridge construction, hovering several feet above the water. Four supernormals with levitation abilities controlled the platform, moving it along steadily until it floated in place, facing the crowd gathering near the foot of the Steel Bridge.

The expressions on the faces of the governor, mayor, and other city officials who'd agreed to lead the ceremony from the supernormal-powered platform made me bite the inside of my cheeks to keep from laughing. According to Uncle Alex, riding on the platform was a gesture of good faith to show the normals accepted our abilities, but the officials all looked a little seasick—either from the motion of the platform or from the knowledge they were being levitated by the four supernormals standing at each corner.

Uncle Alex and Aunt Kate looked calm next to Council Leader Jones and General Stone, who'd both come out from Colorado for the ceremony. The past few months had been hard on the 'rents as they adjusted, not only to life without Uncle Dan but also to their roles as ambassadors to the normal world. My cousins and I barely saw them. Lange handled most of our training now.

My phone vibrated in my hand, and I glanced at the screen. "Hey guys, can someone get to Jack and Anna? They're stuck at the back of the crowd."

Zoe and Lange grinned at each other, Zoe saying, "I think she means us." They dashed off, returning a minute later with Anna and Jack.

"Whew!" Anna brushed back her hair. "I'll never get used to that rush." She smiled at Lange. "Thanks."

"How's Harold?" I asked Jack, who was straightening his tousled clothing.

"He's okay. he's wanted to spend some time with Maude and the others." Jack said.

I remembered the homeless woman who'd blown away most of her camp. "How's Maude doing?"

"Better." Jack pulled out his phone, showing me a video of Maude smiling proudly at a little whirlwind on the palm of her hand.

Maude hadn't been the only transient person who'd reacted to the sight of flying, flaming, or speeding supernormals by trying to use their untrained abilities. One camp had burned to the ground. Luckily, everyone made it to safety. Another man saved his cluster of companions when he teleported them and their belongings all the way to Mount Tabor Park, several miles from the waterfront.

After the battle, Harold worked with Uncle Alex and other healers to help with the lost, confused supernormals, many of whom didn't understand what their powers were or where they came from. Several believed they'd been cursed or had been abducted by aliens.

I'd asked Uncle Alex about it, indignant that these people were lost. He told me, "It's terrible. Smitty thinks that back before we were so reduced in population by the first Benjamin Hallowfield, there was more intermarrying with normals than there is now." He'd stopped with a smile. "Some exceptions apply of course." He was referring to the fact that he and his siblings had all married normals. "But there are some latent strains of the supernormal lineage out there. And those people became stunted because they'd never been developed, most of them having manifested abilities when they were young. Many thought they were going crazy." He shook his head, his eyes compassionate. "We're going to help them. I hope some can be trained to use their abilities and rejoin society."

I shook myself out of my memory of the conversation with Uncle Alex. The platform maneuvered closer to the shore.

"Tough memory?" Zander said to me quietly while my friends and cousins talked to the people around us. Most of them were normals who wanted to learn more about supernormals.

"Yeah," I met his eyes, "but it was my own. Isaac wasn't in my head rewriting my history." A fact I was grateful for every day.

Zander put his hand over mine, "You heard the news about Isaac, right?" We hadn't had much time to talk since he'd flown in with his Great-Aunt Wanda early this morning. He'd been living with her in the little village outside of HQ. He'd spent the past few months being questioned about his time with Mountain of Ash as well as learning how to live outside control of a nefarious organization with plans to take over the world. People were still very impressed he'd managed to hide his hatred of Isaac and the Ashers. His shielding technique was being studied by researchers so they could use it if there were any other mind readers about in the world. "Isaac is locked away, cuffed, and surrounded by the dampening field. His brain waves are being monitored day and night to make sure he's not using his abilities."

"No coma, though," I commented.

"Yeah, Ben told them it didn't work that well on him, that he was still aware and could feel the thoughts of others. And Ben could clearly direct his thoughts since he sent you all those visions." Zander glanced at my wrists, which still bore the scars from the cuffs I'd worn during my confinement. "He said the cuffs work best to cut off powers. But I guess you know that."

I nodded, reflecting on Ben's own punishment. He was cuffed, but he was given a reduced sentence for his role in helping defeat Mountain of Ash. He was confined to a cell, but not placed in a coma. "Yeah, I visited Ben a few weeks ago when your great-aunt took you to meet your cousins on the East Coast." I smiled a little. "He's doing okay. He's glad they're letting him help them learn more about his ability." I stared over the water. "I think he hopes he'll be freed one day." I looked at Zander. "What's your great-aunt say?"

Zander looked uncomfortable. "Honestly, it's going take a long time before the stigma of his power fades. Isaac's actions didn't do much to alleviate people's concerns. Pretty much the opposite, in fact."

I sighed, knowing he was right.

Lange said, "Hey, we should probably get closer to the memorial." He waved a hand in the direction of the covered sculpture. The rest of us followed as he began pushing his way carefully past people.

Anna and Jack clasped hands, smiling at each other as they shuffled through the crowd. Anna said, "Hey Ollie, when do you leave for Texas?"

"Next week. Why?" I was finally going to South Texas to spend a month training my ice ability with the McEveety family. General Stone had been true to his word and arranged it soon after the battle. I was looking forward to the trip but felt strange leaving Portland.

"I want to throw you a going away party." Anna answered.

Governor Lewis's voice boomed over the river and echoed across the throng "Hello everyone!" We hurried to get in place beside the memorial.

The crowd noise dropped to murmurs as everyone's attention focused on the platform where Council Leader

Jones stood proudly beside the governor, who continued to speak, "We welcome you and our guests —" she turned to Council Leader Jones with a serious expression, "— to whom we owe great thanks for preventing the complete destruction of Portland. As we mourn the lives and livelihoods lost, we take the time to acknowledge our gratitude for those who saved countless lives at the cost of revealing their secrets."

Cheers burst out of the crowd all around us, and the governor waited for them to settle down before continuing.

"Council Leader Wanda Jones would like to say a few words," the governor announced.

"Thank you all for coming today as we dedicate this park as a memorial to the lives of everyone who rallied to save this city." Council Leader Jones smiled at the throng. "It was the best of efforts by all types of humanity working together, proving we can live in harmony."

I only half-listened while she talked about the rebuilding efforts in Portland. Aunt Kate had already told me of the plans to create an alliance between normals and supernormals across the globe. Washington, D.C. was going to become the global center for supernormal and normal partnerships.

"...Daniel Brighthall." My uncle's name caught my attention, and I tuned back into the speech. "He was a true hero. He gave his life to defeat the leader of Mountain of Ash, the ultimate sacrifice. Daniel Brighthall embodies what it means to be a supernormal and a citizen of this world." Council Leader Wanda Jones held up a hand. "I call on everyone, all people of the United States, of the world, to work together to build our partnership. As a reminder of what we all lost together, we dedicate this park and this memorial to those who lost their lives and to the families who lost loved ones."

She dropped her hand, the signal to reveal the memorial. Anna, Jack, and Kevin took one end of the drapes, and I joined Zander, Lange and Zoe at the other end. At Lange's call of "Now!", we pulled away the white cloth, revealing a large sculpture of a bridge with figures standing in the middle, shaking hands.

The base of the sculpture was white granite covered in black writing—all the names of the people who died in the Battle of Portland. The names were in alphabetical order—normals and supernormal names intermingled. The only name that was more prominent than the rest was Daniel Thomas Brighthall emblazed across the top. I wondered what my grouchy, uptight uncle would have thought about being the hero of the day. I had a suspicion he would have shrugged it off and added training on how to avoid lightning to our workout routine.

I stepped back to allow the rest of the people to get closer, listening as folks murmured to themselves as they read names of people they knew. The memorial stood in the middle of the brick walkway, so everyone could move around both sides. People were already laying down flowers, paper hearts, and other tokens of love for those lost. Some people cried as they traced fingers over the carved names of loved ones. Strangers shared stories of how their family or friend died.

A woman stood near me, looking sad as she touched a name on the wall. She held the hand of a girl who stared at me with wide eyes. She looked like she was about seven years old. I smiled at her.

The girl said, "Can you show me your powers?"

"How did you know I have powers?" I asked, surprised by her question.

She shrugged. "I saw you earlier. You were doing something with your hands."

"Oh, this?" I cupped my hands together, concentrating on forming a better flower than I'd made earlier. People gathered around me as I focused on building each petal carefully. When I was done, I felt a flush of pride: the ice was recognizably a rose. I held it out to the girl, who took it with a grin. Her mother had been watching while I created the flower. Now she touched it with a look of wonder before giving me a tentative smile.

In a twisted way, Isaac had achieved one of his goals: the world knew about supernormals. Watching the little girl smile up at me through her crystal rose, I thought about the way this new world of normals and supernormals reflected my own growing powers. This world had always been possible, just lying dormant, like my abilities. Now it had taken root and was beginning to grow. And in this girl's eager eyes, I saw a hopeful, better world beginning to emerge.

About the Author

Growing up in Fort Worth, Texas, LeeAnn Elwood McLennan was always looking for any opportunity to read – under the covers in bed, in the car, and in class using the book hidden in the textbook trick. When her father introduced her to sci-fi/fantasy through a book of short stories from Astounding Stories, she was captivated by the possibilities in every word, and her daydreams involved other worlds, magical powers, and time travel. Despite graduating from Clemson University with a degree in English, LeeAnn has spent her career working in computer engineering related fields. She lives in Portland, OR with her husband, Andy, and two cats (number of cats subject to change at any moment).

Special Thanks

Wow, I can't believe the trilogy is complete! I've loved inhabiting Olivia's world for so long; it's bittersweet to step away (for now). That may be why it was difficult to finish *Emerge*. I wanted to write the best ending for Olivia and for my readers. I hope you like it.

Writing *The Supernormal Legacy* trilogy has made me think about what it means to have superpowers. I often invite folks to consider what superpowers they have. You don't need the ability to shoot flames out of your hands to be amazing. Sometimes all you need a courage. Think about it: What's your superpower?

To my amazing writing group – Warren Easley, Alison Jakel, Janice Maxson, Debby Dodds, and Lisa Alber. You are my first critics and I'm thankful for your honest feedback (ok, not always, but I usually get over it). Writing is lonely but you all make it less lonely.

Many thanks to Alexandra Fig for answering my questions about what it's like to be a teenager in Portland. It's a privilege to watch you grow into an amazing young woman.

Thank you Benjamin and Paige Gorman and all the folks at Not a Pipe Publishing for being fantastic to work with and for so much dedication to the world of stories.

Thank you to dedicated editor Sydney Culpepper for going over *Emerge* with a fine-toothed comb. Hopefully I'll improve my use of commas for the next book you edit.

Many, many thanks to Randy Kintz and Marcus Odoms for the gorgeous cover!

Kate Ristau, the dragons are for you, my friend!

To my sister, Sally Beezley, her husband Mark and their son William Maxwell: Thank you for your encouragement.

To my mother, Ann Elwood: Thank you for installing and supporting my love of reading. It was heavenly to grow up as the kid of reading teacher!

To my father, William Elwood: Thanks for introducing me to science fiction and fantasy books! I wish you were around to read my stories.

To my husband, Andy McLennan: I'm grateful every day that you're in my life.

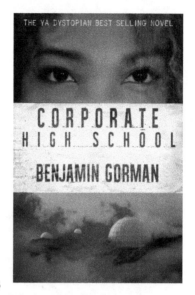

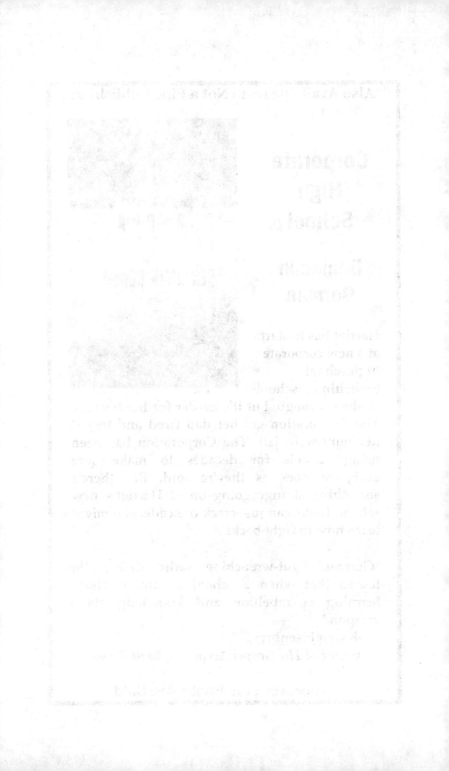

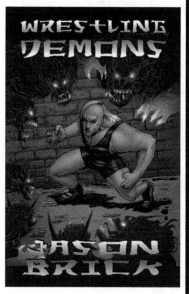

CPSIA information can be obtained
at www.ICGtesting.com
Printed in the USA
FSHW020838130519
58089FS